"One of the best-selling lesbian novels of all time."

—*Rubyfruit Review*

"The story is well-crafted and Forrest uses all her mystery story skills to build up the suspense."

—*Feminist Library Newsletter*

An Emergence of Green

ALICE STREET EDITIONS™
Harrington Park Press®
Judith P. Stelboum
Editor in Chief

An Emergence of Green

Katherine V. Forrest

Alice Street Editions™
Harrington Park Press®
An Imprint of The Haworth Press, Inc.
New York • London • Oxford

For more information on this book or to order, visit
http://www.haworthpress.com/store/product.asp?sku=5370

or call 1-800-HAWORTH (800-429-6784) in the United States and Canada
or (607) 722-5857 outside the United States and Canada

or contact orders@HaworthPress.com

Published by

Alice Street Editions™, Harrington Park Press®, an imprint of The Haworth Press, Inc., 10
Alice Street, Binghamton, NY 13904-1580.

First published in 1986, with additional printings in 1987, 1991, 1993, and 1995, by the Naiad
Press Inc. of Tallahassee, Florida.

PUBLISHER'S NOTE
This is a work of fiction. Names, characters, places, and incidents either are the products of the
author's imagination or are used ficitiously, and any resemblance to actual persons, living or dead,
business establishments, events, or locales is entirely coincidental.

Cover design by Lora Wiggins.

Library of Congress Cataloging-in-Publication Data

Forrest, Katherine V., 1939-
    An emergence of green / Katherine V. Forrest.
        p. cm.
    ISBN-13: 978-1-56023-542-2 (pbk. : alk. paper)
    ISBN-10: 1-56023-542-X (pbk. : alk. paper)
    1. Lesbians—Fiction. 2. Women artists—Fiction. 3. Married women—Fiction. 4. Bisexual
women—Fiction. 5. Female friendship—Fiction. I. Title.

PS3556.0737E4 2005
813'.54—dc22

                                                                    2004024652

❧ With Loving Thanks ❧

To Montserrat Fontes, Janet Gregory, Jeffrey N. McMahan, Karen Sandler, Naomi Sloan—members of the Third Street Writers Group, whose talent and integrity have helped me with this novel and all my work.

To Jean Bjorklund, whose enduring friendship has sustained me and helped me with my life.

❧ Editor's Foreword ❧

Alice Street Editions provides a voice for established as well as up-coming lesbian writers, reflecting the diversity of lesbian interests, ethnicities, ages, and class. This cutting-edge series of novels, memoirs, and nonfiction writing welcomes the opportunity to present controversial views, explore multicultural ideas, encourage debate, and inspire creativity from a variety of lesbian perspectives. Through enlightening, illuminating, and provocative writing, Alice Street Editions can make a significant contribution to the visibility and accessibility of lesbian writing and bring lesbian-focused writing to a wider audience. Recognizing our own desires and ideas in print is life sustaining, acknowledging the reality of who we are, as well as our place in the world, individually and collectively.

Judith P. Stelboum
Editor in Chief
Alice Street Editions

✎ Author's Foreword ✎

From the perspective gained during a two-decade writing career, it's easy to track the trajectory of my growth as a novelist: it forms a direct parallel to the jagged upward line charting the struggles and growth of the LGBT community. The novel you hold in your hands signals a distinct departure in topic and tone from the three books I wrote previous to it, just as it marks an extending horizon line in the advance of LGBT civil rights.

Curious Wine (1983), my first novel, is a classic coming-out story reflective of much of the literature of the day—discovering and coming to terms with our sexual identity. My second book, *Daughters of a Coral Dawn* (1984), dramatized a lesbian ideal while it explored some of our politics: the kind of world women might build when they seize the freedom to create it. My first mystery novel, *Amateur City* (1984), fell somewhat within these same realms in its portrayal of a police detective deeply closeted because she perceives this as necessity. Kate Delafield begins her fictional life insulated from virtually any exposure to her wider community.

Of these three novels, *An Emergence of Green* extends most directly from *Curious Wine* in its candid scenes of sexual discovery between the two female characters; but it departs from that novel and other coming-out stories in the immediate identification by all three major characters of what is happening among them. The quandary for Carolyn Blake and Val Hunter is not to search for the essential nature of their desire nor to flounder over acquiring the language of their attraction; it instead lies in defining its dimension, power, ramifications, and the parameters of their own needs and courage. Nor is there much mystery for husband Paul Blake. From the moment Val Hunter enters his life he clearly understands what is at stake—that the assertive woman who has moved in next door represents the gravest possible threat not just to his marriage but to his entire concept of power-centered masculinity.

As the strands of characterization in this novel were coming together, I was determined not to portray Paul Blake as the standard male villain extant in most lesbian fiction. In fulfilling this vow I introduced his point of view into the novel: I inhabited his mind. He in turn took up residence in my own. He stubbornly resides there still.

Certainly the world and its view of our LGBT community have changed since the time of *An Emergence of Green* in 1984 Los Angeles. Were I to begin writing this novel now, and set it in 2004, it would convey society's greater awareness and grudgingly eroding prejudice, but Carolyn and Val would not be much different in how their encounter transforms them nor in their internal conflicts over what it will essentially mean for them. Paul Blake would be not one iota different. Nothing about who, why, or what he is about has changed in our contemporary context. He is the quintessential American male, the successful, upwardly mobile, self-made achiever—an American cultural ideal.

Here then: the 1984, yet very today, story of Carolyn, Val, and Paul.

Carolyn Blake, just home from work, walked with automatic swiftness through the cool stillness of her house into the bedroom. She heard faint but vigorous splashing from the pool. She froze, her glance raking the room: the gold chains spread over her jewelry case were undisturbed. Whoever was out there taking a dip was not a thief brazenly cooling off after vandalizing the house.

With the release of fear came intense irritation. She stalked into the living room. *Kids,* she thought. *They've somehow climbed the alley wall . . .* She yanked aside the drape covering the glass door leading to the backyard.

For a shocked instant she stared at the shadowy shape in the pool. Before she could drop the drape to run to the phone, the shape rose—dark-haired, in shorts and a T-shirt, pulling herself up to sit on the side of the pool.

As Carolyn unlocked the glass door, the woman stood. In a sudden tight spring she dove, uncoiling straight and clean into the water with a distinct splat. The feet were slightly apart, the splashes from the entry of the shoulders tiny and sharp-edged. Walking across the shaded cement patio and the narrow stretch of lawn to the pool, Carolyn watched the woman come up through the water in a slow coursing, her body like a scimitar—back arched, arms tight to her sides, eyes closed, the face raised and rapt. The slow-motion curving plane to the surface contained such sensuality that Carolyn felt a sharing of it.

Stopping, the swimmer brushed fingers across her eyes. She saw Carolyn on the pool deck and swam with easy breast strokes toward her, and rose to her feet in the shallow end, water running over broad fleshy shoulders, streaming from dark tendrils of hair, dripping from a curling edge onto the nape of her neck.

Carolyn's gaze rose from faded cutoff jeans scarcely reaching strong tanned thighs, to a gray T-shirt glued to large breasts—the T-shirt bearing a legend so faded it was indiscernible—to keen dark brown eyes and a wide full mouth that twitched in amusement.

The woman tossed black hair from her face in a shower of spray. "Six foot two," she said.

Carolyn's laugh was involuntary. "Who on earth are you?"

The woman brushed at a few dripping curls clinging stubbornly to her forehead. "Val."

As in Valkyrie, Carolyn thought, staring in awe. Even the chesty resonance of the voice seemed perfect. A memory tugged at her, elusive and tantalizing; she struggled to retrieve it.

"I live next door."

"Oh. You're Mrs. Hunter."

After a vivid white instant of smile, Val Hunter nodded. She crossed her arms and regarded Carolyn.

Early thirties, Carolyn guessed, observing without resentment the self-possession of the stance. "Do you swim in other people's pools very often?"

"Just yours. Every day, during the week. No one ever uses it, at least in the daytime. It's the biggest in the neighborhood—I've looked. And the cleanest, I might add. I've been swimming here all spring."

"Really." Carolyn smothered a laugh.

"I couldn't see the harm. It seems a shame not to use it when your husband works so hard to keep it nice." She gestured beyond the fence. "I hear him."

"Paul likes to fuss over it. He's never satisfied with any of the pool services. Mrs. Hunter, how in the world do you get past a fence and locked gate?"

"Please call me Val. I hop the fence."

"You hop the fence," Carolyn repeated. "You just hop right over our little seven-and-a-half-foot fence."

"It's a little high," Val Hunter conceded, "but I get a good toehold and leap on over."

The June sun, pitiless San Fernando Valley sun that had long since burned through the protective morning haze, beat fiercely on Carolyn's shoulders. The steamy smell of water that had splashed on the hot cement deck clung to her nostrils. Moisture had formed in a light coat under her hair; she shifted her shoulders in her silk dress as she squinted at Val Hunter. "Does your son swim here too?"

"Of course not. I'd never let Neal do anything like that. You certainly know a lot about me."

"We knew you and your boy moved into the Robinsons' guesthouse in April. Paul talks with Jerry Robinson when they're out working in the yard."

Again there was the vivid white smile. "So you avoid Dorothy Robinson like the plague, too." As Carolyn, disarmed, groped for a response, Val Hunter shrugged. "Lonely prattling old woman. Pathetic." Again she smiled. "You're not usually home at this hour."

Carolyn found refuge in irony. "My apologies. My hours just changed. God, it's hot. June's not supposed to be this hot, is it?"

"Sometimes it can be. Allow me to invite you into your own pool." With large darkly tanned hands Val Hunter gripped the edge of the pool and hoisted herself out in one smooth motion. With three long strides to a chaise she picked up a towel and briefly rubbed her face and hair. "Guess I'll have to find the second best pool. I do want to thank you. I'd decided when I moved on I'd leave a note, a little thank-you gift, tell you how much I enjoyed it."

"Don't stop," Carolyn said quickly. "Why not use it? It really does go to waste."

Val Hunter nodded. "A lot of things people have go to waste. But people have all these ideas about ownership and property rights."

"What time do you like to swim?" Carolyn asked, thinking that Paul was one of those people; he would object violently to anyone sharing their pool. He even pursued hovering insects with vengeful swipes of the skimmer.

"About now, between three and four. In the heat of the day. Neal gets home from day camp around four-thirty."

"From now on I should be home about ten after three. I'll let you in."

"Thanks. Thanks very much. But I don't want to trouble you. I'll just come in my usual way; I'm used to it by now."

Carolyn glanced at her watch. "You have what, thirty-five more minutes? Jump back in. I'm going in the house before I collapse."

"Why not cool off in the pool? Enjoy the sun?"

"I don't swim," Carolyn said, turning and walking rapidly toward her air-conditioning, wanting to change her dress before perspiration damaged the silk.

"If you ever want to learn," Val Hunter called, "I give lessons. Free."

She changed into the bright red Chinese print Paul loved, a shift slit up one side to the thigh. To the sounds of continuous splashing from the backyard she made a vodka and tonic. She pulled aside the living room drape. Val Hunter's arms seemed to rip the water apart with each downward plunge of her body. In the turmoil of her passage Carolyn could see only broad shoulders and wide hips that rose so powerfully and generated such propulsion that the feet, tight together, flipped up out of the water. Again the elusive memory tugged at Carolyn's mind; she could not recapture it.

The swimming stroke Val Hunter performed was misnamed, Carolyn thought—totally unlike a butterfly, a delicate, fluttering creature. . . . At the end of the pool, with a sudden compacting of her body, Val Hunter performed a flip-turn, glided, then resumed her dramatic stroke. Impressed, entertained, Carolyn watched for some time before she dropped the drape back into place.

She switched on the stereo radio and as Irene Cara began "What a Feeling," she turned the volume control up to seven. The music pulsed into the room, filling it to the corners. She felt charged by the music's energy, the heavy beat bouncing off the walls. Fishing a paperback historical romance from under the cushions, she curled up in her favorite corner and in a blissful cocoon of velvet sofa and vibrant music and cold tangy drink, skim-read her novel, lingering only over the love scenes.

At five o'clock the phone rang. She turned down the music, knowing the caller would be Paul. Even before her hours changed he always called at this time to explain why he would be late, refusing to concede after almost a year that eighty-thirty to six o'clock was now his normal working day. She murmured sympathetically, as she always did.

At six o'clock she went out to the backyard and dropped her novel into a trashcan, pausing to breathe the coolness beginning to invade the Valley heat. The pool was aquamarine stillness, its surface slightly riffled. The deck was dry, pristine.

She made a salad and prepared the steaks for the barbecue, the task performed with leisurely and profound enjoyment; usually weekday dinner was a flurry of frenetic activity. At six-thirty-five she poured enough chilled vodka for three martinis, one for her and two for him, and made a bucket of crushed ice. She carried all this into the living room to the bar, switched off the stereo and turned on the channel seven news.

Maybe when he sees how everything's ready now before he gets home, he'll stop being so angry about my new hours . . .

✎ 2 ✎

Val Hunter showered, and briefly toweled and brushed the short
dark hair which would be dry in less than ten minutes in the heat of
her house. Still nude, she tossed her wet shorts and T-shirt over the
line behind the house, and came back into the cluttered living room
thinking without enthusiasm that she should tidy.

She donned fresh clothing, another pair of shorts and a T-shirt, and
tended to her paintbrushes. With her usual patience she rinsed each
brush in mineral spirits, soaking them all in warm water, then rub-
bing the bristles of each on an Ivory soap bar, using her palm to
lather, the soap turning into the bright hues of the paint. After rinsing
the brushes in warm water she repeated the operation until the lather
was colorfree. Delicately, lightly, she squeezed the damp, clean
brushes to reshape the bristles, and laid them out to dry.

With dissatisfaction she contemplated the painting propped
against the box on her worktable; there was nothing more she could
do for several days until the paint dried. She studied the gray mists of
the composition from different angles, bothered by the false light of
the late afternoon falling on the paint—wan and pale citron compared to pure strong morning light.

When she next glanced at the clock she was shocked by the time.
Neal was due home. She propped the painting against a wall where it
would receive light but be out of her line of sight, and dispiritedly vi-
sualized the contents of her refrigerator. Frozen enchiladas would be
fast but unappetizing in this heat. . . . Maybe hamburgers. Neal could
help decide.

"Guess who's the next Pete Rose," her son said from the doorway.
"I got three hits today."

In two strides she was to him, roughly gripping him. His body,
small for his ten years, was sturdy and tanned to dark mahogany. She

pressed her lips to brown hair streaked copper and blond from the sun, and inhaled his earthy smell. She knew not to comment; he never needed to be told he should shower. "You're beautiful," she said. "That's just great."

"Nah." Neal extricated himself and straightened his shirt and running shorts. "My average's up to only two-seventy-six."

She nodded without comprehension. "I'm proud of you."

He waved a self-deprecating hand. "What's for dinner, oh great and powerful Oz?"

Ignoring his habitual reference to his favorite movie, she answered, "Crab legs mornay."

His sneakers squeaked on the cracked tile of the kitchen floor. "Hey, we got lettuce," he called, his head in the refrigerator. "How about a salad? And cheese and salami and crackers? That's a good balanced meal."

"Fine with me."

"I'll shower off and cut up the other stuff if you make the salad. Hey, Ma?" His voice was pleading. "If I clean up the living room could I maybe watch the ball game? The Dodgers are on the road, Fernando's pitching."

She said grudgingly: "It won't kill me not seeing the news for once."

Neal's glance traveled the room. His tone was aggravated: "How do you get this place so messed up in just one day?" She grinned at the retreating back of her son as he went to shower. She dropped more ice cubes into her glass of water and settled herself on the sofa, unfolding the morning *Times* that Jerry Robinson as usual had left at her door after he was finished with it.

Much later that evening she thought of Carolyn Blake. She flipped open a sketch pad. Her drawing was incomplete—a rough pencil outline of details impressed in her memory: a mantle of smooth polished hair—sand-colored, she remembered—reaching not quite to the shoulder, a few strands stirred by the hot dry breeze, and the almond shape of eyes she remembered as green coming out of gray.

⟡ 3 ⟡

Shortly after six-thirty, Paul Blake drove down Heather Avenue looking at his house from the moment he turned the corner. As always, in his mind was a corresponding image of another house: frame like this one, but with dirty white paint peeling from its sagging gray timbers, and a yard sparse from neglect and sere from merciless Chicago winters. This house, his own house, was an immaculate beige frame trimmed in dark brown, landscaped with perfect grass and luxuriant green foliage, used brick generously enhancing the foundation and enclosing a tiny circular garden on the front lawn. He loved the used brick; its richness distinguished his house from all others on the block and more than compensated for the minute front lawn. And that other house, the house of his boyhood, had never had a single proud feature, much less the largest swimming pool in the neighborhood. He pulled into his driveway.

Moments later he was further gratified by the soothing colors of his living room, virginal white sofa and armchair, thick blue-gray carpeting, cool accents of dark blue and emerald combining in carefully placed pillows, vases, paintings. The heavy white drapes covering the glass door to the backyard were closed—odd that Carolyn had not opened them as she usually did. He welcomed the sight of a martini shaker on the bar only in the instant before he remembered why it was there.

Carolyn came out to him from the kitchen, into his embrace. Her perfume was at its most tantalizing—almost worn off over the day and mingling with the personal odor of her skin that he knew intimately. He was pleased by the dress she wore, and pierced by his love for her.

"Princess, you look gorgeous." He always remembered to express his pleasure when she wore dresses, in the continuing hope of permanently discouraging her from her usual pants or shorts. Tonight, he realized bitterly, she wore the Chinese print not to please but to mollify. Her arms tightened around his shoulders and she raised her face. He kissed her lightly; he would not allow himself to be mollified, even slightly.

"How was your day, honey?" she asked.

"Fine. Routine. And yours?"

"It was okay. For the first day."

Annoyed by the caution in her voice, he released her and moved to make drinks, his attention diverted to the television and a discussion of rising interest rates. He had to think for a moment when she asked about the woman next door. "You mean the artist?"

"Artist? Artist? Why didn't you tell me she's an artist?"

He frowned at her tone. "Oh hell, big deal. What do we know about art? Everybody paints. Or writes, or sculpts. What do you care about her?"

"I . . . curiosity, that's all. I . . . saw her today."

He shrugged disinterest. "I've never laid eyes on her. From what Jerry says she's humongous. An Amazon."

"She is tall," she said mildly, taking the drink he offered her. "Taller than you."

He did not respond. He had never admitted to anyone that his five-foot-ten-and-a-quarter height—which he called five eleven if it had to be mentioned at all—bothered him. He watched her walk to the kitchen wishing again that she were just an inch or two shorter, no more than five five, the same as his first wife. Whatever her faults, Rita had looked good with him. Picking up his drink, he went into the bedroom to change clothes.

They went outside into a balmy evening. He ran the skimmer over the pool, grumbling about the rising Valley wind. Each day of this June week had been hotter, the evenings cooling only gradually in the unusual humidity.

Gauging the steaks on the fire, he said, "Ten minutes at least. Think I'll take a swim."

She watched her husband pull off his polo shirt and cotton pants, his shorts. With only sporadic exercise—a little tennis, golf two or three times a month with a customer, an occasional swim—his body was well proportioned and trim, only a suggestion of softness in the belly. His one physical problem, a nonthreatening congenital heart murmur, had been sufficient to keep him out of Vietnam. In the natural light of evening his pubic hair was much darker than the hair on his head, which was full and thick but salted with gray, lighter gray at the temples. "A young Cary Grant," one of the wives had sighed to her at a company picnic. She was proud of his looks.

"Like what you see?" He leered at her playfully. "Woman, take the steaks off the fire for a while."

With an involuntary glance at the fence she laughed and waved at him. "Oh, go swim." As she adjusted the steaks over the charcoal she watched him, his aggressive path through the water, his choppy strokes less efficient than the smooth power of Val Hunter.

His nakedness brought memories of buying the house and her enchantment with the privacy of this fenced-in, shrubbery-enshrouded yard. The first evening in the house Paul had coaxed her into the pool and untied her bikini. The warm water against her nakedness had filled her with unbearable sensuality—a sensuality almost spiritual. In a corner of the pool he had lifted her willing legs around him. But as her hips beat against the cool hard tiles, the water churning in turbulent eddies around her, water had been pumped painfully into her, the pressure on her tissues agonizing. She gasped for him to stop, but he would not or could not. Smothering screams—how could she scream out here for everyone to hear?—she pounded on his chest and shoulders, and when he did stop she wrenched herself from him and stumbled into the house, crying, and again pounded on his chest when he followed. "Why didn't you stop! Why didn't you!"

He caught her wrists, held them away from him, his eyes brimming with tears, his face distorted into gray agony. "I thought . . . you liked it at first, then I thought . . . you'd start to like it . . ." He broke away and left the house, returning after several hours incoherently drunk. That week flowers were delivered every day to her office, and a pearl necklace had appeared among her jewelry on their dresser.

The steaks were almost done. "Paul!" she called.

With an odd feeling of detachment she watched him again as he sawed the towel roughly back and forth over his back, muscles working in the lightly tanned arms. As he turned away to towel his hair she studied the flat curve of his spine, the molded buttocks symbolic to her of the simple efficient beauty of the male body. He pulled on a short terry cloth robe, tying the belt into a neat square knot as he came over to her, smiling, his pale blue eyes calm even after the vigor of his swim.

He kissed her forehead. "The steaks look perfect, Princess."

Again she looked at him as she took the steaks off the fire. After eight years, she concluded dismally, the difference in their ages was more, not less, apparent. She had not grown as he had—this confident, handsomely graying man who seemed more attractive now than ever. At twenty-six she was by comparison still a child.

Freshly showered and shaved, he lay propped on pillows. Carolyn sat at the mirrored table in the dressing area brushing her hair, wearing the peach gown he loved, her body backlighted, the slight swell of her breasts accentuated by the silken cling of the gown. If only her breasts were larger—like Rita's. Rita's had been lovely to pillow his head on, especially after lovemaking. But in all honesty they had been otherwise too pendulous. And Carolyn's legs were lovely—not the long slim fashion model legs, but far superior to Rita's short plump ones.

His gaze strayed over the rich colors of the bedroom; expensive cherry woods and plush gold carpet, bright clown prints on either side of heavy gold drapes. He was pleased.

Who could ask for more, he thought a few minutes later as he stroked her, his hands light on her throat and shoulders. Her mouth was tender, responsive, and tasted of mint toothpaste. He held her on him to run his hands down her back. Her hair, heavy textured silk, lay over his neck and shoulders. He turned her.

Afterward he lay with his face buried in her hair, breathing the sensual fragrance. Her breathing was shallow, rapid; she was stroking his hair, kissing his face, murmuring indecipherably. He raised his head and looked at her. As always after this ultimate intimacy she gazed back out of veiled, impenetrable eyes, maddening in their privacy.

He rolled carefully from her, gathering her into his arms. Yes, he reassured himself, he was good for her; he knew that from how she was when he was inside her. He did make her happy.

"I love you, Princess," he murmured sleepily, nuzzling her, her delicate fingers soothing on the back of his neck. His contentment was disturbed by the knowledge that tomorrow morning she would rise several hours before he did, and tomorrow night she would begin going to bed early as well. But not for long; he would simply wage guerrilla warfare until she quit that stupid job for one with regular hours. Other men might want novelty in their lives, but he did not. He wanted only her. All the change and challenge he needed he could find in his work. He would soon have her in his bed when he wanted her there, just as he had for the past eight years.

Like a warm shroud, sleep descended.

❧ 4 ❧

Stealthily, Carolyn rose. She closed the bathroom door before turning on the light, and with swift automatic skill administered a douche, absently considering that she had not mentioned to Paul the extraordinary presence of Val Hunter in their pool. There was no reason to mention it—no reason to further upset him. She tossed the empty disposable douche into the wastebasket and turned out the light.

She curled up close to him, against the solid comforting breadth of his back, feeling vague arousal as she sometimes did after they had made love. His unhappiness over her work hours could not continue, she decided. A two week trial—then if he was still unhappy she would have to quit.

Quit, she thought wrenchingly. Maybe he would come around . . .

Four-fifteen. She looked at the digital clock with a surge of gladness. She did not have to get ready for work till four-thirty; she would spend this extra fifteen minutes dawdling over coffee and the paper. Paul muttered a sound of protest as she took her warmth from him, then rolled over and sank back into sleep.

The coffeepot was attached to a timer set for seven o'clock when Paul got up. She drank instant coffee and gazed at the darkened shadows of the house in contentment, leafing through the *Times* that had arrived faithfully at some mysterious earlier hour.

At five-twenty she let herself out of the house, pulling a sweater around her shoulders. An awakening pale light, concealing any threat of heat, lay over the Valley, over the joggers androgynous in their sweatsuits in the misty overcast. She drove the Sunbird slowly down Verdugo Road, loving the empty streets, the silence.

That afternoon she arrived home after work wilted by the brief walk to her car in the supermarket parking lot, depressed by reports on the radio of brush fires and first-stage smog alerts. The heat that had arrived that week had settled in, rising in waves from roof and pavement, creating erratic winds that scoured the tinder-dry hills.

She was surprised to hear the sounds from the pool. It was too hot, she thought, to move, much less swim, and the pool would be dirty from the wind, from the ash of fires on the nearby hills.

She drew the drapes aside. The pool looked clean enough; bare of twigs and leaves, but of course Val Hunter was every bit as capable as Paul of handling a skimmer. Carolyn watched her swim, a simple crawl stroke, the head position stationary even during the rotation to breathe, two waves flaring out from the top of the head, both small, one just in advance of the other and slightly the larger. The energy and drive of the body were compelling—the smooth propulsion, the completion of each arm stroke economical and unvarying, each hand entering the water cleanly, coming out cleanly. Powerful thighs generated a rhythmic kick, minimizing body roll, stabilizing the body perfectly. In only eight strokes Val Hunter traversed the forty-five-foot length of the pool and then flip-turned; Carolyn counted again and again.

Val Hunter hoisted herself out of the water at the shaded deep end, dragged a chaise out of the sun and under thick overhanging low fronds of the palm tree. She dabbed at her hair with her towel, then dropped exhaustedly onto the chaise, shoulders heaving.

After a moment's hesitation Carolyn drew open the drapes, slid back the glass door, and stepped down into the heat.

"Hi," she said awkwardly. "It occurred to me it's hard to leap over the fence with a cold glass of something in your hand. Would you like a drink?"

Val Hunter took a deep breath. "You're wonderfully kind to trespassers. Something cold would be great. Anything."

"I'm having vodka and tonic. Would you like that?"

"Just tonic would be fine."

She returned to the pool carrying her own drink and a tall glass of tonic with a slice of lime in it. Val Hunter raised herself on an elbow and drained half the glass. "Oh God that's good." She placed the glass on the cement beneath the chaise. "Neal insists soft drinks will eventually shred my kidneys," she said cheerfully. "Ten-year-olds should be put in camps till they get over that sanctimonious stage."

Carolyn chuckled, then looked away, into the pool. Drifts of silt had formed patterns on the bottom. "The water's dirty," she said.

Val shrugged. "I skimmed out the worst of it. It's still cleaner than the ocean."

"I need to change my clothes," Carolyn said softly. "Would you . . . like to come in out of the heat for a while?"

Val drained her drink. "I'd love to be where it's cool. I'll get out of these wet clothes. Be over in five minutes, okay?"

Before Carolyn could respond Val Hunter had risen, towel in hand, had taken several loping strides to the fence and leaped, grasped the flat top, pulled herself up to hang poised for an instant, then disappeared.

◈ 5 ◈

Val briefly inspected the sparse contents of her dresser drawer, then donned khaki shorts and her newest T-shirt.

What does this Carolyn Blake want? She's an attractive enough person; she shouldn't have any shortage of friends—or at least acquaintances. She probably thinks you're weird enough to be interesting. And as for her, she's neither interesting nor weird, but face it: right now you're bored.

She followed Carolyn Blake into the living room and condemned the room with a glance as she would a bad painting. How could anyone live in this blue-white glacier? Even green tones, normally warm, were frozen by their isolation.

Carolyn asked, "Would you like more tonic? Or—"

"Tonic is fine." She examined the contents of the bookcase—hardcover novels by Roth, Updike, Bellow, Nabokov, Vonnegut, Didion, Pynchon. None had been read, she suspected; the dust jackets looked too uniformly perfect.

"May I sit on the floor?" Val inquired when Carolyn returned from the kitchen. The white sofa and chair repelled her.

"Wherever you like." Carolyn curled up in a corner of the sofa, feet tucked under her.

A graceful young woman, Val thought, settling herself on the floor, her back against the white armchair. *Attractive even in red . . . but how could anyone under thirty change into a dress to relax? And can't she see that red's a completely wrong color for her?*

"I understand you're an artist. Have you been painting long?"

Val sipped her tonic. The question was polite, nothing more. With certain levels of ignorance she was quite willing to divert the conversation; she no longer felt any obligation to defend the history and profession of art. "Years," she said. "Through two marriages and a pregnancy and two foreign wars and domestic crises too gruesome to describe."

Carolyn's voice was soft, shy. "You sound a hundred years old."

"Thirty-six."

"You are? So is my husband. You don't look it. I'm . . . almost twenty-seven."

You don't look it either, Val thought. She smiled. "I don't care how old anyone is. My son is more interesting than most of the adults I know."

Carolyn chuckled. "I hope I can compete with Neal."

Val smiled again, wondering what she was doing here with this vapid woman in her iceberg of a house. "It's nice to talk to an adult during the week. Have you lived here long?"

"A year and a half. We're both from Chicago but Paul was transferred to Alabama for a year, then we came out here. He's district manager for American Tube Supply. They distribute metal tubes in every state in the union."

God, how dreary. And she looks so proud. "How do you like L.A.?"

Carolyn considered the question. "I like the . . . differentness, the feeling of . . . possibility. Yes, I like it. I might be trying not to like it too much because Paul will very likely transfer again. What about you? Where are you from?"

It's a layer deeper than shyness, Val decided. *There may be something in her after all—but she's like a violet that can't take the sun.* "Connecticut. But I've been out here since sixty-eight. Neal was born here." She sipped her tonic. "It's so cool and lovely in your house—the first time in days I've felt comfortable."

"You don't have air-conditioning?" She looked aghast. "How can anyone live here without it?"

"It's hot for June, but I'll adjust. Even in the heart of summer the Valley cools off at night."

"But you must *die* during the day."

"You really do get used to it. Like people in the desert. I don't mind all that much; I love the sun." She admitted, "But all this smoke and ash in the air is miserable. The fan just blows it all around."

"We have a portable air conditioner in the storage room. Take it. We had to buy it in Alabama for the bedroom." She grimaced. "Alabama. I could've danced in the streets when Paul was transferred out of there. Do take it, Val. You can keep one room cool. It's better than nothing."

"Well . . . Neal would love it." She was thinking of increased electrical bills. But maybe once in a while when it got really oppressive . . . "Let me think about it." She changed the subject. "What do you do that you work such odd hours?"

"I'm a personnel assistant at Everest Electronics, over near Glassell Park. Microcomputers. The office and plant are together. My boss decided he should make himself accessible to the night shift plant personnel for at least part of the day."

"Seems a good idea," Val commented.

"He's very creative and bright," Carolyn said with animation. "I love him. I mean, he approaches things with a . . ." She fumbled for a word. "He lost his hand two years ago in an accident, he wears a prosthetic. He's a firebrand liberal; he understands being handicapped in this world. He . . ." The next words were blurted: "Paul hates my new hours."

Val smothered a yawn. "Prefers you in bed in the morning, does he?"

Carolyn answered soberly, "I was stupid enough to take the job without asking him. It's a promotion—not much of one, only a few more dollars—but it meant working directly with Bob Simpson and I was so delighted to be asked I just went ahead and said yes, not thinking how Paul would react."

Another Diary of a Mad Housewife. *God, spare me.* "Maybe you assumed he'd be just as happy as you." Refraining from inquiring how much consultation had gone into either of Paul Blake's transfers, she said instead, "He took you out of Chicago into the middle of nowhere, then out here. You had to quit jobs both times, I assume?"

"I really didn't mind. Well, the one in Chicago I did mind," she amended. "It was my first job with responsibility. But—"

"This job doesn't keep you overtime. You don't have a child you're quote selfishly neglecting for a career unquote—that was Richard's big beef. He was my second husband—" She broke off, seeing Carolyn's fascinated stare. "Don't mind me. I have strong opinions on everything. Your marriage is your own very private affair."

"Is Val Hunter your own name?"

She was startled by the question. "My own name is Carlson, but Neal's father and I were never divorced, only separated. He was killed in an accident two years ago. I decided it was easier all around to keep the name Hunter." She chuckled. "I've always thought Val Hunter sounds predatory."

Carolyn shook her head. "I think Val Hunter is a perfect name for an artist. It has a . . . clean sound."

Val glanced at a clock over a fireplace laid with three perfect logs and lined with white brick surely not meant ever to be exposed to flame. "I'm afraid it's almost time for Neal to come home and criticize my choice for dinner." She had fifteen more minutes—but why remain here with this young and very married woman?

"Take the air conditioner."

Val reflected. "Only if you let me do what I can to repay you. Let me teach you to swim, to gain a little enjoyment from your own pool. I absolutely guarantee you won't drown."

"I'll think about it," Carolyn said after a moment. Her face was closed in refusal.

Val's interest was piqued. "There's a problem," she said gently. "Obviously there's a problem."

"When I was seven, one of the girls I played with pushed me into a park swimming pool. The lifeguard fished me right out but I got a lungful of water and apparently permanent terror." Carolyn had placed her hands on her knees as if to use them for support. "I've never told anyone this, not even Paul. I really don't know why; it's not such an uncommon thing. You—you swim so beautifully; you make it look so easy."

Val watched the hand that smoothed the fabric of the red dress, the face that held a childlike vulnerability reminding her of Neal. "Carolyn," she began, then stopped. "May I call you Carrie? To me it suits you more."

The hand relaxed. Carolyn smiled. "I've always liked Carrie better than Carolyn but no one's ever called me that."

"Carrie, if that had happened to me I'd feel exactly the same as you."

Carolyn's eyes traversed the length of Val's body. "It wouldn't happen to you." She smiled again, an impish smile that struck Val with its attractiveness. "No one would push you into a pool."

"When I was growing up, it would've made so many things easier to be a regulation-size woman like you—I'd have given my soul." She added, "I still would."

"Why? It's so different today. Today you're just a tall, strong woman. What's wrong with that?"

"Our culture. It's fine to be a very tall, thin fashion model—a decorative woman. Otherwise you're abnormal, bizarre. Height's a competitive advantage men still claim as solely their own. I got married when I was seventeen. I needed to prove I wasn't too tall to get married. Poor Andy was nineteen, he thought marrying me would prove he was a man. If he wasn't too sure about it before, he was less sure afterward. You can't imagine how it feels to hear laughter directed at you. And neither of us with the ego strength to withstand those stares, the derision. We were married seven weeks."

"That's terrible, Val. Those were awful times. But now you're accomplishing something of value. Many people never do anything with their lives. You have a *talent*."

Val looked at her sharply. This conventional woman sitting on her white sofa in her secure, affluent world could have no concept of how much that talent had been the saving presence in her life. "How would you know?" she said goodnaturedly. "You've never seen my work."

The voice was shy: "I can tell. You have substance. And your work must, too. Could I ask what kind of things you paint?"

Val was touched, and pleased. "I think my work is generally expressionist, although that's not inclusive." Carolyn looked attentive but blank, and Val changed the subject. "I have an idea how you can enjoy your pool without feeling nervous at all—without even getting your hair damp. Will you be here tomorrow?"

Carolyn took a strand of hair, sliding her fingers along it. "I was going to get my hair cut tomorrow."

"You really are petrified of water," Val said sympathetically.

"No, I really do need to get my hair cut."

"You do? Why? It would look wonderful to your shoulders or below."

"You think so? I've worn it this way for years. Paul . . . maybe I'll think about it. Anyway, it can wait, I'll be here tomorrow. What do you have in mind?"

Val grinned. "Wear your bathing suit. And trust me."

Carolyn looked at her with eyes that were wholly green. "I do trust you. Do we have it settled about the air conditioner? You'll take it?"

"Thanks. You're a godsend."

❧ 6 ❧

Carolyn tried on the bikini she had bought the week they moved into the house. Frivolous, Paul had termed the two pieces of fabric, a bright green floral pattern she thought reflected the fresh daring newness of California. She had intended to buy one more pleasing to him but then procrastinated, the experience of their first night increasing her aversion to the pool. Every weekend after that first night, and often during the week, he had coaxed her until she donned the bikini and climbed gingerly down the masonry steps at the shallow end to splash without pleasure while he leaped off the diving board and thrashed about as if his alacrity could instill enthusiasm in her. Inevitably her passivity affected him; she was finally able to bury the bikini in a drawer, confident she would rarely have to exhume it. Only once, during a Sunday afternoon barbecue for his staff, had he asked her to wear it, his purpose transparent: to show off his young wife to the men he worked with.

Her thoughts turned to Val Hunter. Masculine, Paul would call her; one of those dykey women spawned by the women's movement. But, she reflected, sexual preference was pretty clear here, wasn't it? Even if Val Hunter wasn't with anyone now, she had married not once but twice and had a son. And she, Carolyn Blake, was longtime married. And anyway, there wasn't the slightest hint of sexual interest from Val Hunter and you could always tell, couldn't you?

The bikini fit perfectly, and she felt reassured. She put the bikini back in the drawer.

Such an unusual woman, she thought enviously. Yes, there was that height and the problems Val Hunter had spoken of, but such bearing she had, such carelessness about her clothes, how she walked, how or even where she sat. Utter indifference about her appearance—not a trace of makeup, her hair scarcely combed . . . Bold opinions, easily and confidently given. . . .

Again there was the elusive memory pulling at the edges of her mind, the image of Val Hunter somehow beckoning to her past. Tantalized, Carolyn struggled fruitlessly to remember.

She leaned down to kiss Paul good night, pressing her lips to his forehead. He shifted in his armchair, glanced at his watch. "So soon?"

She eased herself into his lap, sliding her arms around his neck. "It's just an hour before you come to bed too, honey. Just an hour. I never go sound asleep, you know that. Wake me up." Kittenish and flirtatious, she stroked his hair and breathed into his ear. "You've done it often enough in eight years."

His eyes looked intently, soberly, unyieldingly into hers. "I love you," he said. "I love you more than anything in this world."

"And I love you, Paul darling. Give this a chance," she pleaded. "Just a chance to see if we can . . . adjust. Please?"

His mouth was tender on hers, his hands gentle around her waist. "You think about it too," he said. "Think about whether this is really what you want."

⤷ 7 ↩

Awakened by the insistent low buzz of the alarm, he stretched across the bed to switch it off. He had refused to move the clock to the night table on his side of the bed; he would not formalize Carolyn's new hours. He buried his face in her pillow, smelling faint delicate scents of her, remembering lovemaking.

He pulled on a robe and went into the kitchen, poured steaming coffee from the automatic coffeemaker, and carried the cup back to the bathroom. No longer would he sit at the dining room table with the paper and his coffee; he used to do that with Carolyn. And the newspaper, which she now read before he did and left folded beside his coffee cup, he would take to the office with him.

He spread shaving cream over his face, his thoughts straying back to the first days of his marriage when Carolyn would come into the bathroom in the mornings to sit without speaking on the lid of the toilet, knees under her chin, to watch him shave. In those days she had been fascinated with every aspect of his maleness, scrutinizing how he tucked his shirt in and fastened his pants, how he knotted his tie, even how he arranged his genitals inside his shorts.

He had enjoyed her fascination even while understanding that it was not meant directly for him. There had been few men in her life. When Carolyn was nine her stockbroker father had tidied up his affairs, including deeding the house to his wife, cashed his last commission checks, cleaned out exactly half of the family bank accounts, and vanished—Mexico, Carolyn's mother believed—making no subsequent effort to contact his wife or only child. Carolyn's mother soon sold the house and moved into an apartment next to her sister and brother-in-law and their two daughters. These cousins of Carolyn's had become her closest companions—but then they had gone away, the family moving up to Evanston before Carolyn turned twelve.

Although she could speak freely and without apparent pain of the desertion of her father, it was at least as great a betrayal as that of his own mother, of which he never spoke; and he had always understood the disconnectedness in Carolyn. He understood the tenuousness of her roots—and was aware that she did not. Now she lived on the farthest coast from even these roots. Her mother, a vague, nervous, washed-out physical caricature of Carolyn whose fine-edged lucidity made him uneasy, had been in a sense further removed from Carolyn— she had recently remarried. Not only did he understand Carolyn's disconnectedness, he welcomed it; he wanted all her sense of belonging and permanence to come from him.

He was proud of this marriage, his second. He had read that divorced people more often than not repeated their mistakes, seeking out similar marriage partners. Carolyn could not have been more different from Rita.

He thought of Rita seldom—and then with relief and gratitude that she was gone from his life leaving no residue other than memory. Her age, he supposed, had been the most grievous problem. Women, after all, no matter how malleable they seemed, how willing they professed to be in the areas of compromise, were set in their personalities without hope of change once they got into their twenties; and Rita had been twenty-five, he twenty-three.

At the time, she had seemed the ideal woman. Attractive, with a healthy glowing vivaciousness, her primary appeal had been a maternal caring for him; she had flattered and praised and encouraged and catered to him, even eased some of that pain he had carried with him since boyhood, that great wound opened in him by his mother.

But Rita's volubility allowed for no silence, and her unflagging energy became a draining suction. Sex especially was a swamp in which he felt inextricably mired. She needed lengthy intercourse for orgasm, and each time he had to hold on and hold on while she gasped almost almost almost until mercifully she came and he could have his own orgasm, more agonized release than pleasure. Each time he would lie utterly spent while she babbled praise and love, her grateful hands holding his head pillowed into her big soft breasts, until he dropped into black sleep.

Occasionally she wanted to give him fellatio, which he detested but surrendered to out of a shameful sense that he should want it, enduring the act by squeezing his eyes shut to excise the vision of her pendulous breasts as she bent over him, the sight making him feel as if he were being serviced by a whore. Steeling himself, he would reciprocate, a suffocating ordeal of wetness and nauseating odor, while she emitted little shrieks and her body flopped on the bed like a beached fish.

There was no peace anywhere in his life. After he had been married four years and had begun to acquire his first professional success, she wanted to have a baby. After all, as she nagged insistently, she was approaching thirty. Unable to bear the thought of another demanding voice in his life, he put her off with granite determination. She retaliated by pouting and then withholding sex, and when he did not bother to conceal his indifference—indeed, his relief—the acrimony between them reached irrevocable heights. They divorced with outward amicability but with dark hatred between them. A scant, embarrassing three months later, Rita remarried.

The restoration of his single status soon evolved from relief into awkwardness. At work he was now odd man out, automatically excluded from talk of wives and children, a misfit at company functions involving employees' families. He was soon led to understand in subtle ways by men above him that those who blended best into the corporate echelon met certain criteria of conformity. Marriage gave evidence of stability; marital responsibilities created career commitment; married meant normal. Single, on the other hand, meant alienation from the mainstream, potential independence in the workplace. Whatever his professional abilities, a single man was a potential corporate maverick. Single meant not-quite-normal.

Understanding more and more of the intricacies of corporate politics, he studied the wives of the men around him and congratulated himself on his single status. Aside from his own innate talents, he could gain advantage and increased career opportunity by marrying the right kind of woman, and he was lucky to be free to choose a new woman.

He met Carolyn at his cousin Joan's wedding reception. A freshman classmate of Joan's, eighteen years old, possessed of laughable ideals and the endearingly foolish belief that the world was filled with nobility, she was elusive and shy and unaware of her loveliness. He was enchanted by her, drawn to her in an amused and tender protectiveness new to him. The tranquility in her, her central chord of stillness, was like a nourishing oasis in his life. And young as she was he felt challenged by her, by her quality of reserve, an ambiguity he could neither encompass nor fathom.

With single-minded calculation he laid siege. When he learned she was seeing two other young men he was suddenly charged with fear. That he would fall in love with her had not been in his calculations; the possibility that he might fail to win her terrified him.

He knew his maturity was an asset, his sophistication an advantage. Attempting to overwhelm, he deluged her with large and small attentions: dinners, the theatre, flowers, cards, notes, gifts. Physically he was affectionate, but careful not to press after his initial overtures met resistance. Her reticence, entrancing after the clamorous and exhausting demands of his marriage, only deepened his love. At the same time he sensed that the old-fashioned quality of their courtship appealed to her idealism, her romantic nature.

He met her mother, who clucked over him in birdlike eagerness, approving of his professional accomplishments—at twenty-eight he was already senior salesman, eighteen thousand a year plus bonuses plus company car—and his conservative appearance, his seriousness, his maturity, his prospects. Although divorced, he was childless and alimony-free.

He chose the day Carolyn passed all her freshman finals for his marriage proposal. When she did not reply, only looked at him, he was so fearful that he could scarcely control his voice as he added that of course he would want her to continue with college full time until she graduated.

"All right," she answered, her voice uninflected, as if the condition of continuing college had decided her, as if she were agreeing to a business deal.

He did not care. She was his.

They had not yet gone to bed together. "I want to wait now," he told her honestly. "I don't know why it's so important—but I want the marriage ceremony; I want the waiting. I want everything special there can be." She smiled at him then, a radiant smile that seemed to him purest love.

Six weeks later they were married in a small private chapel so banked with flowers he could still call their fragrance to memory. She had turned nineteen; he was twenty-nine. His boss had been best man. His father, visibly uncomfortable in a formal suit, had tugged constantly at his tie as a dog would scratch at a flea. His brother, Rolfe, wearing a cheap gray seersucker jacket over shapeless pants, had attended along with his husky and coarse wife Theresa whom Paul despised no less than he despised Rolfe. Carolyn's mother had of course been there, prim and frightened in her beige lace dress; and the two cousins Carolyn was close to, who were her bridesmaids; and several of her friends from college who seemed to him more curious onlookers than friends.

They flew to New England. The incandescent fall landscape was afterward a blurred memory in him; even the photos Carolyn had taken were meaningless, without any reference points. Desire unlike anything he had ever known had overwhelmed all his senses. Tenderly he touched and loved her, and her shy response continually ignited him. Now that she was fully his, his love plumbed new depths, acquired a new intensity of possessiveness that both astonished and terrified him.

As welcoming as she had been to his caresses, she had seemed at times restrained, had looked at him with something like remoteness.

"I want everything wonderful for you," he told her. "Am I too fast? Too anything?" He pleaded, "Tell me."

"It's me," she confessed. "It's not you at all. It's just . . . nerves."

During their third night she was wetter than usual for his entry, and when he felt for the first time a clasping of him in her, he came instantly, groaning his ecstasy. Afterward she lay with her eyes closed, her breathing rapid and shallow. He asked eagerly, "Good? Was it . . . good?"

"Yes," she whispered, and looked at him. And still there was that distance in her eyes, a veiled privacy. In the ensuing years, whenever he had looked into her eyes after lovemaking the veil was always there, as if something within her was still beyond his reach.

His mother had been a stern and cold woman who thoroughly cowed both his father and his brother. Rolfe had inherited his father's height and sandy hair; he, Paul, had his mother's coloring and her blue eyes. He and only he had been close to her, had been privileged to understand that her forbidding demeanor was the bluff she ran against the meanness and poverty of the world she was trapped in, her means of surviving her all-male surroundings, of enduring a husband as crude as his rough and tumble business—supplying corpses of cars to wrecking yards.

Just after he turned sixteen his mother fell ill. The day after she was given a diagnosis of intestinal cancer she rented a motel room and accomplished her death efficiently—washing down two bottles of sleeping pills with a pint of vodka and without the least trace of sentimentality, her formally signed note reading, THIS IS BEST.

His father accepted the suicide with numb stoicism, inarticulate in this loss as in all other facets of his life except his work. Rolfe, older than Paul by three years, said to Paul, "You and her—the two of you thought you were better than the rest of us. But now after this . . ." Paul had turned and walked away from him, and in the twenty years since that day saw Rolfe only when unavoidable; he could not bring himself to consider forgiving him.

His mother, however, was beyond all forgiveness. Why had she died without any acknowledgment of their special bond, as if she wished to annihilate his connection to her? THIS IS BEST. The manner of her death denied that he had been an exception to those words, denied that he was different, denied his potential in the world, reassigned him to the hopelessness of his surroundings.

His anger and bitterness fueled an unsuspected strength he unearthed in himself—a single-minded obstinance. He thrust pain and futile questions out of his mind and with grim persistence, undeterred by all obstacles including exhaustion, put himself through Chicago State University, working the night shift stacking cartons of cans in a meat packing factory. Vowing that he would work for a Fortune 500

company and no other, he patiently researched and applied to one
company after the other, in alphabetical order. He was hired as an
inside salesman on his fifth interview.

Aside from his wedding to Carolyn, he looked back on his first day
at American Tube Supply as the greatest day in his life. He had
won—had smashed all barriers, defeated all the forces marshaled to
pull him down and keep him at the level of his father and his brother.
Thoughts of his mother—the words THIS IS BEST—still crept into his
mind, to be pushed angrily away. He had risen above what she had
done to him, yet in the ultimate betrayal she was not there to witness
it. She was outside his triumph, his anger, his revenge.

How carefully he had initiated with Carolyn the subject of having
their own child. She had looked at him questioningly, her eyes grave
and accepting. He remained silent, waiting for her to speak. Finally
she ventured, searching his face anxiously, "You're ten years older. I
know you must want them . . . but when I finish college, just a few
more years . . . I know I'm being selfish but it's important to me, dear
Paul . . ."

"Whatever you want, Princess, it's your decision," he said, thinking
that in a few years he would be better able to know if he could ever
share her, whether they would ever have a child.

He knew better than to suggest she did not need a degree, that he
would take care of her, that while the extra income would be welcome
when she did take a job he did not want a paragon who juggled husband and home and career. In the world of his work where he was increasingly valued and finding more and more secure a place, he was
admired and envied—as he knew he would be—for Carolyn's youth
and good looks and subtle sensuality. A fairy princess could not be
more perfect than the woman he had fallen in love with. He did not
want anything about Carolyn to change.

As his career gathered impetus and placed new social and financial
demands on them, she had doggedly continued going to the University of Illinois. After they bought the condo on the Near North
Side—a real bargain but a precipitous drain on his income—she borrowed tuition money from her mother and took a part-time job,
working several hours a morning in the college bookstore. Hoping

she would become discouraged and drop out—or at least postpone her degree—and with the fresh and vivid memory of his own hard-won college degree as justification, he immersed himself in his work, giving lip service encouragement and sympathy but no help with the cleaning and cooking and shopping. If she stopped even briefly, he calculated, it was odds on she might never go back. Her grades declined, she became tired and morose, but still she persevered through the first two years of their marriage, refusing to drop out for even a semester.

As she began the final semester of her third year, he found her late one night slumped over her books, her face gaunt even in the relaxation of sleep, her pen still within slack fingers. Suddenly he was pierced with love and pride in her, proud of her determination and guts. She would make it through to graduation—he would make certain of it. The next day he ordered her to quit the part-time job, and after that he did much of the housework, began to shop for groceries. She had thought him a hero.

The euphoria of her college degree soon evaporated under the cool disdain of personnel managers who examined her résumé and interviewed her for entry-level positions in business.

"This is 1981, they can't *ask* me those questions," she raged at Paul. "It's not *legal* to ask how old I am and if I'm married and if I plan to have children. They can't *do* that! But if I say anything it's good-bye Miz Blake, nice chatting with you!"

One evening as she related the frustrations of that job-hunting day, her voice choked with tears, he made a mistake.

"Take it easy for a while, Princess. Take a little vacation. You've earned it, all those years in college. You don't even have to work."

Her eyes were a bright green hardness he had never seen before, and she said in a quiet voice, looking at him as if he were a repugnant stranger, "I *do* need to work."

He proceeded to compound his error. "I have contacts. Let me make a few calls—"

She shrieked an oath at him and fled into the bathroom and locked the door.

Throughout their marriage her chief weapon during their few serious quarrels had been silence—and even when he perceived himself as totally in the right he always capitulated, her avoidance of him, even briefly, more than he could bear. For the next two days she would not speak, would not hear his apologies and explanations, his efforts to atone and make peace. Afterward he wondered how long she would have maintained unforgiving silence had her anger not been consumed in the jubilation of finding a job at Jorgenson Illumination.

"Not only am I a customer service representative," she proudly informed him, "but they have women supervisors and managers. The salary may not be much but I don't have to type except for filling in the blanks on order forms!"

He swallowed his laughter, hugged her in joy and relief, and took her to bed before she remembered how angry she had been.

She was very good at the job, earning a performance bonus after only four months. A supervisory position, despite her age of twenty-two, was a distinct possibility in a year or so. But then he was offered the promotion, the transfer to Alabama. After her burst of happiness for him, she was desolate for herself—and then as quickly shrugged it off. "There'll be other jobs for me. I just wish I'd had a little more time on this one. I need more experience to get another good job."

In the fall of 1981, in the midst of recession, conservative Birmingham, Alabama, did not welcome into its job market a young married woman freshly moved in from Chicago, judging her a likely transient unfit for anything more responsible than low-rung secretarial work. After two months of futility she took a clerical job, which she hated along with their apartment, the weather, the city of Birmingham, and the South. They made no friends and stayed home most evenings.

When they left Birmingham at the end of 1982 he was regretful; he looked back with nostalgia to their days in this unwelcoming city with its various hostilities. He and Carolyn had been united in their isolation and he had been utterly content.

There was never a question whether he would accept the promotion to Los Angeles—a big promotion, district manager in the company's largest sales region. They could buy a house again—even in L.A.—made possible by the company's relocation bonus package. In his new tax bracket the write-off would surely be necessary. But Los Angeles seemed so much larger a city than Chicago, open and endless, and he did not like the unvarying brightness, the raw newness of the landscape, the alien feel of it. There was an unsettling within him, inchoate, indefinable, as if his life were edging slightly off center, as if he were losing his firm grip over some primary domain of his own interior landscape.

The house in the San Fernando Valley was a zone of comfort; privacy was possible in this vast, flat, anonymous plain of sameness, these enclaves of three-bedroom homes plus swimming pool plus barbecue, each enclave boasting its own shopping mall and each with its wide main streets where traffic flowed swiftly past huge supermarkets and Taco Bells and Burger Kings. But still he watched Carolyn closely, in nebulous anxiety that the vibrations he felt from this bizarre city would change her.

She immediately found a job—the job she currently held—so excited that she would not hear his protests that she faced a forty-minute, rush-hour commute to Glassell Park. When would it ever end, he thought in disgust, this irrational fixation women had about jobs where they did not have to type.

Paul Blake locked his house and walked into his garage, dark suit coat over his arm, and climbed into his Buick for the drive downtown.

On balance, he reflected, the change in Carolyn's hours and the acceptance of the promotion without his consent were mere ripples on the surface of his marriage, but he must be careful. As the saying went, a bird must be held lightly, not tightly. But, he added grimly, not too lightly.

She had surprised him. Still she was capable of surprising him. He had searched those green eyes for eight years trying to see and understand how to touch a depth of feeling—perhaps passion—that he had always sensed was just beyond his view, closed off from him, a privacy that did not involve him. Squeezing his eyes shut for an instant, he retreated from the glimpse of emptiness his life would be without her—that lurking depth of fear that was always in him, even after many untroubled years of marriage. He pulled out of his driveway in a screech of tires.

❧ 8 ❧

Carolyn opened the drapes to see Val Hunter lying at the edge of the pool on a dark blue inflated plastic raft, a bright green raft beside her. She had been swimming; her hair and T-shirt and shorts were dark with wetness. Carolyn slid the glass door back and stepped from the cool dimness of her house into a Valley afternoon that gripped her in its hot dry fist and blinded her with its brightness; as she walked from the shadow of the house into the sun her bare skin felt blistered.

Val sat up, greeted her with a grin and a wave. "What could be safer than floating on a raft? Neal and I use these at the ocean." She gestured. "The green one's yours, Carrie. Good choice of bikini—green's your primary color."

"You of all people I definitely consider a color expert." She was pleased by the odd compliment but embarrassed by the pallor of her skin in comparison with Val Hunter's burnished tan. She thought of Paul's opinion of her bikini and asked mischievously, "Do you think my suit is frivolous?"

Val was carrying the green raft to the shallow end of the pool. She cast a puzzled glance over her shoulder. "A bathing suit should be serious?"

Smiling, Carolyn descended the three steps at the pool's shallow end. Waist deep, she splashed water over her arms and chest, shuddering at the cold unpleasantness on her sun-heated skin. As her body grew more acclimated she waded around in unwelcoming foreignness, feeling the water pull on her legs, dragging her steps.

"We need to be careful today," Val said, eyeing her. "You don't have a trace of tan. We'll stay in the shade."

"That's the deep end," Carolyn objected.

"Don't worry, you'll be perfectly safe. I guarantee it." Val waded over to her, steering the green raft. "Go back up the pool steps. I'll hold the raft, you slide on."

The raft was solid support, the front section tilted to form a pillow. "Good," Carolyn said with a sigh of relief. She paddled carefully, then more bravely.

Val climbed out, tossed in her raft, dove in after it, hoisted herself onto it, and paddled over to Carolyn, who was laughing delightedly as her own raft bucked in the turbulence Val had created.

"Sold a painting today," Val said. "Second one this month."

"That's wonderful. Congratulations. Do you do pretty well with your work?"

Val laughed. "Not even close. I belong to the great common denominator of artists—few of us in any field ever make much money. I'm always surprised at what sells, though. I never offer Susan anything I don't think is good, but very often what I consider my best work sits for months."

"Who's Susan?"

"My agent. And friend. She has part interest in a gallery just off the beach in Venice. She comes from money; she can afford to indulge her tastes—fortunately for me. She shows women artists exclusively, which hurts her business and her prices. Men do rule the world of art, and the majority of them ignore the artistic vision of women. They give validity only to masculine experience."

She inspected Carolyn's shoulders. "You've already got a pink flush." She seized Carolyn's raft and with her free hand paddled vigorously into the shaded end of the pool. The hand remained on Carolyn's raft. "Okay? I've got you."

"Fine. I feel perfectly safe."

They drifted into a wall; with a casual kick of a foot Val propelled them away. "Two years ago, Carrie, I had to borrow money from a friend to take Neal to Atlanta for the cremation services for his father. It was one of the low points in my life. Richard's child support had been erratic, to put it kindly, but at least it did come once in a while. I'd had lots of jobs of course, all of them low paying—there aren't many opportunities for a woman trained only in the fine arts." Holding Carolyn's raft firmly, she pillowed her head on one arm. "But Richard left insurance. Amazingly enough. Two policies, both small, but I've managed to keep the money intact. I'm one of the few people besides the rich that high interest rates have helped. It's not easy, not by a long shot, but I'm damn lucky. The interest pays the rent, a few other expenses. Unless there's a catastrophe the money'll be there for Neal when he's ready for college. I don't live in terror like I did before. Ever been poor?"

"Not really. My father left when I was nine and we had to move to an apartment, but we weren't really poor . . . But Paul was. He never talks about it."

Val nodded. "A child can feel so ashamed. Let me tell you, when you have no money you fear everything. Every little rattle in the car makes your heart stop—you can't survive in this town without a car. I'm happy I have Neal, but a child is an obligation like no other. Just when you think you can finally buy him a decent pair of pants or take him out for a meal, electricity goes up or some appliance breaks."

She sighed. "There were times I'd pray to sell a painting—I didn't know how long I could put food on the table. Money you can count on, even just a little, can make such an incredible difference . . ."

Intently listening, Carolyn tried to imagine herself alone, with a child.

Val said, "I'm starting to sell; it's beginning. We're going celebrating tonight. Neal's favorite place is the Sizzler." She closed her eyes. "It's been more than a month since the last time . . . I can already taste my steak . . ."

Carolyn was silent, watching Val's contented face, thinking that two nights ago she and Paul had gone to a Ventura Boulevard restaurant with prices high enough to buy ten dinners at a Sizzler.

Carefully, she adjusted herself on the raft, pillowing her head in her arms, comfortable in the silence that had fallen. Drowsy, smelling the heat of this day and drinking in the fragrance of the cool water, listening to the slap of water on the side of the pool and the shaking of the heavy palm fronds above her in the light breeze and the faint distant drone of an aircraft, she studied through half-open eyes the hand that lay close to her in both protection and repose. A big hand, and well-shaped. A hand that was somehow graceful, with fingers slightly tapered, the tips blunt, the fingernails large, square, serviceably pared, with dark traces of paint trapped in the cuticles. Tanned hands, strong and capable, but soft: she could see the plump cushioned pads on the underside of the fingers. She could imagine a slender paintbrush dwarfed by this hand, held with delicate grace in this hand . . .

Val groaned and opened her eyes. "God it's peaceful, but I know it's time to go."

She paddled vigorously to the steps at the shallow end, Carolyn in tow, slid off her own raft, and held Carolyn's while she climbed off.

"I really enjoyed it, Val. I'm sure you have a few minutes more. Let me get you something to drink before you leave. Come in."

"Carrie, my clothes are wet."

"You're fine," she said firmly.

Later she put Val's drink glass in the dishwasher and left her own out on the sink as she always did. That night she explained that she had bought the rafts to float in the pool after she got home from work. For as long as possible she wanted Val Hunter to be exclusively hers, beyond any criticism or judgment of Paul's.

"One raft would have been enough," he complained. "Didn't they have better colors? They're cheap-looking." He picked up a library book from the top of the Plexiglas bookcase. "What's with these?"

She had gone to the library after Val left. She said casually, "They're about art. As you pointed out the other day, I don't know the first thing about it. I decided to find out."

His eyes drifted over her, returned to the bookcase. "They're all banged up and dirty. Why don't you buy some new ones at the bookstore? They'd look good on the coffee table."

Relieved, she said, "Honey, that's a waste of money till I know what kind of books to get."

"Just trying to keep you happy, Princess. What's for dinner?"

७ 9 ल

For the next two days Carolyn was delayed in leaving her office, only half an hour, but arrived home each afternoon to look with keen disappointment at the shimmering surface of her empty pool. She could not call—did Val even have a phone?—nor could she go knocking on her door; their relationship lacked sufficient weight.

On Thursday she arrived home at her usual hour; again the pool was deserted. Changing into shorts and a blouse, she reflected dismally that of course she was inconsequential in Val Hunter's life; how could she be anything else? Val Hunter was independent—look at how she dressed, took care of herself. Val's life was totally unlike her own. From the stereo Billy Joel rocked into "Uptown Girl" as she restlessly paced the living room.

There was a tapping at the front door, followed by the doorbell chime. She switched off the stereo and then peered through the peephole. With sharp gladness she saw it was Val.

"Missed you the last two days, Carrie. Would have been here earlier, I was out sketching today, I don't know what was wrong with the Ventura Freeway, never did see any accident. Thank God I drive a Volks or I'd be out there still, waving a towel over my radiator." After a brief survey of Carolyn's white terrycloth shorts and light cotton blouse, Val looked down at her own clothes: paint-smeared jeans and a sleeveless V-neck gray T-shirt. "Sorry, I look like hell."

Carolyn was looking at her admiringly. "You look terrific. Like a working artist. Come in, let me get you something to drink. You look hot and tired. And thirsty."

"No, I—well, just for a minute. But not in the living room—I don't want to smear ochre over your blue carpet."

Carolyn led her into the kitchen. "I'd be grateful if you'd do that to the sofa."

Val leaned against the sink and drained a glass of ice water, refilled it from the tap. "Why did you buy that sofa if you dislike it so?"

"Paul thinks it's elegant and I suppose it is. I thought I could get used to it. I don't think he really likes it much either, but we won't do anything till we get another house. A bigger and better house," she added with more than a trace of sarcasm.

"With a bigger and better pool for you not to swim in." Grinning, Val poured her remaining water into the sink and rinsed the glass. "Why don't you come over today? To see some of my work?"

She followed Val down a narrow concrete path, moss growing between its wide cracks, to the small house of yellow stucco overhung by two date trees and surrounded by patches of thick ivy and many broad-leaved plants encroached upon by weeds. Ferns crowded the shade along the fence that divided this house from Carolyn's backyard. The whine of insects permeated the quiet. A few white butterflies darted among sparse marigolds poking their heads out of the weeds that reached into the path and brushed at Carolyn's ankles as she picked her way along, careful of her footing in her wedge-heeled sandals.

"It's very private back here," Carolyn offered.

"I've learned why privacy is so prized by the rich. Most of us in our entire lives never learn what true privacy is—never experience it." Val opened the unlocked door of her house.

The living room would fit into less than half of hers, Carolyn estimated. It smelled of paint and turpentine, and was dominated by two huge abstract paintings of red and green hues covering virtually the entire expanse of two walls. A bay window with useless gauze curtains tied to its sides allowed dappled light to wash the room. Beside the window, on a battered and paint-smeared table, was a large canvas propped against a box, flanked by a chaotic jumble of paint tubes, brushes soaking in glass containers, cans of oils, sketch pads, pencils, and other paraphernalia Carolyn could not identify. The room was furnished with a worn tweed sofa not much larger than a loveseat, an equally worn armchair with a minute wooden footstool, a scarred bookcase overflowing with paperbacks and topped by a small television set, a card table covered by a vivid red print cloth and apparently serving as a dining room table. The only source of artificial light appeared to be a pole lamp in a corner, its metal shades aimed downward at the armchair. Sketch pads and sections of the *Los Angeles Times* were stacked on a coffee table which was a simple square of pale, flimsy wood.

"There's not much to see," Val said. "It's pretty small, especially the kitchen—which could be even smaller, as far as I'm concerned. Look around if you like."

Carolyn glanced into a room the size of her own walk-in closet, its flooring buckled linoleum, and crammed with a small refrigerator and stove and sink, a few cupboards.

The bathroom was tinier, with a shower and no bathtub. Bright blue shag covered the floor. Two thin, gaily striped towels hung from metal rings.

"Neal has the big bedroom," Val said with a chuckle. "I don't care where I sleep. I think it's important for a youngster to have privacy, don't you?"

"It was important to me when I was growing up."

Neal's room contained a single twin bed and a dresser, a small desk of gray metal which looked freshly painted. Sports posters and banners festooned the walls. The room was immaculate, almost austere in its neatness.

"He'd kill me if he knew I was showing anyone his inner sanctum." There was warmth in Val's husky voice. "I create such havoc wherever I go; I think he's overcompensated by being a neat freak. This is my room, Carrie. It wasn't meant to be a bedroom, but it's good enough."

The narrow room, which was surely meant to be a closet or for storage, was filled entirely by a twin bed and a two-drawer nightstand with a gooseneck lamp, and by canvases that sat on the floor along the walls.

Carolyn walked back into the living room with Val and stood beside the worktable. "I like your house." Seeing Val's amused smile she protested, "I really do. It has a nice feeling, a warmth. A . . . comfort. A casualness."

"Casual we are," Val said cheerfully. "I'll show you the work I have here, which isn't much. Mostly work that's drying or that doesn't fit in with what Susan's showing right now." Carefully she took the canvas leaning against the box on the table and placed it along the wall.

"Can you tell me what that one's going to be?" Carolyn eyed faint jagged lines vaguely suggesting intricacy, the tones sand colored.

"It's one of a series of figurative paintings I'm doing right now. Neal and I took a trip into the Mojave and found just wonderful things. This one's a fascinating plant, it looks like green-red mist on the desert sand. The tiny flowers and fine tracery of stems make me think of the human body with its connections of veins and arteries and blood vessels—the sand holding it could be human skin. I'm laying film over film—I'm looking for an opalescent glowing effect and I want the brush strokes to show. It's still taking shape in my head and very interesting to think about. I can't do anything more till it dries."

"I see," Carolyn said. Until this moment she had thought it possible that Paul was right—Val Hunter might be a dilettante. She said, "I thought all painters used an easel."

"Never had one. A box on a table works perfectly well as long as it holds the canvas still and you have the best light on your work. I get good strong morning light through this window—it's the best kind. Besides, any extra money, there are always so many other things more important . . . Neal's been wanting to go to day camp every year and I've never had the money till now." She shrugged. "I've been painting this way for years. He's a boy only once."

Carolyn surveyed the jumble of supplies on the table. "Looking at a painting, you never imagine all the things an artist has to buy. Canvas, paint, brushes, a palette—"

"No palette," Val interrupted. "This is my version." She reached to the end of the table under paint-stained cloths and unerringly fished out a piece of plate glass with beveled edges, the underside painted white. "I just scrape it off when I'm finished. It works beautifully, I'd never have any other kind. And except for watercolors I buy the basic ingredients and make my own paints. I really prefer to now. But there are a thousand other things you always need. I use a lot of sketch pads and good pencils; I do a lot of sketches to make color notes. And frames and turpentine and varnish. I sometimes use a palette knife— that means quantities of paint that would put a house painter to shame." Carolyn picked up several tubes of color and examined them curiously.

"I'm still learning things about color," Val said. "Different approaches, techniques, ways of emphasis. To this day, as well as I've learned the discipline of preparation and concentrating fully on a concept, sometimes an entirely new idea takes over and I have to begin all over again. And starting over costs money and time. Quality materials are so very expensive . . . not like when I was first learning and could afford to experiment with student-quality paint and cardboard for canvas."

"I had absolutely no idea," Carolyn murmured, running her fingertips over the soft pliant bristles of several paintbrushes.

"A few years ago was the worst, when inflation was so bad. Prices just skyrocketed. I didn't have Susan's gallery then and I was scrounging to have my work shown anywhere—laundromats, anywhere. For a while I even had to stop working till there was a little money again. . . . Either that or sell my body for paint, which believe me was a temptation. Imagine me down on Hollywood Boulevard—a six-foot hooker."

Val lifted a large canvas that leaned against a wall facing into the light and propped it against the box. "This is another in the series I'm doing. It's finished."

Carolyn felt enmeshed in the painting, as if she were caught in the multitude of tiny shapes tinged with pink and green against a riotous background of wiry dark green. The detail of the painting was dense, the images covering the canvas from edge to edge without break.

"Manzanita," Val said, frowning at the painting, chin between a finger and thumb. "This particular kind grows along the California coast."

Carolyn said faintly, "I feel like I've fallen into the bush." She was frustrated by her inability to articulate her perceptions.

"You do? That's wonderful." Val looked genuinely pleased. "Susan likes this entire series and this one in particular. She says it's like a Pollock, and I guess it does have that barbed-wire effect."

Swiftly, Val removed the canvas and replaced it against the wall. Her upper arms in the sleeveless T-shirt were lighter tan and large, the muscles firm and smoothly working as she pulled canvases away from the wall. "Here it is. This one's almost finished."

Carolyn blinked at the feast of color—red, yellow, blue, and white hues and tones. "It looks so . . . joyful," she managed to say, again angry with her inadequacy, her eyes drawn to the rich yellows and blues, following and exploring the color patterns.

"I like how you react to my work," Val said immediately. "This is a fusion of desert flowers. It was very hard to do. To me the desert has always been like a starving entity that goes on an incredible binge in the spring, as if to compensate all at once. I wanted to show the profusion, the sheer extravagance."

"Warm," Carolyn murmured, "the painting is warm."

"Thank you. That's what I was hoping to achieve with the reds and yellows. But balance was such a serious problem with so many color tones . . . Color is energy; colors act and react with one another. There were more decisions than usual about composition. I do love the red flowers," Val said, smiling and indicating a section with blossoms shaded rose to reddish purple, the stamens long and white and tipped with scarlet, the branches profligate. "It's called a fairy duster. Remarkable, isn't it? And this one with the brilliant leaves and inconspicuous flowers is Indian paintbrush."

"Did you . . . do you paint from memory?" She wondered if the question was foolish, if any question she might ask would be foolish.

Val hesitated, "Well, when my work isn't representational, actual color isn't relevant—it's just one of the many elements you synthesize in creating a painting. I usually sketch and make color notes and then let things percolate in my head till it feels right to begin. But for this series I took pictures. I have a terrible camera but I matched my snapshots with high-quality photos in books about desert flowers. That's how I learned their names. I want to do more of these paintings, focusing on light and shadow. I'll need to look very closely at the actual flower for those, too."

She pointed again. "This flower's called blue sage. This one's baby blue eyes. Aren't the names marvelous? The white with the bluish band down each petal is a desert lily. See the ruffle-edged leaves? And this lovely yellow is a woolly marigold. And this is desert sienna."

"It's wonderful. It's a wonderful, wonderful painting." She could think of nothing more to say.

"Thank you. It does need more work but it's almost there. The yellows come forward too much, the blues need to be brought up a bit. Now I'll show you a real change of pace—from an artist who ordinarily loves bright color." Val came out of her tiny makeshift bedroom with a painting perhaps five feet long and three feet high, and propped it against the box.

A succession of gray tones lay across the canvas, beginning at the top with deep gray which was not opaque but seemed somehow impenetrable, and dissolving into successive bands of lighter grays which became a pearl mist that ended abruptly at bold gray-black brush strokes of solid squarish shapes. Thin needles of color knifed down through the gray bands, into the gray-black, the needles of silver, blue, blue-purple.

Carolyn stepped closer to the painting, needing to shut out her surroundings, and in the stifling heat of Val's house rubbed a sudden chill from her bare arms. "I don't know the first thing about art," she finally said. "All I can tell you is I truly love this."

"What is there about it that touches you? Can you tell me?"

"I don't know. . . ." Looking at the painting, searching for words, Carolyn answered slowly, "The peaceful quality . . . the way the grays combine. It makes me feel mellow. Like I do on rainy days."

Val's smile was intense with pleasure. "You do know about art. Rain—our rain, Los Angeles rain—was exactly what I was trying to convey. The distinctive way it rains here, how it doesn't cloud up but grays over, darker and darker, then lightens and rains."

She indicated the gray-black shapes at the bottom of the painting. "This is the horizon line with the suggestion of our endless, mostly flat city. Susan likes this one but won't take it, it's too much of a departure to hang with my other work." Val chuckled. "She's hoping I haven't gone into what she calls a gray, uncommercial phase. She's not enthusiastic about a series of paintings I'm working on at the beach house either, but—"

"Beach house?"

"Her parents have a small place in Malibu. In exchange for checking things out every week while they're in Europe, Neal gets to play volleyball on the beach and I get to work on a series of ocean paintings."

"Seascapes? How wonderful."

"No, not seascapes," Val said with a grin. "Sorry to disappoint you. Better talents than mine have tried to capture the ocean. I don't think anyone has—at least not enough of it. I'm painting the *effects* of ocean—surfaces of rocks, the scouring of high tide, things like that."

Carolyn was staring at the painting. She asked impulsively, "How much do you charge for your work?"

"It's negotiable, like all art. Whatever the traffic will bear and depending on Susan's opinion, and the size of the canvas. Most of my work is fairly good size and Susan asks in the four- to six-hundred-dollar range, before gallery commission."

Carolyn closed her eyes for a moment. She said recklessly, "I want this one. I want to buy it. I love it. I want to own it."

"It's yours then. But I won't sell it to you."

"What? I want to buy it. You know I can afford it; you can't just give your work away—"

"Of course I can. I can do anything I want with my work. And I refuse to be any more in debt to you than I already am. I've been using your pool for months. Your air conditioner is a lifesaver, it's making it possible for me to work better and longer."

Carolyn sighed. This was crazy. "Anything I've given you isn't that much and isn't important to me at all."

She continued to argue, but Val parried her points with good-humored grins and shakes of her head. "All right," Carolyn conceded. "Can you tell me a good place to have it framed?"

"I'll do that—don't argue. It doesn't cost much. I always make my own frames. It's not difficult and I enjoy it. Besides, who better than the artist knows how it should be framed?"

Carolyn asked in resignation, "When can I have it?"

"It's finished drying but needs to be varnished. Let's say Monday."

Val glanced at her watch and was startled. "I haven't even thought about dinner. And Neal's due home. I want you to meet Neal. I think you two would like each other."

Carolyn was pleased, as if she had passed an important test. But she hesitated. How would she explain this to Paul? Any of this? "Of course," she said. "Soon."

"How about some evening?"

"Sure." She wanted to flee, to sort through what she had done before Paul came home. She changed the subject, not wanting Val to pin her down before she had time to think. "I'll have the painting Monday for sure?"

"I'll varnish it in the morning when the light's good. I see no problem. . . . Yes, Monday."

"Good." She edged toward the door. "I'll see you tomorrow in the pool?"

Val smiled at her. "Monday. Neal and I are going to the beach house, then backpacking in the San Bernardino mountains."

≫ 10 ≪

Val pulled a sketch pad out of the pile on the coffee table, the same pad she had used for her first penciled impression of Carolyn Blake. The latest drawing was of Carolyn on the white sofa in a silk shirtwaist dress, her feet drawn up under her, her head tilted slightly to the left in what Val knew to be unconscious habit when Carolyn was listening. A hand rested on a knee, and Val spent some time on the tapering fingers and the thumb that was in interesting apposition, a wide angle out from the fingers. She filled in details of the dress, the folds of soft silk, her pencil straying back up to the throat, lightly sculpting and accentuating the curve.

She turned the page, and in a few strokes Carolyn stood with her feet close together, arms crossed, her hands clasping the inside of her arms; as she had stood in this room only a few minutes ago looking at paintings. Several lines completed the shorts Carolyn wore, but Val lingered over the legs, the long curves, the slenderness of them.

Again she turned the page. In close-up she emphasized delicate bone structure, the rounding at the end of the nose and at the center of the chin, the fine breadth of forehead. She feathered in an irregular hairline at the temples, a suggestion of eyelashes not readily apparent because of their blondeness.

She held the sketch at arm's length, appraising not her work but the subject. Carolyn Blake was by no means conventionally pretty, yet she was exquisite.

With tender strokes she finished the soft lines of the throat. The sketch was now asymmetrical on the page but still her pencil descended. Under her hand slender shoulders and then small breasts took shape, shadowed, suggested by a top piece of the bikini, cleavage clearly visible.

The image of Alix filled Val's mind, and Val's pencil stilled.

—Sometimes when a person wants another for so long, the want can go away. And finally the want of you has gone, Val. I'll always love you but I don't have to have you anymore. You know it, how I wanted you. And I know you could have loved me. Even with Bette and my other lovers, knowing you could love me kept me hoping, kept me tied to you. You never allowed yourself to love me.

—I do love you, Alix. I never wanted . . . more.

—You did. The year we lived together we never went to bed but there was everything else. How you touched me, how you looked at me.

—What was real for you was a phase for me. Experimentation.

—I see you better than anyone in your life, Val Hunter. Better than both your husbands, your parents, anyone. I know how you think, I know your self-control. You make something not exist by denying that it does. One day you'll admit what you want—to yourself, if to no one else.

—I'll admit nothing. All the choices I've made, even if they turned out wrong, seemed best for me. I have a choice about everything. Look at me, Alix. I'm independent. Free.

—Free? You've let everyone else dictate how you've lived. And when you finally couldn't stand it anymore you withdrew completely. Soon you'll be totally consumed by your art because there isn't anything else. Maybe you'll even devour your son.

It had been six months since she last heard from Alix. "Why Houston?" she had asked her.

"Because Helen came out to her parents and they want nothing to do with her. She wants to be with friends in Houston. There's a large gay community there. And because I need to get away from you—to finally break the tie."

She would hear from Alix, of course. They had been supreme presences in each other's lives since the year they lived together. Alix—tiny, blonde, desired by men who expired like moths against her brilliant cold flame—was right. Val knew Alix loved her, and the depth and sexuality of that love. After Alix had turned in anger from her to other women she had never taken any of Alix's lovers seriously, including the current Helen. Val had basked in Alix's love; she missed it. If a man could ever love her like that . . . What Alix perceived in her and was attracted to was the androgyny all good artists must possess, nothing more . . . It was the reason for her own attraction to Alix.

That Helen's parents had disowned Helen was additional proof, if more was needed, that a lesbian lifestyle was a complication anyone should avoid who had any choice in the matter. She certainly had a choice. Bad enough to lack anything resembling a fashionable female body let alone the height and size and physical strength and deep voice and aggressive personality to go with it. Bad enough that because most people assumed she was a lesbian she had to wear her two failed marriages and her production of a son like a badge. Why on earth should she seek further ostracism?

Neal came in. She closed the sketch pad, slid it in among the stack on the coffee table, and leaned forward for his hug. She followed him into the kitchen, listening to his chatter with one level of consciousness, thinking that she should have Carolyn Blake come over soon. Neal would love Carolyn.

❧ 11 ❧

Carolyn walked down the path beside Val Hunter's house, her thoughts a confused jumble. How would she handle this with Paul? Not only was it impossible to maintain the secrecy of her friendship with Val, but how would she explain the painting? She regretted her impulsive act only in the moment before she remembered the gray peace of the painting and her feeling as she stood before it in the heat of Val Hunter's house. No, she wanted that painting to hang in her house. She was lucky to have a chance to buy it—and she *would* buy it, no matter what Val said—and she was lucky to be able to afford it. But how to handle this with Paul?

"Why Carolyn, hello! What a surprise to see you over here!"

"Hello," she said tightly to Dorothy Robinson, annoyed at being startled, that her thought process had been interrupted.

"You've been visiting Mrs. Hunter, how lovely. She and her boy are so nice. Don't you think so?" She took a step closer to Carolyn, the point of her sharp nose quivering like the antenna of an insect. "Do you know them well?"

"No, not well." Carolyn edged away from her, backing down the path. "I've got to run. Paul will be home soon—"

"You must come over, Carolyn, you and Paul. You will, won't you?"

"Of course, Dorothy, but with each of us working different hours, well, you know . . ." Impatient and exasperated, she finally made her escape.

"I've bought a painting from Val Hunter." She had decided that the best approach was direct—like the clean simplicity of a Val Hunter dive—but during the conviviality of dinner time.

He was gnawing on a chicken wing, watching Peter Jennings report on the Reverend Jesse Jackson's visit to Cuba. He looked away from the TV screen and toward her, blankly. "You did what?"

"I bought a painting. From Mrs. Hunter. Next door."

"The Amazon? You don't even know her."

"We've talked a few times," she said as casually as she could.

Dabbing at his lips with a napkin, he studied her. "Oh? You've never mentioned it."

She shrugged to convey that she had not considered it important.

"It seems odd that you didn't mention it. Talking to an Amazon who paints strikes me as unusual enough to be worth mentioning. Now I see the reason for the art books. I don't see why you wouldn't tell me."

She was irked as much by his characterization of Val as by his inquisition. "Do you tell me everything that goes on during your day? You hardly mention anything at all. You're never interested in my job—"

"Why did you buy this painting? An act of charity?"

Anger flared. "She's very good. She's a wonderful artist. Her work is displayed in a gallery."

"Oh?" He looked taken aback. "Which one?"

How could she have been so stupid? She hadn't thought to ask. "Venice, I don't know where."

"Venice," he repeated. "Where all the loony tunes roller-skate."

She said crossly, "Does she have to hang in the Metropolitan? I like her work. Isn't that good enough?"

"How much was it?"

Swiftly she gauged her husband. Val had said: Whatever the traffic will bear. "Four hundred," she said.

"Four *hundred?* Carolyn! You might have consulted me!" He stared at her.

"Oh, Paul." She did not feign her disgust. "I spend almost that much on each of those dresses you insist I wear to your office parties."

"That's different. This is something for the house. What if I don't like it?"

"I don't think you'll mind it. It's a study of rain—really quite unobtrusive. It'll fit in very nicely in the living room."

He said sarcastically, "So you've even decided where it should hang."

"Honey," she said in her most conciliatory voice, "let's not fight. If you don't like it we can hang it in the garage." *Not very damn likely,* she thought.

"Four hundred. For an amateur she's pretty proud of her work."

Anger flared again. "She is *not* an amateur. I told you her work is displayed in a gallery. She sells her work. I sell my work. You sell your work. Are we amateurs?"

"I don't know anything about this so-called gallery and neither do you. Maybe she's just giving you a line. And if she sells her work only to you, she's an amateur."

"You're so quick to sneer and judge things—"

"I'm not prejudging anything," he said in a tone edged with ice. "Not till I see this painting you went ahead and bought without even a thought for my opinion. It must be these new hours of yours—you've been testy and strange ever since you've been on them."

His voice softened. "Why don't you invite Mrs. Hunter over, maybe for dinner? If you're that impressed with her, I'd like to meet her."

Nonplussed by this unexpected tack she blurted, "I don't think you'd care for her."

"Now you're the one who's prejudging."

"She doesn't seem your kind of person, that's all," she said lamely, feeling suddenly that she had lost control. "There's her son too, he's only ten—"

"Invite him too. Wednesday's the Fourth of July—invite them over, we'll barbecue. The kid'll love the pool. Okay?"

"I'll ask her," she said reluctantly.

The next day during her lunch hour she drew four hundred dollars from their bank account, and back at her office consulted the Valley yellow pages. After work she drove out along Laurel Canyon to an art supply store. Afterward she stopped again at the library and checked out several more books. She had the remainder of this afternoon and all weekend to read.

On Monday she changed into shorts and a blouse and walked out to the pool to greet Val. "So how was backpacking?"

"Hot as hell. But great." Val had emerged from the pool and was toweling her hair. "How was your weekend?"

"Boring," Carolyn admitted after a moment of reflection. "Will you help me with some packages in the car? Then can I come over and get my painting?"

As she looked into the trunk of Carolyn's car Val said accusingly, "What's all this?"

"A gift. If you can give me a gift I can give you a gift."

"No. You can't do this."

"Of course I can. I can do anything I want." Carolyn chuckled, enjoying herself. "I'll take these packages if you carry the easel."

Carolyn lowered her packages to the work table in Val's house, staring at the painting propped against the box, framed in a paper-thin band of silver. "It's perfect. I love it more now than when I first saw it."

"I think the framing is right, it extends the painting to the edge. And the varnishing went well—only took one coat."

"Is that unusual?"

"No, just lucky. Often there's a flat spot or some matte areas and you have to give it another coat." Val was opening a package. "Holy Christmas morning," she said softly, "will you look at all this. Sable brushes." She picked one up, stroked the bristles with sensual delicacy.

"The woman at Carter Sexton said that painters always need brushes, and sable is best. I told her you made your own colors; she said to get basic colors and lots of white, dry pigments and linseed oil. So everything here is her suggestion—the watercolors and watercolor paper, it's their best. And the roll of linen canvas."

"Even a carrying case." Val's voice was a purr of pleasure. She had unlatched the wooden case filled with tubes of watercolor. "I've always needed a decent case to carry supplies when I paint somewhere besides here."

Carolyn watched, smiling, as Val touched the tubes of paint with caressing fingertips. Impulsively she hugged Val, and was surprised by the softness of her body; she had expected muscular solidity. "Can you come over for a few minutes and help me hang my painting?" She knew exactly where it would go—across from where she usually sat on the sofa, so that she could glance up and see it.

"It's interesting," Paul said.

Carolyn clearly understood that he disliked the painting. "I think so too," she said relentlessly. "I think it's wonderful, I've never seen a painting I like so much."

"That's going a little overboard, don't you think? I don't know that it looks best in the living room—"

"I definitely do. I love it, Paul," she stated, defying him to deny her the pleasure she felt in this painting. "I *love* it."

He nodded. "I'm starved."

As she served their dinner she tried to recall another time she had successfully asserted herself on any issue of importance during their marriage. She could not remember any. She could not remember trying before.

At dinner, as they watched Peter Jennings report on the Reagan administration's unhappiness with the Reverend Jackson's activities in Cuba, he said, "Tell me, are all Mrs. Hunter's paintings like that one?"

She replied carefully, "What do you mean, 'like that one'?"

"Modern." He grinned, trimmed a piece of lamb neatly from the bone. "Does she paint navels in the middle of foreheads?"

She said coldly, "Is that your sole understanding of modern art?"

"Come on, Princess. I was just trying to be funny."

She knew better; she knew he had not really accepted the painting in the living room and this was an indirect attack on it.

"Forgive my levity," he said sarcastically. "I should have realized you're an art critic now that you've read a few books."

She remembered the pride she felt during the past weekend when she looked at examples of cubistic art in her books and suddenly understood why the concept had been so daring and exciting—that it had led the entire revolution into modern art because artists for the first time had looked at an object as it would appear from different angles, in different places, at different times. She said, "I'm only glad I don't have your sneering ignorance."

He contemplated her.

She had always disliked this aspect of him, this feeling of being under the microscope of his gaze in cold, evaluating analysis, as if he had laid his emotions aside like a scientist. "I've never closed my mind to anything," he finally said, his voice uninflected. "Did you invite her for the Fourth?"

She had decided that she would wait, and if he did not mention it again . . . "I'll ask her tomorrow."

She lay on her raft next to Val in peaceful, quiet companionship. She had applied suntan lotion so that she could remain in the sun longer.

"I've been reading about different forms of art," she said. "I know expressionist art comes out of emotion and it's individual and personal art—but from what I've seen, your work isn't abstract. Yet you say it's expressionist."

"I love artists like Rothko who work with pure color and elemental shapes. And sometimes I use distortion to show greater intensity of feeling. But often my work is figurative, even representational, like the desert scenes you saw the other day. But it still comes out of my emotion. . . . For example, I might choose to paint the bark of a tree red."

"Why?" As Val chuckled she said, "I'm sorry to be so dumb."

"You're not being dumb. It's a good question, the kind Neal asks. Makes me check my premises. I remember reading somewhere that the only ones who can really force us to reevaluate our lives and perceptions are children and artists. Carrie, let's say the tree I'm painting is dying against a sunset sky. It's sunset for the old tree too, the end for it, just like the end of a day for us, with a glorious red that actually means death."

"I see," Carolyn murmured, thinking that she truly did see.

Val chuckled again. "If you ever wanted to see people skewered for dumb questions you should have been in my art class in New York.

You could ask Kolvinsky anything, but if he thought your question was stupid he just wouldn't answer."

Carolyn laughed. "Did he ever refuse to answer you?"

"Frequently, the old bastard." She laughed along with Carolyn. "Kolvinsky taught me, though. Opened my eyes like never before to color and light. I see the unique colors of the California landscape thanks to him . . ." She trailed off. "Died three years ago. I'll never forget him." In soft reminiscence she continued, "Tiny man, spiky gray hair like nails in his head. Always wore a clean white shirt, sleeves rolled up to his elbows, plaid ties with stains—God knows what they were. Terrible old baggy pants, looked like he'd stolen them from a bum. Always wore the same brown shoes, paint stains all over the toes. Always at me to sleep with him, never gave up. I guess he was fascinated with the idea of bedding a woman a foot taller than he was. The old bastard," she repeated, chuckling in affectionate memory. "The only thing he was really wrong about was where you could work. He insisted a painter had to be in New York or Paris."

"Did your parents send you to art school?" She realized she knew virtually nothing about Val's background.

"Just the year in New York. Otherwise I've pretty much scratched for myself. Dad was a wildcatter—about as perilous as professional gambling. It was feast or famine in my family. Mostly feast when I was growing up and mostly feast for my brother Charlie—he's six years older and has a degree, a mining engineer. Takes after Dad, been all over the world, in Brazil since April. Anyway, when I was old enough it was famine time again. Dad did manage to pay for the year in New York."

"What about your mother?"

Val sighed. "She's still in Connecticut. Lives with two spinster relatives. Dad retired five years ago on his Social Security and military pension. Came out here to be with Neal and me. She wouldn't come." She sighed again. "I don't know if it was all those years of being on the edge with Dad, but she's a born-again Christian now and thinks Dad and I are heathens and I'm a tool of the devil because I'm bringing up Neal without God . . . you get the picture. I've always embarrassed her. My height was something she couldn't fix—you know, like giving someone a nose job. And she hated the whole idea of me becoming an artist." Val's smile was wry. "All things considered, I'm glad Mother's in Connecticut. Mother thinks modern art is mostly fraudulent and quite possibly pornographic."

Carolyn was looking at her sympathetically. "That's such a shame. Your own mother so narrow-minded when she should be so proud. I think art is exciting. It is to me . . . I'm learning how to look at it."

"Art *is* exciting, Carrie, not because it's my profession. It tells us who we are and where we are, makes sense of life as life actually is. I think that's why there's so much resistance to it."

Concealing a smile, Carolyn said, "Some people's whole idea of modern art is navels painted in the middle of foreheads."

Val laughed. "It's interesting how strongly some people reject a portrayal of the human body rearranged. It's a gut level reaction—as if their whole sense of identity is threatened."

"Who's your favorite painter, Val?"

"Oh God, I don't know." Val squinted at her in the brilliant sunlight. "I couldn't choose one. Well, maybe Cezanne, he was the first to bring a whole new experience of seeing. . . . And the great colorists—Matisse might be the greatest, but then van Gogh brought the whole spectrum of color to full strength. . . . And Gauguin, his simplification of form and all that emotion . . . Turner, of course. Klee, his theories of color like musical harmonies . . . Marin and Wyeth for watercolors . . . Kandinsky . . . DeKooning, his draftsmanship and subject matter are so incredible. . . . O'Keeffe, Frankenthaler—"

"Enough," Carolyn said, smiling. She closed her eyes and drowsed, sleepy and contented in the sun. When she opened her eyes it was to an expanse of blue and the pool marker a distance from her that read nine feet. "Val," she uttered without thinking.

"Right behind you." Val paddled quickly up to her. "I dozed off."

Carolyn reached to Val's raft, took her hand. "Go ahead and doze off again. I've got you now."

Val's eyes closed. Carolyn lay still and peaceful, drifting on slow currents. Val's big hand was unexpectedly soft, and Carolyn was aware as she dozed of its warm protectiveness, the cushionlike flesh of the fingertips.

When she opened her eyes, Val was looking at her. "What does your husband think of the painting?"

She knew she had hesitated too long in answering. "I like it more than he does." She was relieved by Val's easy smile.

"Art is purely subjective, Carrie. People disagree all the time about all the art forms."

"Paul hasn't had much exposure to art," Carolyn ventured.

Val said lightly, "I hope disagreeing about my painting won't start a war between you."

Val lay with her eyes closed again, trailing Carolyn's hand through the water between them. Her fingers traced the shape of the hand, over the fingers and fingernails, over the wedding ring.

Carolyn said, "Paul wants me to ask you and Neal over the evening of the Fourth. For a barbecue, to swim . . ."

Val did not open her eyes. Her lips turned up in a mischievous quirk. "Oh? Will you be there too?"

The two laughed together. Val said, her eyes amused, "I know all about husbands, Carrie. Neal will enjoy the pool. I'll do what I can to pass inspection."

ꝺ 12 ꝗ

"Has anyone ever told you you're tall?" Paul joked.

"Never." Smiling, Val shook hands with him.

Carolyn was astonished by Val, who wore a white dress—sleeveless simplicity, tied at the waist by a twisted cord of bright colors—and sandals fashioned of several thick strands of hemp. In the V-neck of the dress, which was cut down to her cleavage, hung a medallion of shell-thin squares and rectangles, red and yellow and blue—the primary colors of the spectrum, Carolyn now knew. Her only other ornament was a ring, two intertwined gold wires. Her eyelids were lightly brushed with muted rose eyeshadow. An application of lip gloss heightened the natural color and fullness of her lips. Her dark eyes and bronze skin seemed to glow with an attractiveness generated from vitality and health and strength. Gazing at her, again Carolyn was tantalized by the elusive memory from her childhood.

In crisp white shorts and a yellow polo shirt, Neal Hunter seemed to Carolyn small for ten, with a physical delicacy quite unlike his mother. Shifting the bathing suit he carried to the other hand, he shook hands with Carolyn, then Paul.

Paul looked unusually handsome, Carolyn thought. His hair had been freshly cut and styled, the gray at the temples given fluffed-up prominence from blow-drying. He stood straight and trim, the softness of his midsection concealed by a loose, powder blue jacket-shirt over dark blue khaki pants.

"Val, what are you drinking?" Paul stood in the cool of the living room, his back turned deliberately to the new painting. He had decided that no amount of politeness could persuade him to praise it; he would not mention it.

"Tonic. No more than a splash of vodka, please." Val wondered if her dismay showed. Those ice blue eyes surely mirrored an inner coldness. And that impervious face . . . He was so wrong for Carolyn. But then, she thought wryly, she had seen many unlikely pairings—such as herself with her own two husbands. This instant assessment might be wrong . . . although her first impressions were rarely wrong.

His tone was bantering: "A splash of vodka? Two Excedrin would give you more kick."

She was annoyed; she was always irritated by people who made condescending jokes when others did not care for alcohol. She answered lightly, "One Excedrin is my limit. I'm a real sissy."

Carolyn said, "Let's go into the yard. It's cooled off nicely."

"Go ahead," Paul said. "Neal and I will be right out with the drinks. Won't we, pardner?"

"Yes sir," Neal said.

Neal doesn't like him either, Val thought. Walking into the yard with Carolyn she heard firecrackers begin in the distance, faint concussions, then sharp volleys of sound. From several houses away a dog began frantic barking, immediately echoed by other barks and howls.

"Val, you look very nice," Carolyn said softly.

Val's glance encompassed Carolyn's print skirt and peasant blouse. "You too." She said impishly, "You thought I'd show up in my cutoffs."

Carolyn laughed. "It would've been okay with me."

"I have two dresses for emergency occasions. Both identical. This white one's for casual, the black one's for dressy."

Carolyn laughed again. "What a wonderfully simple approach to life."

"Val," Paul said from behind them, "your vodka and tonic. No more than an eyedropper of vodka—Neal can testify."

He was stabbed by their easy intimacy; Carolyn's laughter, her comfortable gesture of sliding her arm through Val's. He handed Carolyn her drink and set the pitcher of martinis down on the picnic table, then poked the coals of the barbecue as he considered Val Hunter with brief, measuring glances. Almost all women he met looked at him at least once in sexual awareness, but she had not; there was no acknowledgement of his masculinity, not even now when she was boldly appraising him as he walked to a lawn chair, her brown eyes perceptive and impartial, her big strong-looking hands—man-sized hands—dangling casually from the arms of the director's chair that was his, the one he always sat in when he and Carolyn were in the yard. How could so grotesque a woman—a giantess, a freak—be so confident, so poised? It's a cover-up, an act, he told himself without conviction.

There were indefinable but pronounced alarm signals in him. He was unprepared for her. He disliked her intensely.

"Carrie's so proud of your success," Val Hunter told him.

Carrie. She calls her Carrie. "She's very high on you, too. You never know about artists these days—either they're painting soup cans or wrapping ribbon around an island."

Would he like my opinion on modern business practices? Be polite, Val warned herself. *For her sake. Work at it. He looks bright enough, even for an iceberg. He might be willing to learn something.* "Much art today focuses not on the subject but on a statement about the subject. Painting a soup can might be a comment about assembly lines. Or our throw-away society. As for Christo's work—"

"I'm sure there's justification." He would not sit here and be lectured in front of his wife and this woman's kid. "I'm sure the artist feels justified. But I don't think you can really blame people for feeling that a lot of art is just junk. Nobody likes it but a bunch of fag critics. A lot of people can't understand all the fuss over Picasso. Who can relate to a painting that shows an arm over here, a head over there?"

She crossed her legs and smoothed her dress, her eyes drifting away from him. It seemed a dismissal, a disdainful closing out of him. He stared at her legs. They were large but shapely and so heavily tanned that he looked closely to see if she had shaved. She had; there was a tiny drop of blood on one shin. *Probably doesn't unless she has to,* he thought with a surge of venom.

She was smiling at him. "All art seeks its own audience." Her smile disappeared. She shrugged. "Some people's sole understanding of opera is that it's nothing but screeching. Books are written for a certain audience. So is music. Paintings are created for a specific audience, too. As for Picasso, what is there to say? He's a giant."

"*Guernica* is considered the greatest masterpiece of the century," Carolyn interjected, quoting from her books, her voice vibrant with enthusiasm.

Val nodded. "It's the most powerful depiction of war and suffering yet created. He opened new ground for every serious artist of our century."

Paul felt betrayed by Carolyn's siding with this woman. "Look, I'm college-educated. All I ask when I look at a painting is to know what I'm looking at."

Val nodded again. "Fine work is being done for people who want literal art. But how much literal reality do we need, other than movies and TV and newspapers and photography? Serious art today is what artists know about reality, as well as what they see. That's the basis on which they should be judged."

Carolyn was nodding. Paul said doggedly, probing for an opening, a concession to his viewpoint, "I still want to understand what I'm looking at."

"Then try to look at the why of it, not the what of it. Great art, no matter what the form, is complexity reduced to simplicity. A novel like *Ulysses* takes work on the part of the reader—"

She was delivering another damn lecture. He opened his mouth to interrupt but Carolyn said, "Paul, I want to hear this."

Val addressed Carolyn, having given up on Paul Blake. "Any time you say yes to a work of art, you validate the artist. Artists in any medium are happy for whatever value is found in their work. Artists like to reach a comprehending audience, but that happens rarely. And I truly believe," she added, "that a fully realized work of art has no definitive interpretation, anyway."

Neal asked, "Is it okay if I go swimming?"

Poor Neal must be bored to death, Carolyn thought. She said, "Why don't I go in the pool with you?" She was proud that Val was so easily holding her own with Paul. She would give both of them more opportunity to become better acquainted without the distraction of her own presence. "I can float around on my raft and keep an eye on him." She caught Val's amused glance and grinned. "Or vice versa."

Paul mentally cursed Neal Hunter and his lousy timing. He would not have the opportunity to rectify his position with this woman in front of his wife—at least not immediately. "Go ahead," he said in an easy tone, refilling his martini from the pitcher. "I want to listen to Val more. Besides, I haven't seen you in a bathing suit for weeks, Princess."

Princess. Save us, Gloria Steinem. The man calls her Princess.

"Let me take care of putting the potatoes on the coals," he said to Val. "In the meantime, think about justifying how a bunch of colored squares can be beautiful."

He got up and went to the barbecue, and watched from there as Val Hunter's eyes followed Carolyn and Neal into the house. He scrutinized Val Hunter carefully: it seemed to him that she was looking—staring—at Carolyn, not her son; but he could not be certain.

He returned and Val Hunter uncrossed her legs, stretched them out before her. Somehow this gesture was more offensive to him than when she had crossed them.

She answered his question. "Art may be the most subjective of all the art forms." With him, she thought, this was surely true—no one is more subjective than a blind man who will not see. "For some people, viewing work such as Rothko's squares can be a highly aesthetic experience. It requires a discriminating sensitivity to interaction of color, the distinctions between hues and values of color, the way color areas seem to change in relation to other areas, knowledge of the way the artist has controlled all these factors."

He was a fool. He had made the basic tactical error of encountering this woman on her own turf. Perhaps she was spouting the rote theories of the art world . . . but she felt comfortable and secure, this independent woman who was without a man. He should be more conciliatory, make more effort to see what kind of woman she really was, what influence, beyond selling her work to Carolyn, she might have.

Meaningless small talk was a waste of this opportunity. He cast about for a subject. He said, "I heard on the news the latest Supreme Court ruling, the Jaycees can't keep females out anymore. Another victory for you women."

To his surprise she laughed, soft, amused laughter. Then she said, "A victory?"

"What would you call it?"

"A joke."

Carolyn and Neal came out of the house. Carolyn's glance was quizzical. He answered with a smiling nod and covered his affirmative signal that all was well between him and Val Hunter with a low whistle: "Princess, you look gorgeous."

He turned back to Val Hunter. Obviously, politics would hardly do as a conciliatory subject. He sipped his martini, refilled it from the pitcher, and glanced over to watch Neal Hunter and Carolyn lift the two rafts leaning against the fence and carry them to the pool, Neal dwarfed by his dark blue raft.

From the steps at the shallow end of the pool, Carolyn slid onto her raft, looking over to see if Paul had noticed her new expertise; but he seemed intent on his conversation with Val Hunter. Well, that was good. She turned her attention to Val's son. His sun-streaked hair was much lighter than his mother's, finer textured; but his eyes were Val's eyes, dark brown, alert, perceptive.

"Ma says I have to call you Mrs. Blake unless I'm asked not to."

"If you want to call me Carolyn, then you can," she said firmly.

He cast a glance of pure triumph at his mother. He stood next to Carolyn's raft, his body submerged except for the bony shoulders she found so endearingly vulnerable on young boys. She smiled at him. "I understand you go to day camp. Why don't you tell me about it?"

"Know anything about sports?"

"Hardly anything," she confessed.

He crossed his arms and said matter-of-factly, "Then you won't be interested."

She remembered Val's remarks about the sanctimoniousness of ten-year-olds, but she smothered her amusement, sensing that laughter would be a mistake. "Then let's talk about something you'd like to talk about."

"Okay." His eyes were bright with challenge. "I think your living room looks like it comes from the Emerald City."

This time she did laugh, knowing it was all right to do so, unable to prevent herself in any case. "Well, I definitely know this isn't Kansas. It may even be Munchkinland. But home is where your heart is."

"Hey," Neal whooped, "that's good."

"It's my favorite movie," she said, thinking that it might very well be; at this moment she could not think of any she loved more. She added with a grin, "Who knows? I might even like sports if I only had a brain."

He was beaming, rocking her raft back and forth in his exuberance. "Are you a good witch or a bad witch?"

"A bad witch, of course. What fun is it to be a good witch? But if you're not careful you'll dump me in the water and melt all my beautiful wickedness."

"I like you," Neal said, and slid onto his raft.

He said to Val Hunter, "You must find it difficult raising your son by yourself."

"Actually, less difficult." She chuckled, rattled the ice cubes in her drink, took a swallow. "I don't mean that to be facetious—Richard died two years ago." She held up a hand to prevent his offer of condolences. "He left me for good five years before that. Even when he was with us he was a drifter, never staying long on any job. He was in a high-demand profession—chemical engineering. He left whenever he felt like it, went wherever his feet took him."

Paul said enviously, "That was great—for him."

"To be footloose—that seems to be prime male mythology. It's understandable, I suppose, in young men or women. But for all of us, romanticism should be tempered by some maturity."

"Think you'd like to marry again?" he probed. He felt probed in return, her swift glance gauging him. Then her eyes became remote, focusing on the palm tree facing her.

"Marry again," she repeated, as if testing the words. "I see no reason why. But there are few absolutes in this life." *Why do men always ask,* she thought, *and women seldom do? And why do I always have to be careful how I answer men?*

He realized that if he asked would she like to live with someone, he would invite the same evasiveness. "Don't you think a male presence is important to a boy's development?"

More ground that was totally familiar. Give the same old safe answers you always have, she told herself. But she said, "Maleness by itself doesn't make for a good role model, Paul. You'd have to know my two husbands to understand," she added in an attempt at humor. "Neal has good models in his grandfather, several of his teachers. His baseball coach is a splendid, gentle man."

Splendid? Gentle? That's masculinity? "But Neal's home life is all maternal," he said. "All the divorces today, these new moral standards, how can young boys get the proper idea of masculinity?"

The target was too exposed, too inviting. "That so-called proper idea of masculinity is what's wrong with this world."

He felt in control, as if conducting a job interview in which the candidate had suddenly begun giving only wrong answers. "So you believe in androgyny? Unisex?"

She shrugged. "I can't attach value judgments to those labels— I really don't care. As long as those roles aren't forced on anyone, either." Logically, her answer was correct; why did she feel uncomfortable with it?

"You mean you wouldn't care if your son turned out to be a faggot?"

She winced less at the term than at the withering tone. "Any parent would prefer to have life made as easy as possible for a child. But children do go their own way; I certainly did. I doubt that I'm anywhere close to what my parents expected. Are you?"

"I don't know what my parents expected, but it was much less than what I've accomplished. I grew up dirt poor and put myself through college."

"When I was college age, opportunities were so limited that there was very little reason for women to bother going to college."

More poor me. God, he was so tired of hearing poor me from women. He took a drink from his martini and said aggressively, "The changes in the past ten years are astounding. I've seen so many women and minorities moving into positions never open to them before—"

She knew better than to argue, she knew enough to mouth the usual safe things, the platitudes. Don't upset him, don't alienate him—not if she expected to keep Carolyn's friendship. But all her life there had been a reason not to speak her feelings or knowledge: She needed a job, or to be accepted into art classes, or to have her work looked at. To take care of Neal. Always there had been a reason, and always the same price . . .

She said, "I've heard this conversation from so many men. You think we're doing so well. Stop talking to other men, stop looking at the tokens around you. Read the statistics. There's been almost no gain for blacks since the Civil Rights Act. Women as an economic class are even worse off than before. In four years this government has made a direct frontal attack on every gain minority groups have ever won, from abortion to—"

"Crap," he cut in, reckless with anger. "Don't lecture me with that feminist bullshit. If you women had your way we'd take some black washroom attendant and make her company president, make some secretary chairman of the board. Women want everything now, without competing for it, without earning it. You want to turn this country into a socialist swamp. Gender gap, my ass. We aren't against women, we want qualified women, like the one on the Supreme Court—"

"You should be proud of that one," she interrupted acidly. "You have a man on the Supreme Court now who looks exactly like a woman."

"You say that because she doesn't agree with all the bleeding heart liberal crap. Sanity is coming back to this country, political balance, the pendulum's swinging back—"

"Pendulum," she repeated. "Such a nice bloodless word. Now we learn the truth. You'll give us all the lip service we can swallow about being born equal and having equal opportunity, but you're keeping the power. You'll never give any of it up. Women have to understand their own power, women will have to take it themselves—"

"Crap," he spat. "You feed this bullshit to my wife?"

His question sobered her, calmed her. "Actually, we've never even talked about these issues."

He took another swallow from his drink. This uncontrollably widening channel of anger in him, was it from the vodka? He did not care. "What *do* you talk about?"

Again, instantly, her fury rose to its previous height. "Ask her."

"I will. What do you *want* with my wife?"

She faced him belligerently. "Meaning what?"

"Meaning she's married and you're not. Meaning she's married and damn happy about it. Meaning since you've got all this feminist shit down pat, are you a lesbian too?"

She remembered Gloria Steinem saying: *Are you my alternative?* She mustered all her sarcasm. "Not before this evening."

Neal had been sitting on the steps in the shallow end, water up to his neck, watching Paul and Val. He came dog-paddling up to Carolyn. "Ma's really mad about something."

Alarmed, Carolyn stared at Paul and Val. They were leaning toward each other; Paul's face was tight and closed, but seemed calm; Val was obviously making several points to him, ticking them off so forcefully that each finger bent back as she jabbed at it. Carolyn watched for a few more seconds. "I don't think so, honey. They're arguing about something but—"

"Ma's really mad. I can tell."

Neal dog-paddled back to the pool steps. Carolyn steered her raft after him.

"The whole trouble with women like you," Paul said, "is simple." He grabbed his crotch. "You don't have this. You want one. Deny biology till you turn blue. Only *men* can fuck—you got that? Women don't have the cocks to do the fucking that needs to be done in this world. They know it and you know it. Most women don't want what you feminists think they want. The women's movement is over. Women have had a good look and they don't want it."

"How would you know? You're a Neanderthal who still thinks everything should be done with a club or a cock." She pointed scornfully at his crotch. "You're *stuck* with that."

"If I'm a Neanderthal, you're an Amazon—and that makes you a *myth*. I've worked with women, *normal* women, in the North and South and now out West for *twelve years*. Thank God none of *them* were feminists. You're the only feminist I've ever *met*."

Out of her rage came the clear thought that she had never hated anyone with as much passion as she hated this man. She said in a low, deadly voice, "I'm not the first feminist you've met. You've met hundreds. Thousands. Do you think the slaves who said 'Yes Massa' loved their masters? Do you think there aren't millions of women every day who say 'Yes sir' or 'Yes dear' and in their hearts hate their lives and hate—"

"Not *real* women. You call yourself a real woman? Look at you. Look at—"

"Paul!"

His rage was jarred by Carolyn's expulsion of his name, another concussive sound amid the firecrackers exploding in the yards around them. He turned from Val Hunter. The red haze of hatred in his vision took in his wife.

"Ma, let's go." Staring at him, Neal Hunter backed away.

"You poor little bastard," he said to Neal. "God only knows what your dyke of a mother's doing to you—"

"Paul!"

Val Hunter rose and moved swiftly toward the house, the hem of her dress strained to its utmost by the length of her strides, Carolyn running after her.

Val Hunter stopped at the glass door. A hand reached, touched, clasped Carolyn's bare forearm. "I'm truly sorry, Carrie. Good night."

He did not hear his wife's reply; he was outraged by the familiarity of Val Hunter's touching Carolyn, by that offensively familiar nickname.

Val Hunter released Carolyn, disappeared into the house, her son in her wake. Carolyn whirled around and came toward him, her eyes narrowed slits, her fists clenched.

"That Amazon bitch. How could you possibly like that bitch, that—"

"You bastard." Her voice was flat, glacial. "You can't *stand* me having a friend of my own. You can't *stand* it that I did one thing on my own, that I had the gall to buy a work of art—"

"Art, my ass. That piece of mud hanging on the living room wall is no more art than—"

She picked up the chair in which Val Hunter had been sitting—his director's chair.

"Carolyn!" he screamed as he understood what she would do.

She swung the chair viciously at the barbecue. Foilwrapped potatoes and burning coals were strewn all over his manicured lawn, sizzling like lighted firecrackers.

"Christ, oh Christ." He leaped for the garden tools he kept at the side of the house. "Jesus, look what you've done!"

๑ 13 ๑

Val tried to explain to Neal. "It's like blending yellow and red and blue—it comes out black or gray. People can be like colors—fine by themselves but put them together and they're ugly."

He said fiercely, "I should've popped him one when he said you were dykey." Still in his bathing trunks, he stood militantly in their living room, feet spread apart, hands on his hips.

She fluffed his hair, grinning at the image of her son wading into Paul Blake with his small fists flying. "Do you even know what that word means?"

"Ma, for crying out loud." He gazed at her in disgust. "Don't you remember Mr. Steinberg?"

She remembered when Neal had come home from school to talk only of the English teacher who had asked his students every hate reference they knew to groups of people, writing each word on the blackboard as it was volunteered. "I bet we came up with fifty," Neal had declared, obsessed with his effort to convey the awesomeness of that list, the ugliness of those words, row upon row of them, beginning with *kike, hymie, hebe,* and *jewboy,* which Mr. Steinberg himself had written.

"Listen pal," she said to Neal, "it's the Fourth of July, remember? Why don't we go watch some fireworks? Let's drive out to Devonshire."

She felt infected by her hatred of Paul Blake. She needed to get out of the house, as if open space and fresh air could relieve the festering. She would not dwell on the events of this night.

"You wearing that?" He was looking at her dress in disapproval.

"Is the pope Baptist? Last one to change clothes is a Winged Monkey."

"Surrender, Dorothy!" Neal raced for his room.

Later, on the Ventura Freeway, with fiery flowers bursting and fading in the night sky, and Boy George singing softly on the radio, Neal said soberly, "Carolyn's a good lady, Ma. I really like her. Why'd she marry such a creep?"

She returned to her analogy. "Some colors might not mix, sweetie, but others do just fine together."

He shrugged and turned up the radio.

But it was incomprehensible to her as well. She called up the image of Paul Blake, and in the choking fullness of hatred that rose with the image, tried to analyze her emotion. She thought of her trip into the Mojave with Neal, and the solitary diamondback they had watched patrol its harsh terrain with easy, confident menace. While Paul Blake might not be as soulless as a reptile, he was the clear embodiment of the many men she had known whose arrogant superiority mocked her and the value of anything she said, thought, felt, created, accomplished. Men who expected to dominate and control, who viewed independence or rebellion with an amused tolerance others might give to a child, or an idiot, and viewed more serious threats to their dominance with wary condescension, as if dealing with mental aberration.

Why had Carolyn subjected herself to such a man as Paul Blake? Val conceded with a moue of distaste that Paul Blake did have an aura of sexual confidence; he had conveyed that when their eyes had first met—not as invitation or comment on her as a desirable woman, far from it—simply as a statement. Many men were hopeless sexual performers, a condition even more likely when they were young. To Carolyn at the age of nineteen perhaps a mature Paul Blake had seemed the ultimate sexual sophisticate. God knows, Val reflected, it had taken an older man to give her the only sexual reassurance she had ever known.

Perhaps it was Henry Ingall's stature—five feet seven (why, why did she always attract short men?)—and his age—fifty-five to her twenty-four—which had given her a feeling of confidence instead of the usual tension and apprehension. She had relaxed with him, and climaxed three times, all of them after intercourse, reaching orgasm easily each time from manual, then oral stimulation. "This is what you like," he told her back in those days when women were trapped in the theories of Freud and Kinsey. "You're remarkably responsive and that's all that matters. Don't feel guilty about what you like; there's nothing wrong with it and don't let anyone ever tell you differently." That assurance had been gratifying but useless in the sexual battles of her two marriages and subsequent affairs. If she confessed her needs, men perceived her—or themselves—as inadequate. After she made the same dismal discovery again and again, it had become easier to accept whatever was offered.

Perhaps her clash with Paul Blake had occurred because she would not massage another male ego in the presence of her maturing son. Or maybe she had reached a place in her life when she did not care enough anymore to pretend to anyone—even if it meant losing the friendship of someone she'd come to like. And perhaps the truth was none of this—she simply had met someone she loathed so much that all the barriers had been pulverized in that closed circuit of hatred containing only her and Paul Blake.

No matter how much consciousness raising had seeped into the larger world, Carolyn Blake would cleave to Paul Blake because that's how it worked, how it still worked. Except for the pitiful rebellion of changing her working hours, Carolyn Blake had given no indication that she was other than a dutiful wife. And that had to be the real reason she had married a man ten years her senior—to have someone to obey, a husband and father figure to tell her what to do.

But I'll miss her. How very much I've come to enjoy her . . .

"San Diego Freeway's coming up," Neal said, snapping his fingers to a Michael Jackson song.

"Right you are," she said, and changed lanes.

❧ 14 ❧

Carolyn flung herself onto the bed in the guest bedroom to stare dry-eyed at the ceiling. She could hear Paul in the yard cursing as he searched out the flaming coals she had scattered; he was so close to her window that if she lifted her head she would see him. She did not want to look.

Val blames herself, I'm certain she does. Whatever was said has to be his fault. I may not know her well enough to be sure, but I do know him.

Suddenly she rose, straightened the yellow print bedspread, and then her own skirt and blouse, and walked out of the house.

Twice she knocked on the door of the darkened guest house, and soon made her way disconsolately up the path. Jerry Robinson had come out of his house and stood in his driveway, peering at her with his watery, timid blue eyes. "Mrs. Hunter and the boy, they left a few minutes ago."

"Thank you."

"Heard you folks in your yard a bit ago. Seemed like some commotion."

Nosy old man, she thought furiously. "Nothing of any consequence," she said, and brushed past him.

"You and Paul, you come over soon now," he called after her.

Paul sat on the sofa watching television. "I suppose you've been over there apologizing." His tone was aggressive, heavy with resentment.

"They've gone out," she said tensely. "I didn't have a chance."

"I don't want to hurt you." He spoke with clear precision. "But there are things you don't realize. I'm sure she's a dyke. What she really wants is—"

"Shut up! That's enough!"

His voice was a lash: "Don't raise your voice to me."

"I'll do what I damn please! Don't you say one more word!" Her shout escalated to a scream. "Val Hunter is my friend. It was your idea to meet her—"

"I don't like her, Princess. I can't help it. I just can't stand her."

He had spoken with surprising softness, almost apologetically. Disarmed, she lowered her own voice. "You have no right to dictate my friends."

"I'm not trying to. I can't stand that particular woman." He grinned with obvious effort. "Could you try someone else?"

Partly mollified, she adjusted her tone but said stubbornly, "She's my friend and she'll continue to be, if she's willing after the evening she spent here—"

"You're convinced everything that happened was my fault. But I took so much shit from her—"

She stalked over to him, her anger a flame. "Tell me all about taking shit, why don't you. Lake Michigan wouldn't hold all the shit I've had to take from the stupid leering clowns at your office parties. Smile, you tell me. Be gracious." Her voice had risen sharply, her words approaching incoherence. "What's good for the goose—if you need lessons how to take shit and smile—"

He held both hands over his head in surrender. "So be it. Can we make peace?" She sat at her end of the sofa, frustrated and still furious. "Are we going to have dinner?"

"I'm not hungry," she said unforgivingly. She was looking at the gray painting on the wall, trying to calm herself. He went into the kitchen, quietly made himself a sandwich.

Later that silent evening, he followed her into the guest bedroom. "Aren't you carrying this a bit far? Did I commit a capital crime?"

"I want to be alone. Is that a capital crime?"

His expression was both wary and baffled. He nodded, and left.

Her anger slowly dissipated; she thought of returning to their bedroom. But she was fully stretched out—spreadeagled—enjoying the unaccustomed freedom and spaciousness. Irresistibly, she drifted into sleep, pushing away any thoughts of him. The final image in her consciousness was Val in her white dress, her tanned body radiant with health and strength.

The next afternoon Val was not in the pool. But she answered Carolyn's knock immediately, standing in the doorway in her usual shorts and T-shirt. Her smile was quick, and wry. "I don't know how to break this to you, Carrie, but your husband and I have fallen in love."

Carolyn's attempt at a laugh was weak. "What can I say? I don't understand what happened or why—"

Val shrugged. "Bad chemistry."

"You don't really know him—he's different from what you saw. When I first met him he was so needy, like a lost little boy. It's still there in him—" She broke off. It was useless to explain what Val could not see. Perhaps no one except herself really saw Paul. "Val . . . I hope we can still be friends."

Val nodded. "I'm glad you still feel that way. We'll do the best we can under the circumstances, okay?"

She saw that Val did not give her credence, that the words were rote politeness. Carolyn said quickly, "Do you have a barbecue? Can I invite myself over for dinner tonight? I'll bring the steaks we were supposed to have last night. How does that sound?"

"It sounds good." Val grinned. "Neal will be very glad to see you again. Can we go back to your house? I think I'd like a swim."

Carolyn called Paul at his office to explain. "I'll leave some chicken cordon bleu warming in the oven, honey," she said softly, in a peace offering; the dish was one of his favorites.

"Fine, Princess," he said calmly. "See you later."

✎ 15 ✎

Three years into their marriage, when Carolyn was twenty-two, she had become less communicative. She would not—or could not—explain other than, "I just feel like being quiet."

He suspected an affair. There seemed little opportunity, but he knew from a few joyless liaisons during his first marriage how easily such things could be managed. As her moodiness persisted his suspicion grew into obsession, culminating with the hiring of a detective agency. Reassured about her fidelity, remorseful over the waste of money, he called himself ridiculous for his suspicions; and as her periods of quiet continued, he gradually became used to them.

At this moment he could better understand an affair; it would be easier to contend with than this Val Hunter business. And he could find ways to make a male rival sorry he was ever born.

He excoriated himself for scuttling the best chance to solve the Val Hunter problem. If he hadn't had so much to drink, hadn't let his contempt for the woman lead to loss of self-control, he could have befriended her; then it was only a matter of applying a tactic from the world of business: finding the right buttons to push. Little by little he would have stripped the ground out from under her. Often the simple use of caricature laid all the groundwork. Gargantua, he would have called her—smiling of course, as if he meant the nickname to be affectionate. Paula Bunyan.

He put aside the sales forecast he was reviewing and studied his desk calendar. July 23—nineteen days since the Fourth of July, since this whole mess started. Twice a week without fail she was going over to that house in the evening. For just an hour, she said each time. But it was usually an hour and a half; and last Thursday it had been two hours. She had explained: "Val and I want to listen to Geraldine Ferraro's acceptance speech."

"I know it's a historic moment for women," he had replied, "and I want to hear it too. With you, Princess."

She shook her head. "You don't feel the way I do, the way most women feel right now. If you could hear the women at work—" She added with finality, "You wouldn't vote Democratic unless Reagan switched parties."

"You've never even cared enough to vote," he pointed out.

"This time I do," she had said softly, and left the house.

He picked up the report again, and once more laid it aside. What did she want from that woman? What did she need? Why these evening visits, why couldn't they talk over the back fence? To spend time with Neal, she had said, because I love him and I can't invite either one of them over here. And Val is working. But artists could work anytime, midnight if they wanted to. Carolyn had said something about her own housework. But how much time did cleaning and cooking actually take? Not long, with just two people and every labor-saving device money could buy. How much dust could two people create? And Carolyn was spending more leisure time in the sun. She was tanned, and getting darker all the time.

There was no escaping the fact that Carolyn wanted to be with her. No rationalizing the issue. Why? What did they talk about? Carolyn was still checking out those scruffy library books—how much was there to learn about art, or to talk about? Certainly he was as intelligent as the Hunter woman, his job was easily as interesting—and paid a hell of a lot more besides. He did not talk about his work much, but Carolyn did not seem that interested.

He slammed a palm on his desk, scattering the pages of the report. He didn't need any more of this, goddammit. He needed calm in his life, to feel comfortable again with his own wife. To have things the way they were before. Hard enough to stay on top of things in his work without this, and everybody knew the next territorial manager would be himself or Dick Jensen; Will Trask was watching them both with those gimlet eyes of his.

There had to be a solution—there always was. Wait it out? He could do that, but for how long? These nineteen days had been interminable; the thought of that Amazon bitch laughing at him excruciating. And he was by no means blessed with patience.

What did people do to bring more glow into their marriages? Inject some element of change, that was what.

Ludicrous as it might seem, he probably should start thinking of Val Hunter as if she were a man. Grit his teeth and act as if he were competing for Carolyn again, just as he'd had to do before he married her. Distasteful as it might be, there were advantages in approaching the problem this way. He could do things for Carolyn that Val Hunter could not hope to match.

Again he looked at his calendar. In sinking realization he saw that he was trapped, for at least three more weeks. The Olympic Games began this coming weekend; the athletes were already arriving. From all reports traffic would be horrendous. His own company had made contingency plans for bus and carpooling, had encouraged all employees to go on vacation. You wouldn't be able to get anywhere in town, get a restaurant reservation, anything. His shoulders sagged.

Still, it never hurt to check around, to ask. Never automatically accept things as they appear, he reminded himself—that basic rule of sales also applied to life. You never knew when you might find that unexpected chink in a piece of armor that appeared impervious. . . .

He reached for his intercom, then changed his mind. Margie couldn't be trusted with this. She was too passive, too willing to take no for an answer, which was why she was a secretary and not in sales where she wanted to be—and why most women couldn't make it in business. Most of them were like that.

No, he would make a few inquiries himself, see how hopeless the situation really was.

ᘛ 16 ᘚ

Carolyn and Val had not spoken for a long, comfortable time. In the water between their rafts Val's fingers slowly traced the entire shape of Carolyn's hand, front and back, between her fingers, over her fingernails. Val's eyes were closed; her face, turned toward Carolyn, was still and peaceful.

Carolyn studied the wide forehead, the thick dark eyebrows and lashes, the generous beak of nose with its slightly flared nostrils, the full mouth. Most people, Carolyn reflected, would say that the sensual mouth was her best feature, and it might well be her own favorite. The lips were expressive, like the big soft hand which held hers. She loved Val's hands, hands that were always confident and sure, whether they were stacking dishes or folding clothes, stretching canvas or constructing frames, delicately cleaning brushes or sketching in one of the numerous pads Val kept in easy reach around the house. Val had not allowed her to see those hands in the actual process of painting: "Carrie, I can't have you see my unfinished work . . ."

Carolyn took her hand out of Val's to turn over onto her back, luxuriating in the sun as the raft floated out of the shady end of the pool. Feeling a strong sense of well-being, she stretched, gazing down at herself in satisfaction. Tanned to deep gold, she felt buoyant pleasure in her body, a recent and altogether new pride. Wanting Val's hand again, to feel its large softness enclosing her, she reached to her. For some time longer she dozed, aware only of the soothing drone of an aircraft, and the hand that clasped hers. She opened her eyes to see Val looking at her.

Val smiled. "Your hair's growing."

"Is it too long yet?"

"Not nearly." Val released Carolyn's hand and shook water from her own before picking up a strand. "There's more curl on the ends now. You're young, you should look young. Don't be in such a hurry to catch up to Paul, to anyone around you." She rolled the strand in her fingers. "Your hair's the color of drying sand."

Val rarely commented on her appearance, and Carolyn was reluctant to let the moment go. She murmured, "Wet sand doesn't sound very appealing."

"Not wet sand, drying sand. Meaning sand with sun on it. It's a color so difficult to get right. . . ."

They floated in silence again. But Val's fingers continued to move slowly in Carolyn's hair. Carolyn said lazily, eyes closed again, "Neal's so excited about the Olympics."

Val chuckled. "We'll see two events. I'm taking him to the women's marathon, he's taking me to the men's. The price for both is exactly right—free." Still chuckling, she propelled their rafts to the shallow end of the pool. "Will you be over tonight, Carrie?"

"Sure thing."

Paul arrived home on time—an unusual occurrence—and after kissing her, placed his briefcase ceremoniously on the sofa. "Let me get our drinks, Princess. We have something to celebrate. I have a wonderful surprise, I've been working on it all day . . ."

She arrived at Val's at eight-thirty. "I couldn't come any sooner," she said disconsolately, walking into the tiny cluttered living room. "Where's Neal?"

"At the corner buying milk. We ran out." She was frowning at the package in Carolyn's hands. "Not something else for him."

"Just another puzzle—"

"On top of the one the both of you are putting together, on top of the Monopoly game you bought last week, and the baseball glove, the airplane assembly kit—"

"Oh stop." She was moving around the house in her agitation, picking up newspapers, tidying.

"You stop. Friends do not come to my house and clean. What's gotten into you?"

Carolyn dropped the newspapers she had gathered up. "Oh God, Val, I've got to go to the Bahamas."

Val threw back her head and laughed. "Let me get you an aspirin."

"I don't want to go," Carolyn said vehemently. "I don't *feel* like going. But if you could've seen him. A whole briefcase loaded with brochures. He's planned everything—hotels, side trips, a night in Miami, even our clothes. He called my boss to make sure I could take the time off."

Val was grinning. "So, when do you go?"

"Friday!"

"Friday?"

Carolyn flung herself down on the sofa. "I can't stay over here very long, he'll be too hurt. He's like a little boy over this trip." She admitted sheepishly, "I couldn't have come over at all except I told him I wanted to brag a little." She saw a gratifying soberness on Val's face.

"How can you leave Friday?" Val said. "That's when the Olympics begin. How could he—"

"His travel agency told him they have all kinds of space on flights out of L.A. People aren't flocking into town nearly like anyone expected. And we're going to some island, I don't remember the name, it's not as big a tourist draw as Nassau. The only problem was the hotel in Miami, but he has a business connection down there, so—"

"Hi, Carolyn!" Neal slammed the door in his exuberance, gave his paper bag to his mother, and hugged Carolyn. "Where've you been? Hey, is this a present for me? Did Ma tell you we saw the Olympic torch?"

"Yes," Carolyn said, hugging him back, "but tell me all about it anyway; she probably left out something good." She grinned at Val, happy to be here.

Val smiled. "Carrie, stay a few more minutes," she coaxed. "He'll soon have you all to himself . . ."

❧ 17 ❧

Val pulled a sketch pad from under a stack. The pad was nearly full, and she leafed through it slowly: Carolyn, in a sundress, walking toward the pool carrying drinks. Carolyn, wearing shorts, sitting in a deck chair, legs gracefully crossed, applying suntan lotion to her arms. Carolyn on a raft, lying on her stomach, an arm under her head, dozing; then lying on her back, a hand shading her eyes from the sun; leaning on an elbow toward the artist, smiling,

Val selected a number one pencil, refined lines in Carolyn's body on earlier sketches; she knew how to draw that body now. On a fresh page Carolyn's face took shape again, this time with an expression of pouting gloom. Val smiled as she sketched.

Later in her narrow bed, she assessed what had occurred in the now-silent war between her and Paul Blake. If he had been playing a waiting game, he had lost patience. Carolyn lacked full knowledge of their unbridgeable mutual hatred, but even so, continuing this friendship in spite of her husband's displeasure was surprising. She seemed to be gaining in resolve, assertiveness. At twenty-six, part of that might be simply the maturing process . . . After all, Val reflected, while she herself had always stood out in her differentness, she had not actually emerged as an individual nor gained any control of her life until she was Carolyn's age. . . .

But now Paul Blake was definitely laying claim to his wife. Taking her away for two weeks of tropical moonlight and romance, where he would wine and dine and fuck her into submission. And probably it would work. Val turned over and stared into the dark shadows of her room.

The black ocean was rimmed with a profusion of lights, the shore-line of a tropical island. Carolyn's arm was around her; her head rested on Val's shoulder as they stood on the deck of the ship and gazed at the lights. Val's hands circled Carolyn's waist. Wordlessly, Carolyn turned. Val drew Carolyn to her, caressed down over the curve of hip . . .

Val sat up in bed. Her body was heated, her pulse swift. Her first conscious thought was of Alix: Thank God Alix was in Houston. If she were here, could somehow know about this dream, she would laugh her head off.

Val looked at the clock: five-thirty. It seemed somehow perilous to remain in bed. She rose and glided silently into the shadowy grayness of her living room. There was a suggestion of dawn in the lightening sky, and she sat on her sofa to stare out the window at the inky shapes of leaves, and at the fence separating her from Paul and Carolyn Blake.

The dream was explicable; it was an amalgam of circumstances. She was aware of Carolyn's body because she had been sketching it. Not only that, she had just finished an interpretation of it on canvas. Because she was re-creating Carolyn's body, she was imbued with a sense of it. True, they did touch more than most women, but that was because of Carolyn's water phobia, and only their hands touched. . . . Except for today. But anyone, male or female, would enjoy the lovely tactile sensation of that long silky hair. . . .

I am a sexual being, she told herself. With years of only intermittent and mostly unsatisfactory sex. Everyone knew masturbating didn't do it all. A head of cauliflower could look like a sex object after a while.

There was really no problem; nothing sexual would happen between them.

This would be their last day together before he took her away. . . . Except for a few final touches, the painting of Carolyn was finished. She would show it to her. Why not? Carolyn would not know the painting was of her; it was too abstract.

৯ 18 ৵

Her eyes were drawn to a seamless blending of simple harmonies, sensuously curved lines of randomly varied shades of green. Lacking mathematical regularity, the curves were of exquisite symmetry, flowing to the edge of the canvas, laid against a golden background, an echo of sunlight. Carolyn's gaze was drawn upward to a patch of green, a shade soft yet compelling. She saw that it was a stylized eye, looking out into its own self-contained distance. She stared again at the endlessly flowing, graceful lines.

"It's like a musical composition. As if you took pieces of music and . . ." She faltered.

"I don't mind that comparison at all." Val's voice was soft.

"The greens vary so in the curved lines . . . There's a pattern everywhere except in the color changes—"

"It's meant to convey layers, depths. Unexpected, unpredictable layers and depths."

Immersed in the painting again, Carolyn murmured, "God, I'd like to have this. . . ." When Val did not respond, Carolyn turned to her.

"Carrie, it's still drying." Val seemed taken aback. "It needs to dry for a while. Then, to be varnished. And I think I still might want to change something."

She looked at Val, puzzled. The speech pattern had contained a clumsiness she had never heard from Val. But she clearly understood that Val would keep this lovely, lyrical painting. "As long as I have visiting privileges," she said lightly.

Val's smile was sudden. "You can't possibly drag home any more paintings of mine, not even to avenge the Bahamas. What are you, crazy?"

Obligingly Carolyn chuckled, then immersed herself again in the painting.

"Even Michelangelo would be flattered." Val's voice was soft, warm. "Come on, we've got a few minutes—let's go float in your pool."

Proud of her new boldness in the water, Carolyn slid off her raft and clung to the side of the pool at the deep end, near the ladder. She could now submerge her body in water over her head, so long as she had the side of the pool or the raft to cling to.

Val swam over and gripped the side of the pool to face Carolyn. "Enjoy the water where you're going, Carrie," she urged. "I understand it's one of the really beautiful places in the world."

Carolyn placed her hands on Val's shoulders, feeling their breadth and strength as a new and equally secure anchor. She touched her cheek to Val's. "I'll really miss you and Neal."

She felt Val's body come up against hers, felt Val's arms slide around her, and too late realized what would happen. Moments later she surfaced, still in Val's grasp, trying to stop laughing so that she could stop coughing. "You crazy woman, one of us had to hold on!" She clung to Val until her coughs subsided.

Silently, Val assisted her out of the pool. She pushed wet hair off Carolyn's face, smoothed drops of water away with soft wane palms.

Carolyn said, "I'm okay. I really am."

Abruptly, Val released her. "I'm sorry."

"It was just as much my fault—"

Val stepped away from her and seized her towel. "Carrie, take care." With several swift strides she reached the fence and vaulted over.

❧ 19 ❧

He worked late, cleaning up his in-box. He walked into his house carrying an elaborately wrapped box. With a mock bow, feeling slightly foolish, he presented it to Carolyn. Surprised, laughing in delight, she placed the box on the bar and removed the huge red bow and silver paper. She held up by its spaghetti straps a sheer nightgown the color of eggshell.

As he saw her widening eyes, her pleasure, he felt less guilty. Margie had done a wonderful job. After all, he had told her what to buy, and with all that had to be done before he could leave his job for two weeks he hadn't had any time to spare. "It's been too long since I bought you anything like that, Princess."

"You've never bought me anything like this." Stroking the filmy fabric, she walked toward the bedroom. "It's the first thing I'm packing. But it's too expensive, too pretty to wear to bed."

He sat on the side of the bed; she leaned down to kiss him. He pulled her down with him. "Honey, we have to pack," she protested as he kissed her throat.

"In a minute."

She stole a look at the clock. Ten to eight. If she were next door she might be playing a game with Val and Neal, maybe cards. And loving Neal's playful competitiveness, his uncomplicated honesty, the uncluttered seriousness of his mind, his joy in her attention to him.

"Paul," she whispered as he groaned and came. "Dear Paul." He lay motionless as she stroked the disheveled gray hair at his temples.

They were packing. By now Neal would be getting ready for bed. If she were there, she would be curled up on the sofa talking with Val, or watching the early channel nine news, or asking about art, or maybe talking about her own job. Sounds of baseball, or perhaps rock music, would emanate from the radio in Neal's room. Another comfortable evening of blending into the two lives in which she had been absorbed as one of their own.

"Was it something I said? Or did?" Paul asked. "All the sparkle you had when I got home seems to be gone."

With guilty vehemence she protested, "Honey, what we just did was a little tiring. I didn't take the catnap you did."

"I want to make you very happy this vacation," he said softly. He snapped the fasteners on a suitcase and carried it into the living room.

Her friendship with Val—this new, deeply felt pleasure in her life—how could she remove the one abrasive grain of sand, his glum, passive acceptance, his pained martyrdom?

Perhaps if he was reassured in every way of her love . . . Perhaps when she returned, if she could see just a little less of Val . . . Maybe, with herself as a conduit of goodwill, over a period of time the hostility between the two of them could break down. Maybe, just maybe it was possible.

If he was that determined to make this vacation wonderful for her, she would do her best to make him happy as well—in every way. These next ten days she would concentrate all her being on him, his pleasure, his happiness.

❧ 20 ❧

"Just the beginning, darling." Watching the limousine driver stack their luggage in the trunk of the long blue car, he regretted that he had not thought to request traditional black. And he wished that Val Hunter lived in the front house instead of the back one, so that she might see him taking Carolyn away.

"First class all the way, Princess. Nothing but the best from here on." Waving the driver away, he held the limousine door open for her.

Late into the night in Miami Beach, in still, balmy air, they strolled barefoot along the ocean edge. Since their early days together he had seldom mentioned his boyhood, and he related again stories whose pain and harshness had so faded out of her memory that they acquired fresh poignance as he spoke. Later, she wore the nightgown, and in moonlight that cut a swath in the ocean below their balcony she welcomed him with a responsiveness that brought his lovemaking to swift and passionate heights. The next morning she woke to his hands again on her body.

They flew in a nine-passenger Cessna to the Bahamian island of Eleuthera, holding hands as the dark blue sea under the tiny plane turned translucent green. That evening, in the bar of the Winding Bay Club, feeling like expatriates, they shared the opening ceremonies of the Olympic Games with several dozen raucous, cheering strangers, all of them Americans. As a smiling Bahamian waiter replenished her rum drink, Carolyn watched dramatic aerial shots of glistening Los Angeles with tearful pride in her newly adopted city, and when at last the American athletes marched joyously into the Coliseum behind their flag to the buoyant strains of "The Stars and Stripes Forever" she wished with all her soul she were home.

Blue-green seas of crystal purity, blinding white sand, swiftly changing cloud formations in hurtfully blue skies—everything evoked memories of the vivid color in Val's paintings. Carolyn strolled perfect, unpeopled beaches with Paul, waded in the transparent water gazing at tiny, luminous, swiftly fleeing fish, collected seashells at low tide, lay with Paul in the sun.

Eager to explore, they rented a car and with it a quietly courteous guide who took them over unpredictably surfaced roads and through villages of brilliantly hued, neat houses built next to delapidated shacks and ancient buildings dating back two centuries or more. They stopped at other island resorts where Carolyn explored the modest gift shops. They rode along unmarked roads through a profusion of flowering foliage to emerge on the white or rose-tinted sand of an immaculate Caribbean-facing beach, or, on the other side of the island, on windswept cliffs overlooking the crashing Atlantic.

She went on their excursions with enthusiasm, hoping to exhaust him, or, failing that, to exhaust herself so that she could truthfully plead tiredness when she could not bring herself to another crescendo of response to his lovemaking. Time alone with him in their beach-front cottage—whatever the hour of day or evening—meant love-making; her tissues were becoming more and more tender, her insides recoiling as from an invasion.

In the evenings they had dinner in the club dining room, to the sound of murmuring conversations and taped music of the Caribbean, with an occasional pop tune she remembered issuing from the radio in Neal's room after he went to bed. After dinner they would stroll back to their cottage, the coconut palm fronds dancing in the breezy, balmy air, his arm around her, his hand possessively stroking her hip. And soon she would lay listening to the ocean and the wind in the palm trees as she caressed him, as his fingers insistently stroked, seeking wetness for his poised penis. Then the groaning question: "Do you feel me?" "Yes . . . yes, Paul darling . . ." "Better than on our honeymoon . . . Never this good . . ." Kissing her throat, her ears, her face; the final piston thrusts, his descent into sleep.

Washing herself then, patting cool water on her tissues, a soothing welcome comfort between her legs.

Five days into their vacation, early in the morning they were to take a Bahamasair flight to stay overnight in Nassau, she awakened with fierce itching and burning. She examined herself; her vaginal lips were bright angry red.

"I'll check at the desk about getting a doctor," Paul said, his tone uneasy, his forehead creased in concern.

"I don't think it's necessary." She laughed in her embarrassment. "It's not like that infection I had four years ago, remember? There's no discharge. It's just that—" She laughed again. "We've been . . . well, let's wait a day or two, please? I'd be mortified to have a doctor tell me—"

"Okay," Paul said immediately. "But we'd better stay here. You'll be too uncomfortable to—"

"Yes," she said. "Maybe we could get a cab to the nearest pharmacy. I'll pick up some ointment. I'll be fine."

Later that morning, relaxed on the patio of their cottage, she savored the beautiful clarity of the water, the salt smell of the soft air. There would be no invasion that night, perhaps for two or three more nights.

That afternoon they strolled down to the club's tiny gift shop, located in a frame building near the beach. She bought Neal a white Winding Bay T-shirt and several decks of cards with scenes of the islands, the bright blues and bleached whites of the Caribbean. She had already bought him, in other gift shops, a brilliant blue T-shirt emblazoned with a great white shark, and an assortment of shells.

"You're really crazy about that kid," Paul observed dryly. He pointed at a tall black woman strolling gracefully on the walkway beside the gift shop, a basket of fruit balanced on her head. "Can't you just see his mother doing something like that?"

"Honey?" The eyes she turned to him were neutral, her voice seemed detached. "Would you have loved me if I'd been six feet tall?"

"Sure." There had been only the barest hesitation. "I *would*," he added.

"What?" Her thoughts had withdrawn from him; she examined a tray of gold chain bracelets.

"Love you if you were six feet tall."

"Oh. That's good." Did Val ever wear bracelets? Probably not. . . .

That night, feeling guilty at her sense of relief, she suggested to Paul, "If you want to make love, honey, I could—"

"No." His tone softened. "It seems too much like masturbation after the real thing."

As she turned over to sleep, she reflected that perhaps he was as weary as she of their bouts of sexuality. Her body her own for the night, she fell deeply, pleasurably asleep.

For the next two days, no longer feeling a compulsion to initiate activity, she luxuriated in the beach sun, sitting on their patio reading novels she had picked up from a bookshelf in the front office. With Paul off playing golf at the Cotton Bay Club, she would stroll the grounds of Winding Bay and talk with the Bahamian known as the dive master, the club's resident expert on the island's waters. Soft spoken but gregarious, he showed her perfect specimens of the myriad shells taken from the hundreds of miles of island beaches and talked about the history of Eleuthera from the days of Columbus.

As she began to relate this new knowledge enthusiastically to Paul, he commented, "Do be careful who you talk to when you're here alone."

"Oh Paul," she said reproachfully, "this place, these people aren't anything like where we come from. We have yet to see a policeman on this entire island!" He did not argue further, but she stopped telling him about her conversations with the dive master; she did not want him disturbed. Soon the vacation would be over. She was happy.

In the morning two days before they were to return home, as they lay in bed, Paul slid down and lifted her gown and with great solicitude examined her.

"It looks pink and pretty again." He patted very gently with a fingertip. "How does that feel?"

"Much better. Fine," she insisted, feeling ridiculous with him peering between her legs. "I'm just fine, honey."

He came to her then and she took him in her arms. Soon he unfastened his pajamas.

She moved away from him. She murmured, "Instead, why don't we kiss each other . . . here." She stroked his firm penis.

When he stared at her without speaking she said awkwardly, with embarrassed defensiveness, "You told me once you wished I'd initiate things once in a while. I'm initiating. I think we could be a little more venturesome, don't you?"

"I don't want you doing that to me." He smiled then, and propped himself on an elbow and caressed down over her stomach. "But I'd do anything in the world you think you might like . . ."

He felt, she decided a few minutes later, like he was poking at her with a stick. She stole a glance down at him. He lay rigid, his eyes squeezed shut, his face a rictus of distaste, his tongue a poker-stiff extension to her.

Frozen with shame, she grasped his hair to pull him away. "That was lovely," she whispered.

He climbed out of bed pawing at his mouth. "A hair," he rasped, and went into the bathroom. Over the running water she heard him brushing his teeth, gargling.

Getting back into bed he asked, "Try it again?"

Shamed, pierced by his willingness to please her, she said, "No honey, you were sweet and nice."

He took her into his arms. She tasted toothpaste on his lips. Emptying her mind of thought, she concentrated on pleasing him.

❧ 21 ❧

Just as in the early days of their courtship, laying siege to her had worked once more. Twelve days together and only one mention of Val Hunter—and that by him. With tomorrow the last day before the flight home, she hadn't even bought the Hunter woman a gift.

I've won. Even before I bring out the heavy artillery, I've won.

Maybe all this time he'd basically misjudged the situation, the Hunter woman's influence. Maybe it was actually the boy who claimed Carolyn's affections. If not totally understandable, it was possible—and so tonight's heavy artillery would be that much more potent. Women's notions about things were often beyond him; that's what made them so baffling, so mysterious and maddening and wonderful. . . .

He lay in bed dozing, complacent, hearing Carolyn moving about the bathroom. Sex half an hour ago had been an effort that drained him, but the orgasm—so intense he'd lost awareness of everything but the clasping velvet of her . . .

Carolyn came into the room. He said drowsily, "Princess, why don't we take it easy today, work on our tans?"

"Fine, honey. But I want to see the dive master, maybe you'd like to come with me. He has a special shell to show me; he's been cleaning it. I think I might want to buy it."

He shrugged. "Sure." He watched her with pleasure, breathing deeply as he remembered. "It was good."

She turned around and unsmilingly regarded him. "Do I really make you happy?"

"After the vacation we've had you're asking that?" He was bewildered by the question.

She turned and smiled at him in the mirror as she began vigorous brushing of her hair.

"Women!" he exclaimed humorously. "So help me God I'll never understand women." He watched her brush tangles efficiently out of the curling ends of her hair. "When are you going to cut that hair?"

Her eyes drifted to him, then away. "I don't know," she said, her voice vague and distant. "Sometime. . . ."

After lunch Carolyn glimpsed the dive master outside the gift shop. Beckoning to her, he unlocked a door next to the gift shop and entered. As she and Paul walked down, the Bahamian emerged, his massive hands filled.

Paul glanced at the shell's outer coat of lustrous pinkish white ridges, unimpressed. Smiling, his fine teeth very white in his dark face, the Bahamian turned the shell over and held it out to Carolyn. Paul stared, surprised.

The flared, fan-shaped edge was glowing salmon-brown, darkening into sable-brown ridges deeply etched as if they had been made by the teeth of a comb, deepening in richness that spoke tantalizingly of even greater richness within the inner spiral of the shell.

"It's stunning," Carolyn breathed. "It's just wonderful. . . ."

"Take it, touch it," the Bahamian said in his lilting accent. "It is one of our finest, a glorious shell."

Carolyn received the shell reverently in both hands, her fingertips caressing the deeply etched grooves curving into the inner chamber. Her eyes never leaving the shell, she said to Paul, "It's referred to as Queen of the Sea. . . . Mr. Cartwright told me all about it . . . or tried to. . . ."

She looked up at the Bahamian, whose muscular arms were folded across the pale green print shirt of the Winding Bay Club, and returned his smile. "I want it," she said.

"Ninety-five dollars, Mrs. Blake," the Bahamian said softly.

Carolyn nodded. "I want it," she repeated.

"Wait a minute, Carolyn," Paul said. "I agree it's unusual. But shouldn't we talk about this? I mean, it's—Where would it go in the house?"

"Queen of the Sea, how perfect," Carolyn murmured, her eyes distant. "I want it for Val," she said.

"Ninety-five dollars," Paul repeated with a touch of vertigo. "A shell, I don't know that a shell is worth—"

"It is," Carolyn stated. "Mr. Cartwright has been telling me quite a lot about shells. He's been very generous with his time." She extracted her traveler's checks from her shoulder bag, then turned her green eyes on Paul. "There really isn't a problem, is there?"

"I'm sure it's cheap at the price," he managed to say. Again there was the sensation of vertigo, so pronounced that he reached to the side of the building for support.

The champagne, he thought. Too much champagne for their end-of-vacation dinner. His sexual excitement built but would not peak; his body broke out in heavy perspiration. Climax when it happened was more merciful than ecstatic, a bludgeoning reminder of the insatiable Rita of his first marriage.

"You've never been like this before," Carolyn murmured, dabbing with a pillowcase at the pool of moisture between his shoulder blades and in the small of his back.

"I'll shower," he said, breathing with effort.

"You will not. You're fine."

After all his exertion she seemed only slightly short of breath. But then, he was rarely awake for this long afterward.

"You're fine," she said again.

"Darling?" He rolled over onto his back, pulled her on top of him and took her face in his hands. After all the glorious intimacy of their vacation, the intimacy they had just shared, this was the moment.

"Darling, I've been thinking for some time about this, I'm convinced this is the right time for us to have our baby. Now. I want a baby with you. A girl. With green eyes, like yours."

Carolyn's eyes looked unwaveringly into his. "Not yet, Paul."

She took his face into her own hands; he released her and closed his eyes. He felt her cool fingers caress his cheeks as she spoke. "You're only thirty-six—I realize now how young that really is. You're younger to me now than you've ever been. We have plenty of time." She said softly, soothingly, "And I'm just twenty-six. Only twenty-six, honey. I want my career, I want the chance to get more established so

I can do things later if I want to, not have to begin all over again like when we left Chicago. You can understand that, can't you?"

"Mmhmm," he uttered, looking away from her to adjust the pillow under his head.

She rolled off him and took his hand, held it in both hers, pressing it into her breasts. "It's all right then? It seems best right now."

"Mmhmm." He lay quietly.

"Paul?"

Breathing deeply, feigning sleep, he did not answer. He felt her slip out of bed, moments later heard water running in the bathroom.

He lay with his fists clenched at his side. Hotness stung his eyelids.

She had said: *It seems best right now.* That was what his mother had claimed. His mother had stated: THIS IS BEST.

❧ 22 ❧

She had been attentive, physically affectionate with Paul all day. Uncomfortable with public displays of affection, she nevertheless snuggled her head into his shoulder and held his hand from the time the Cessna took off to return them to Miami. She knew very well she had hurt him badly, that he had feigned sleep for hours; his breathing patterns were too familiar to her.

She had been more wakeful than he. She knew that if he had wanted a child any earlier—anytime before she had met Val—she would have acquiesced. It was from Val and the difficulties of Val's life that she had learned how circumscribed her life would be for years to come with the responsibility of a child. Yet Paul was nearing forty; it was his right to be a father. But her life and her career would be limited—not his. The options in her life would drastically narrow, just as they had for Val.

Val had told her, "I'm at my best as a regional painter, but I would have spent at least a year in Europe." There had been a hunger in her face. "And I wouldn't have spent so many years discovering what I wanted to paint and how to study my craft."

Carolyn had asked, "If you had to do it over, would you have . . . had a baby?"

"Oh God, yes. But if I could have waited till I was closer to thirty."

They landed in Miami. An hour later, on their nonstop flight to Los Angeles, Paul stared fixedly out the window of the jet. Knowing how transparent her efforts were to please, she said again, "I had such a lovely time, it was all so very beautiful."

He looked at her then, and smiled, and lifted her hand to his lips. "I love you, Princess. More than anything."

She pulled his head to her, kissed him.

Everything will be fine, she reassured herself. *He'll come around to understanding that another year or two won't make that much difference.*

By early evening she had finished unpacking; her gifts for Neal and Val were piled on her dressing table. She called Val from the bedroom extension, realizing that she had never spoken with her on the phone.

The sound of Val's low resonant voice struck her into sudden shyness. "Hi," she stuttered, "uh, hello—"

"Carrie, welcome home. I was hoping you'd call. Neal wants to say hello, then I'll ask you about—"

"Listen," she said, gazing at the stack of gifts, the carefully packaged Queen of the Sea. "Why don't I come over for maybe fifteen minutes? I brought back a few things. . . ."

She came into the living room, the gifts in her arms. "Honey, I'll be right back. They're leaving for the weekend," she lied, "otherwise I won't see Neal till next week—"

He glanced up, then continued to sort through his mail. "I'm tired. Probably jet lag."

"Lie down for a while, honey," she said sympathetically. He smiled, pulled two issues of *BusinessWeek* out of the stack of mail.

Neal was running around in his new shark T-shirt singing, "I'm the king of the for-r-r-est. . . ."

"The sea, you dummy," Val said affectionately. She was looking at the glowing shell in her hands. "Carrie, it's so incredible, so extraordinary. It would have been so easy for you to give me something I need. I'm so happy to have this wonderful treasure . . ."

"I have to get right back." She was flushed with joy at the pleasure she had given.

"Hey, I haven't even told you about the Olympics!" Neal shouted. "You can't go!"

"Stay just a little longer, Carrie," Val coaxed. "After all, he's had you for two weeks."

∽ 23 ∾

Only slightly stooped by his sixty-seven years, his white hair still full and thick, Jerry Robinson was comfortably retired, spending much of his time fishing at Lake Piru or playing pool with his cronies at this Lankershim Boulevard beer bar—icy cold this night from its aggressive air-conditioning—where he had brought Paul.

After considerable forced jollity with the bar habitués Jerry introduced him to, and after buying Jerry four beers, Paul judged him sufficiently relaxed, and led him to a corner table.

"Jerry," Paul said, making rings with his beer mug on a table shiny with varnish, "you mind me asking what you're getting for that guest house?"

Jerry blinked at Paul. "I don't mind, Brother. Three hundred is what."

Jerry addressed any man he liked as Brother. Paul detested the habit. But he smiled and nodded. "I figured you wouldn't ask what it's worth, Jerry. You've got a good heart. That Hunter woman, she a good tenant?"

"Keeps to herself."

"That only lasts so long. You know women." He chuckled along with Jerry and then asked, "What about the kid? He bother you or Dorothy?"

"Nah. I was worried at first to tell you the truth. Me and the wife don't like being bothered, you know. But it was Dorothy that said to let them rent. They've been okay. He's a good boy. Quiet, good manners. You don't see much of that in kids today."

"It's a wonder." Paul's eyes were caught by the glint of silver, a religious medal visible in Jerry's open-throat Hawaiian shirt. He emphasized his next words: "With a weirdo like that for a mother."

"Weirdo?" Jerry looked at him in rheumy-eyed alarm.

"Well, we had them over for dinner—"

"Dorothy mentioned she's seen Carolyn coming over quite a bit in the evenings."

"Carolyn's very fond of the boy." With effort, he kept the defensiveness out of his voice. "I'm sure he could use some mothering."

Jerry was looking at him, his watery blue eyes sympathetic; and with a rush of rage Paul realized that Jerry assumed he and Carolyn could not have children. He opened his mouth, then clamped his jaw shut.

Jerry said, "You don't think he gets much mothering from Miz Hunter? She seems to take real good care of him."

"Some people can put on a good show, I don't have to tell you that. She says she's been married but Carolyn—" He broke off and glanced apologetically at Jerry as if he had caught himself before revealing a confidence. He continued, "These artist types, well . . ."

Jerry nodded sagely.

"Even if she did have the kid under a mulberry bush, it doesn't make him any less a good kid, right? But that Hunter woman, she's full of strange ideas, Jerry. The night she was over to our house she said right in front of her son she didn't believe in much of anything. Hardly a God-fearing woman, would you say? Ever see her take her kid to church on a Sunday morning?"

As Jerry gaped at him, Paul pressed his advantage. "She doesn't need a man's presence around for her son, she said that, too. God knows what kind of sissy that boy might grow into with a mother who thinks like that. A lot of these women nowadays, they think they don't need men at all."

Jerry nodded. "The wife and I were talking about that just the other night."

"I'm glad Dorothy still agrees with you about things, Jerry. That Hunter woman gets hold of Dorothy, God knows what kind of stuff she'll pump into her. It'd be terrible after all these years if Dorothy got dissatisfied with everything you've both had together."

Jerry gaped at him again. "The wife—I know Dorothy, she could never feel like that."

"Every day on my job I see women out to convert any woman they can get their hands on. More so now that we've got Reagan in and some sanity back in this country. But they've got this Ferraro woman up for vice president now. You sure as hell can't keep Dorothy chained up while you're here or gone fishing, now can you?"

Jerry swallowed beer and swirled his mug, agitating the remnants. Paul signaled the waitress, a hard-faced bleached blonde, for another round. They drank in silence, Jerry contemplating his beer, Paul content to let his words ferment. He felt heavy-headed from the beer.

"Wish I could think of a way to get rid of her," Jerry finally said.

"Well," Paul said carefully, hiding his elation, "there's always a way. You need the house for some reason. Maybe a relative?"

"We don't have any relatives, not close by."

Paul smothered a snort of disgust. "She doesn't need to know that."

"I'm no good at making stuff up, lying to people, you know. They know it when I do."

"Look, Jerry. Why do you need a reason? You're just making one up to spare her feelings. It's your house, man. Don't we still have property rights in this country?"

"By God you're right, Brother!" Jerry clinked Paul's mug with his own and took a deep draught.

"You get three hundred for the place," Paul said, his head thick from the beer, trying to sift through his thoughts and gauge Jerry. "Tell you what. You're getting her out of my hair as well as yours—before she hurts either Carolyn or Dorothy. When the Hunter woman moves out I'll give you a hundred for your trouble, pay the rent till you rent it again."

"That's crazy." Jerry shook his head vigorously. "No way I need you to do that, Brother."

They argued good-naturedly—comrades now—before Jerry agreed he would accept a case of Moosehead beer for his trouble, that Paul would take him to the next Raiders game. They sealed their bargain with a handshake and another round of beer.

"I really think you could get three-fifty for the place," Paul told him. "I know you could get it."

"I dunno. It's awful small, Brother. No bathtub, carpets only so-so. And the kitchen—"

"Three and a quarter, then. Ask that much. You can always come down."

"You're one mighty smart fellow. Always told the wife that."

Paul suggested, "I don't think you ought to go into much detail about this with Dorothy."

"Don't worry about that. The Hunter woman doesn't have much to do with Dorothy. Anyway, the wife always goes along with what I do." Jerry rose, and with a belligerent swagger made his way to the men's room.

Paul contemplated his wavery reflection in the shiny surface of the table. He raised his beer mug. He murmured, "Congratulations, Brother."

❧ 24 ❧

Astounded, Carolyn was staring at Val.

Val chuckled dryly. "I must've looked just like you do when Jerry Robinson told me. He wouldn't look at me, Carrie. I asked if Neal had done anything, and he acted like he wanted to crawl into a hole. Everything I said, he repeated that business about wanting the house for a relative."

"I'll talk to him. Better yet, I'll ask Paul to. They talk out in the yard, they—"

"No." Val's tone was decisive. "I don't care about his reasons. I don't want to be anywhere I'm not wanted. He told me to take all the time I need to find another place. I intend to. Will you help me?"

"Of course. But this is ridiculous. I don't understand—"

"There's nothing to be done. Put it down as one of life's little X factors."

Ignoring Paul's indifference, his increasing irritation, she insisted on talking about Jerry Robinson.

"In the year and a half we've lived here the only relative who visited them was that brother from Hawaii, remember? The Robinsons insisted we come over and meet him. He won't rent to any relative—"

"How do we know? There may be another relative." His voice was sharp, exasperated. "What the hell do I care?"

She said coldly, "I'll be spending a lot of time helping her. It won't be easy finding the right place for an artist."

"I'm sure," he said with heavy sarcasm.

But it was only ten days later when Val said, "This is it, Carrie. Look at the light in here, all these big windows. A little ramshackle but it's cheap compared to what we've been looking at and it'll clean up, don't you think?"

"Yes," Carolyn said, her throat thick with misery at the three shabby rooms converted from previous office space above a down-at-the-heels drugstore, with noisy traffic below them on heavily traveled Magnolia Boulevard. She had loved the tiny yellow house . . . "We can fix it up, Val, make it comfortable."

With Carolyn helping, Val moved in at the end of the month, the last Sunday in September. After Neal went to bed that night, Val flung herself onto the sofa. "Carrie, if I'm this tired you must be exhausted."

"I'm fine." She would not admit that she had never worked so hard, had never been more tired in her life. "You did four times as much as me. You'll be sore tomorrow . . . Come over," she urged. "The pool will be good—"

"Too much to do. Why don't you come here? I'm on your way home now. I promise not to make you work. We'll have more time together."

"You're right," Carolyn said thoughtfully, happy with the idea of more time with Val. "There's usually some advantage in any change—even if it doesn't seem like it at the time."

"This place is brighter, more open," Val said tiredly. "To tell you the truth, I was having occasional attacks of claustrophobia in that little house."

When Carolyn returned from getting a drink of water, Val was slumped down in a corner of the sofa, asleep. It wouldn't hurt, Carolyn decided, for her to sleep in her cutoffs. She lifted Val's feet; Val curled her length into the short sofa. Carolyn found a blanket in the big box of linens, covered her gently, and let herself out of the flat.

Monday, after visiting Val, Carolyn slowed her car as she recognized the orange and white polyester pants of Dorothy Robinson; she was carrying two bags of groceries. Carolyn regarded her pensively. If the Robinsons did not actually intend to rent their place to a relative, then why had they evicted Val? She pulled over and picked up Dorothy Robinson.

When Paul arrived home she was standing in the living room, arms crossed. He did not appear to notice that she had not answered his greeting; he folded his jacket carefully across the back of the white armchair and came toward her. "Lenny was telling me today about a house," he was saying, "three blocks from him in Encino, the owner's desperate. We might—"

"You rotten son of a bitch."

He halted in midstride.

"*You* did it to Val. *You.*"

"What are you talking about?"

His blue eyes were calm, but she had heard all she needed to know in his voice. She had irrationally hoped that Dorothy Robinson was somehow wrong.

"Is this how you look when you're screwing somebody in a business deal? This cool and innocent?" She could not control the trembling of her body nor the reflection of it in her voice. "Jerry Robinson lied to Val Hunter but he doesn't lie to his wife. Dorothy Robinson didn't know about it until after it was done. She thinks it's dreadful how you and Jerry got rid of a woman who hadn't done anyone any harm."

He did not reply. The remoteness of his eyes reminded her of a science fiction movie she had seen the night before, with people whose eyes were blank, their bodies taken over by aliens.

She said, "I see now how it's been. It's not only my friends or the hours I work, it's my entire life. It always has been. You own me. I didn't really know it before because it never really mattered before."

"That's not true. Everything we had together before was wonderful. We were happy before, remember? I don't know what crazy things she's put in your head." His voice was sure, held conviction. "I have every right to protect you from her."

"Protect? *Protect?* You're crazy."

"That Amazon's turned you against me. Put nothing but garbage in your head."

"How could she possibly threaten you? We're married. You're my husband. She's another woman. I'm not your slave, I—"

"Just listen to me, Carolyn. She's not just another woman. She wants you for herself. I know you don't believe this, but that female Paul Bunyan is a dyke. She's trying to get you into *bed* with her."

"She's never done anything, she's—" For a moment her jaw worked in soundless outrage. "I've never been unfaithful to you; it's never even occurred to me. Obviously you think I'm capable of screwing anything, man, woman, or child."

His mouth was a thin white line. "All I know is ever since that Amazon came along we've had half a marriage."

"Half a marriage?" she said grimly. "I'll show you what half a marriage really is."

She marched into the bedroom. It took three trips to move her clothes into the guest room.

✋ 25 ✌

Clouds of cottony mist swirled around them as Carolyn turned to Val, her green eyes wide and needful, her bikini-clad body glowing. Carolyn lowered her head to Val's shoulder, her hair cascading silk. Carolyn's arms held her, Carolyn clung to her; marble-cold flesh warmed under Val's hands. Carolyn raised her face to her . . .

Awake, Val pushed the blanket aside, welcoming the morning air on her heated body.

Only in dreams did she have such images, she reminded herself, her pulse slowing; never in her waking hours did she have such thoughts. . . . Undoubtedly these dreams were the result of the power of suggestion planted by Alix. Or simply misplaced guilt over Alix.

She addressed Alix sternly: *Not all love is sex, not all touching is sex. I have all the touching from her I want or need. I have her warmth, her affection, her trust. You were a phase, Alix. These dreams are a phase.*

In the gray of the room she picked up her watch. Six-thirty. She rose and shrugged into her old woolen robe, grateful for cold mornings and mild days after the searing heat of September. It was early but she had work to do preparing the paintings for travel. And what should she wear? Her newest jeans and the good white blouse, she decided. She was selling her work, not her body. Carolyn would be dressed well enough for both of them; they wouldn't be thrown out of the snooty city of Santa Barbara. . . .

Of all the events of the past week, Carolyn's accompanying her today was the most intriguing. Smiling, Val remembered the circumstances, how she had been bantering with Neal: "Far be it from me, a measly mother, to expect a trip to Santa Barbara and a visit to the beach house afterward to compete with a Sunday in front of Granddad's TV."

Neal had retorted, "Granddad understands all about the Cubs maybe going to the World Series and Walter Payton breaking Jim Brown's rushing record and Dallas being on the tube besides."

Carolyn's query had been soft: "Would you like me to go with you, Val?"

"Well . . . sure," she had replied, quickly recovering from her amazement. "But I do need to stop at the beach house, Carrie. Pick up some paintings—"

"I can spend the day with you," Carolyn had said in the same quiet voice.

What in the hell was going on with the Blake marriage? Never mind all of Carolyn's excuses about wanting to help fix up the flat; she had been spending astonishing amounts of time there. Carolyn's moods had been pendulum swings between frenetic chatter and dispirited silence. It had taken sharp reining in of her concern and curiosity not to inquire, not to probe—to wait for Carolyn to talk when she was ready.

Val squeezed toothpaste onto her brush. Maybe Paul Blake was playing golf or going to a football game or some other stupid male weekend ritual—but even so he must be in a terminal rage knowing where Carolyn would be this day, whom she preferred to be with. Maybe, she thought, peering into the mirror with a toothpaste grin, he even suspected a lesbian affair.

How ironic that for the first time in her life she liked the idea of someone thinking she was a lesbian—as long as that someone was Paul Blake.

She tossed aside the robe and stepped into the bracing cool spray of the shower. Clearly, something was amiss in the Blake marriage. While she wished Paul Blake nothing but ill—and one day surely Carolyn would discover that she could not be married to this man— she could not take any satisfaction in any situation bringing Carolyn real unhappiness.

๑ 26 ๑

Sitting at the table, sifting through the multitude of sections that comprised the Sunday *Times,* he drank coffee and ate the English muffin Carolyn had prepared for him, and listened to the sounds of her preparation for leaving. Before, over the weekends, she always took her bath in the evening, an hour or so before they went to bed, and came out to him wearing a robe and smelling deliciously of bath scents, to curl up on the sofa. Bathing on a weekend morning . . . to go off like this without him . . .

Not since the death of his mother had he been so helpless, so unable to act. Every night since Monday she had slept in the guest room. As usual she had prepared his dinner, but left it warming in the oven; he had worked late all week because he could not be in the house with her. Could not bear her chill formality when she was there, yet could not bear his anguish when she was not there—when she was with Val Hunter. He did not even know where Val Hunter now lived.

"I hope you're not wandering around this late at night in a dangerous part of the Valley," he had said at midnight on Wednesday when she came home. It was both a warning and a probe for information. But she had not replied.

Three times this week she had been gone late into the night, as if she no longer cared about her own lack of sleep, as if he no longer deserved the slightest consideration. Each night he waited up for her. They did not exchange even brief news of their workday; they did not mention—or even allude to—their quarrel. Careful about continuing to demonstrate his own affection, he touched her in the casual ways he always had—an arm around her when he came into the kitchen for ice—all the physical habits of all the days of their marriage, hoping to convey that this part of his love for her was too ingrained in him to change, regardless of the degree of their estrangement.

He had lost essential, crucial control. He was in the weakest position he had ever been in with Carolyn—he held a poor hand of cards, and must play them carefully. No matter what the cost to him in pain, the next move must be hers—or he would lose more than he could ever recover.

Ride it out, he told himself, as he had told himself every day that week. When the cards were this bad, you held them close to the vest, and bluffed. There was nothing else to be done.

This would blow over. It had to. A friendship of only a few months duration against years of marriage? Correct balance had to reassert itself. His side was weighted with eight proven years of loving and caring.

He'd overreacted to the Hunter woman. Used an atom bomb when anything else would have done as well with less fallout besides. He didn't believe today's psychobabble, but Carolyn was indeed going through a life phase, some kind of hysteria peculiar to women. A little fling at independence was what she actually wanted, so let her get this out of her system and then they would go on as before.

He had to stand firm and soon everything would be all right again, everything would gradually return to normal, like it was before. In the future he would be more careful—give Carolyn more leash. When they got transferred out of this loony bin of a city—and he would do his best to make that happen soon, even accept a lateral transfer—he would be certain to immediately seek a wide circle of acquaintances, have more social life. She would have her women friends, all she wanted. But there would be no more Val Hunters.

Whatever the attraction in this relationship, it would pall. Val Hunter was perfectly capable of sexual aberration—the woman was masculine enough to wear a suit and tie—but Carolyn was a completely normal woman who was only temporarily fascinated by a freak. If Carolyn was confused right now, she would eventually belong to him again. Because there was real substance here. He had a close friendship himself—twice this past week he'd talked to Harve in Chicago, betting that the Cubs would reach the World Series—and no friendship, no matter how close, could challenge the powerful bonding of a good marriage.

Yes, ride it out. Be patient. Behave like a saint. No, like a martyr who was allowing a willful wife to do anything she wanted. As soon as Carolyn relented, as soon as she decided to be conciliatory, he'd figure out ways to soothe all her ruffled feathers, make everything up to her, solidify his marriage once and for all. They would be closer than they had ever been . . .

Gazing across the living room dimmed by closed drapes, in the silence of his house he strained for any sound of her. A wave of chill brought gooseflesh to his arms, and he admitted his fear: To love was the ultimate risk. One he had taken blindly, without knowledge of the stakes. Was this what his mother, with her death, had tried to teach him?

He had not learned—had not even seen the warning. He had loved again, and this time with every molecule of his being. To lose Carolyn . . . he could comprehend such a loss no more than he could comprehend his own death.

Carolyn came into the room and he looked at her, his chest tight with pain. She wore a short-sleeved shirt the color of lime, one he had not seen before, and dark green denim pants. Without makeup—just the barest touch of lipstick—she looked very young, her blow-dried hair thick around her face, the ends curly and unruly. He could not remember when she had ever looked more beautiful to him.

He said with difficulty, "Take your car. That heap she drives, you'll be lucky to make it around the corner." He thought he saw a softening in her face, the beginning of a smile.

"I'll suggest it," she said. "You look tired."

"Long tough week." He managed a smile. It was as much as he was willing to concede.

"I'm tired too." She leaned over to quickly kiss his forehead, her hands braced on his shoulders as if to resist if he pulled her to him. "Be back this afternoon."

The scents of her bathing filled him with anguished longing. He clasped her waist; but his hands moved gently on her as he kissed her forehead. He would not be so dishonest to wish her a good time. "Be careful," he said.

As she walked away he closed his eyes, thinking of her silky nakedness pressed into him, her arms holding him.

❧ 27 ❧

Looking at her with pleasure, Val let Carolyn into the flat. It was nine o'clock; she had already taken Neal to his grandfather's. She planned to be in Santa Barbara half an hour before Hilda Green's gallery opened at eleven.

"Paul wants us to take my car," Carolyn told her. "I promised him I'd mention it."

"The Bug's all packed," Val said easily. "I don't want to move the paintings again."

Fuck you, Paul Blake. My car's good enough for your wife, taped upholstery and all.

Still struggling to subdue her anger, Val picked up a small wicker basket. "Some fruit, cheese, apple juice. Neal packed this—he thought we might get hungry coming back."

Carolyn chuckled. "He's amazing. You look nice, Val."

She grinned, her good humor restored. "You look cute." She pulled a Windbreaker from the closet; Carolyn should have worn long sleeves. It would be cool beside the ocean.

Hopestead Gallery was in a wooded enclave on the outskirts of Santa Barbara, one of a dozen specialty shops of white clapboard with roofs of stained wood shingles and a landscape of bark chips and tiny fir trees. "Fancy schmancy," Val murmured. "This probably won't take long, Carrie."

"I'll be strolling around," Carolyn said, eyeing a pastry shop from which delicious odors wafted on the crisp morning air.

In answer to Val's knock, a white door with amber bottle-glass panes swung open to reveal a gray-haired woman in a plum-colored silk dress. "You must be Val Hunter. Come in. A friend of mine has one of your paintings . . ."

An hour later Val found Carolyn wandering through a gift shop. Carolyn spotted her, ran to her, embraced her. "It's good news, I can tell."

Val hugged her back. "Yes." She took her arm, the flesh cool to her palm. "Come on, I'll tell you in the car."

Weaving through heavy Sunday traffic, Val spoke excitedly. "So she's agreed to take six and then we'll see. But she's very confident. She wants to branch out from carrying local artists, to upgrade the gallery, she told me. Upgrade it, Carrie. She'd already decided to carry my work on the basis of a friend's opinion in L.A. and from those lousy photos I sent her."

Carolyn reached to her, covered the hand that lay on the gear shift. "Finally things are starting to open out for you. Neal will be so proud."

Val clasped Carolyn's hand. "I'm so glad you're with me."

"Val—a curiosity question. What percentage does a gallery take when it sells your work?"

"Thirty-five is common. Susan takes thirty. Hilda Green wants forty."

"That much? But that only leaves—"

"Less than you think," Val finished with a chuckle. She squeezed Carolyn's hand. "All the planning, the actual work itself, not to mention materials—I must make about twenty cents an hour. But . . ." She grinned joyously at Carolyn.

The car began to labor and she took her hand from Carolyn's to shift into high gear. "Hilda Green's gallery may be small but she has an active clientele. She thinks my work should be priced at no less than a thousand dollars."

She reached for Carolyn's hand again. For the next hour and a half, her mood pure exuberance, she talked to Carolyn and managed to wend her way through the traffic on Highway 101 with one hand on the wheel.

The house in Malibu was two stories of weatherbeaten gray wood, cheek to jowl with the other modest houses nowhere near the Malibu Colony, their only glamour a limitless sea and sky.

Consulting a card, Val punched a code on a panel just inside the front door to turn off the burglar alarm. Carolyn glanced first at the dominating flagstone fireplace flanked by two picture windows. The house looked out over waves sufficiently strewn with boulders to discourage surfers, a beach rocky enough to deter sunbathers. A long sofa faced the sea; bookcases lined the side walls, one containing a TV and record player. An imposing grandfather clock of burnished cherrywood stood in a far corner, its ticktock perforating the crashing of the surf, its single chime drawing attention to the time: one-thirty. Plants hanging from wicker baskets enlivened the beige and brown colors of the room. Carolyn walked over to examine photos on the dining room wall, evidently interested in the people who owned this house.

"It's wonderful here," Carolyn said. "A dollhouse, perfect for two. But it seems really damp and chilly."

"The upstairs louvers are open," Val said. "It's been so hot they've been open all summer. Get the Windbreaker out of the car while I close them."

"I'm okay. I want to come upstairs with you."

As Val pulled the louvers closed Carolyn glanced at the large bedroom containing an early American four-poster bed, a walk-in closet, a bathroom with an oversize tub.

Downstairs again, Carolyn went to the window. Far out on the horizon hung a gray curtain of mist, but the day was clear and bright and the tide was high, green waves breaking powerfully over dark rocks with plumes of pure white spray. They stood for long minutes, not speaking. Carolyn reached for Val's hand, then released it to slide an arm around Val's waist. Val's arm circled Carolyn. There were slight tremors in Carolyn's body.

Carolyn said softly, "I am cold. I should've worn something warmer."

Without hesitation and without thought Val turned and took her into her arms, held her to warm her. Carolyn's head touched her shoulder; Val felt the texture of her hair against her throat. For a moment they stood motionless, Val knowing only that she must warm Carolyn; her arms tightened around the soft body in her arms. Carolyn uttered an indecipherable sound.

Val's hands caressed the planes of her back, the narrowing curve of waist. Thought emerged then: *Stop.* But irresistibly her hands curved down over her hips, cupped them.

"*Val.*"

The word was spoken with such sharp clarity that Val released her and stepped back so quickly that Carolyn stumbled and then caught her balance.

Val stared at her.

Carolyn's eyes were wide, and filled with consternation.

Val turned away. She thought: *It's all over, I've blown everything.*

✌ 28 ☙

I knew this. The words hung in Carolyn's mind as if written there. *Paul knew this. And I knew it too.*

"Val," she said, surprised at the calmness of her voice. "Would it be all right to have a fire?"

Val turned back to her, her expression dumbfounded. Then she glanced at the fireplace. "I guess so." She added more forcefully, "I don't know why not." In two strides she reached the hearth and knelt on one knee beside the basket of firewood.

Carolyn took a woolen lap robe from the sofa, unfolded and spread it over the carpet before the fireplace to create a smaller, more informal setting in which to talk. Her movements were automatic and instinctive; her mind churned.

The fire was quickly established; Val stood before it with a poker, jabbing at a log—unnecessarily, Carolyn realized.

"Val," she said. She sat down on the blanket and extended a hand to her.

Val sat on the far edge of the green plaid blanket, crossing her blue-jeaned legs yoga style. Carolyn moved to her on her knees, took her hand. The hand was unresponsive.

"Val, we—" With an abruptness that was pure instinct she ordered, "Val, look at me."

The eyes that were raised to her were those of a child expecting a blow. Blindly Carolyn reached to her, took Val's other hand, rubbed both hands in hers, warming them. "Val," she said huskily, "we've been touching for months."

Val did not answer.

I don't know what she needs from me. "Val, can you tell me . . . how you feel?" *God, I'm groping through a minefield.* "Can you tell me what you . . ."

118

"I . . ." Val cleared her throat. "I don't know." Her low voice was off-tone. "I actually don't know."

In silence, Carolyn felt the clear truth of this answer, because it was her own answer as well.

My wanting to be with her was more than friendship, more than guilt over what Paul did to her. But I don't know what I've needed all this time, what I was looking for. . . .

"What difference does it make?" Val's voice had strengthened; her eyes were fixed on the fire.

Carolyn said slowly, "I'm not sure how I feel either. Not . . . consciously. But . . . we've been touching for months. And I've—" She faltered; she was going to say, *brought everything on.*

Her hands tightened on Val's. The way through this had to be with honesty. "Val, I've always been the one who's done most of the touching." The next words broke from an unsuspected depth, an uncapped wellspring: "Because there was something between us and I felt it."

Val did not answer, but her eyes met Carolyn's.

Carolyn held the searching gaze. *I'm not afraid. I wouldn't hurt her. How can she hurt me?*

"Carrie."

She was startled by the sound of her name, and reluctant to come out of her mental process.

Val said, "I've never . . ."

Again she was startled, again by her recognition of truth. The only way any of this could have happened was through mutual innocence.

"I know," she answered. "I would have . . . seen it."

Val's hands released hers. Val reached for her. Carolyn tensed with expectation; involuntarily she closed her eyes. She felt Val's hands in her hair. Val lifted her hair from her shoulders, held it as if weighing it.

Awkward, uncertain what to do with her own hands, she placed them on Val's shoulders, feeling warm solid flesh through the silky fabric.

Soft hands cupped Carolyn's face. *Val's hands.* The knowledge surged through her: *Val's hands.*

Carolyn looked into dark eyes, compelled by their depth and intensity, unaware that her own hand had moved into Val's hair until the crisp curliness wound around her fingers.

Val's eyes were heavy-lidded; she was looking at Carolyn's mouth. As if by hypnotic command Carolyn lowered her own eyes to Val's mouth, focusing on the full sensual shape of it.

She did not know if she had been pulled toward Val or if she had pulled Val to her, but Val was the one to draw away. Still experiencing the gentleness, the softness, the chasteness of the lips that had so briefly touched hers, knowing only that she wanted them again, Carolyn's eyes again focused on Val's mouth.

Under the slow questing pressure of her own, Val's lips became velvety yielding. She held Val's shoulders to brace herself, and stared at her mouth. "Do my lips feel like yours?"

Seeing Val's perplexed look, the beginning of a grin, she realized the absurdity of the question and laughed. Val joined her in tension-breaking laughter.

"I don't know. Do mine feel like yours, Carrie?"

Both hands in Val's hair, she held Val's mouth to hers. Her own lips parted, and tentatively, lightly, she touched Val's tongue with the tip of her own, and then took her mouth away, pierced by the profound intimacy of the connection. Her arms circled Val, her body yearning toward her.

A fireplace log noisily shifted; as it fell in a crash and shower of sparks, the women broke apart. Val rose to tend the fire.

Carolyn watched her in a prickling of excitement—uncertainty mixed with eagerness. In this exploration of newness she felt safe and in control.

Val came back and sat close to her, her eyes calm, steady. But as Val's hands came to her hair again Carolyn realized that Val was hesitant to touch her. She took Val's hands away, held them.

Val asked, "Are you okay?"

"Yes," she answered. "Are you?"

She slid her arms around Val, then yielded to Val's arms gathering her into softness, into the rich soft contours of her body.

She was aware of the rhythmic thunder of surf, the ticktock of the grandfather clock and its chiming of two, then of the quarter hour, then the half hour. Suffused with warmth from the deep pleasure of Val's arms, she lay on the blanket, her back to the fire, her head on a soft pillow. She traced the delicate shape of Val's ear with her tongue and felt Val quiver.

Val shifted, propped herself on her elbows, her body curved over Carolyn. Carolyn's arms circled her; she caressed Val's shoulders, down her back; she slid her hands up under Val's blouse, the bra a barrier over the smooth warm flesh. Carolyn unhooked it, her arms drawing Val onto her, the released breasts another spreading softness on her body. She slid her palms over the smooth planes of Val's back, sinking her fingers into the soft flesh.

Val lifted her body; Carolyn filled her hands with creamy heaviness, curving and pliant, overflowing and incredible. As if wanting only the sensation of Carolyn's hands on her breasts, Val lifted her body fully from her. Tautness had quickly formed under Carolyn's palms; she released the rich full breasts to gently take the nipples between her fingertips.

The clock chimed three o'clock. Carolyn lay breathing the fragrance of the sun from Val's tanned skin and rolling her face in Val's breasts, absorbing in unending greed the pliant round smoothness. Again her lips closed around a swollen nipple; again she took it into her.

Val pulled her up into her arms. Her kiss was aggressive, her tongue swift thrusts. Without gentleness a hand moved down over Carolyn's throat and inside her shirt. The nipple tingled and hardened before Val's fingertips touched it.

The hands on the buttons of Carolyn's shirt were impatient. Carolyn thought: *Poor small breasts, not nearly the feast hers are . . .*

The big, soft hands cupped and caressed Carolyn's breasts; Val kissed her, her tongue stroking as slowly in Carolyn as it had slowly and sweetly stroked her breasts. Still kissing her, Val gripped Carolyn's hips, pressing them up into her. Her hands came to the belt of Carolyn's pants.

Val rose to close the drapes. In the gray of the room Carolyn lay nude, watching Val, hearing the crackling of the fresh log Val had tossed on the fire, the faint barking of a dog on the beach, the thunder of surf.

Val knelt beside her, pulling off her jeans. Firelight made copper-gold highlights in her dark hair, gold tones on her skin. Carolyn's glance slid away, then boldly back: The triangle of hair was a curly black thatch. The wide hips were fleshy globes, large and powerful, stark white etched into the dark tan.

Memory pulled at her, forcefully tugged at her mind. Something she had seen in a place that was green . . .

Val came to her; the big soft hands were warm on Carolyn's body, moving so caressingly down her that Carolyn closed her eyes to feel her body shaped by them. *Val's hands,* she thought; *the beautiful hands of an artist. . .*

Val's body was arched over her, close but not touching her, and Val's hands moved under her, to clasp and lift her hips. She pressed Carolyn up into her, between her thighs. Carolyn pulled Val onto her. Val's body was warm and strong, and like silk, like cream. Enveloped in softness, Carolyn clung to her, gripping Val's back, gripping her shoulders, arching into her, pleasure rolling through her with each stroke of Val's tongue within her.

She had taken her mouth away from Val's to breathe. Between her legs Val's palm was warm, unmoving; Val's swift breathing matched her own. Her body jerked as Val's fingers found her; she was astonished by her own wetness. She shuddered as the fingers began to stroke, and she heard the sound of Val's breath catching in her throat.

Urgently Carolyn rotated her hips in the rhythm she needed; then stopped; Val's fingers, a perfect pressure, had taken the rhythm from her. Carolyn spread her tense, quivering legs fully open.

She tried to hold the tension in her, then to hold a tiny part. But it drained out of her; and her body sank back onto the floor. Breathing deeply, she opened her eyes, soothed by the hand that lay, warm and still, between her legs; by Val's lips tender on her face, and the rhythmic surf that seemed now a part of her.

So easy with her . . . so very easy . . .

How was it that Val would want to come? But Val's mouth came to hers, sweetly sensual, searching. Soon, like a glass refilling, desire rose again, sensations slowly emerging to vividness and more penetrating than before, as if the patterns laid among her nerve ends were widening. At the first touch of Val's fingers her pleasure was deeper, and she knew that what she would feel again would be much stronger. Dimly, just before she came, she heard chimes of the clock, but not the number.

She said thickly to Val, "I want you to . . . to . . ."

But she was overpowered again, by the lips that dominated hers, by hands that caressed with tantalizing sureness, by fingers that came to her again and this time moved slowly, unhurriedly.

Afterward, drugged with lassitude, warm in Val's arms, she stared over Val's shoulder into the gray of the room—gray that enveloped and overcame.

Sharp popping of a log in the fireplace awakened her. The pervasive warmth of her body blissful, she sank back toward sleep, then realized that her head lay on Val's shoulder and Val's arms held her, one hand moving almost imperceptibly in her hair. The blanket was pulled up around her; the fire was reduced to embers.

She lifted her head to stare at Val. "How long did I sleep?"

Val smiled, touched her cheek. "About twenty minutes."

"I can't believe . . ." Carolyn propped herself on an elbow. "That's terrible."

Val smoothed Carolyn's hair back. "Some people might consider it flattering."

"I didn't . . . you didn't . . ." She looked away in embarrassment. "What time is it?"

"A little after five."

"It can't be!"

"It is. We need to get back."

"But you . . . we didn't—"

"I'll take a raincheck." Val's smile was gentle, amused.

The languor of her body had begun to dissipate. She was not ready to leave, did not want to. She cast about for an excuse. "Can I take a shower? Is that all right?"

"I don't see why not."

Staring at Val's powerful nude body, Carolyn followed her up the stairs to the bathroom.

"I need to keep my hair dry," Carolyn said. She pushed this first thought of Paul firmly out of her mind.

In the thrumming of warm shower spray, she stood on tiptoe with her arms around Val, her face pressed into Val's shoulder. Finally Val reached behind Carolyn to turn the shower taps off. Carolyn said heedlessly, "Couldn't you leave Neal with his grandfather just a little longer?"

Val wrapped her in a large white towel. She dried herself, then took Carolyn's hand and led her downstairs. Suddenly she scooped Carolyn off her feet and stood holding her, chuckling. "Humor me," she said.

Carolyn wound her arms around Val's neck, enjoying and admiring the strength of the woman who held her. Something about Val's strength. Again the elusive memory nagged at her.

Val knelt and gently placed her on the blanket in front of the fire. The room had cooled. Val added another log to the fire and poked it into flames.

Carolyn watched her, hypnotized. The memory she had been trying to recapture for months struggled to break clear.

And then she remembered, and was stunned by the power of the memory. Six gigantic bronze sculptures in a park in Chicago when she was nine. Enormous, magnificent, mighty statues of female bodies. Sculpted by whom? It had not occurred to her then to wonder.

"Why are they so big?" she had whispered to her mother, awed by the powerful hips and thighs of the bronze women towering over her.

"They're supposed to be, that's all," her mother said, her voice terse, disapproving.

Carolyn's gaze was finally drawn to a plaque imbedded in the ground. "What's a fertility symbol?" she asked her mother.

"You'll know when you grow up," her mother said darkly, taking her by the hand and tugging, pulling her away as Carolyn stared longingly backward.

She had put the statues out of her mind. She could not bear her mother's threat of what she would one day learn about these great, round, glorious sculptures of women . . .

Val walked to her. In wonder, and in anticipation that contained a touch of fear, Carolyn stared at her. She seemed overpoweringly female.

Val sank down beside her, and as if she were unwrapping a gift, opened the towel, smoothing its folds, her dark liquid gaze in leisurely contemplation of Carolyn's body. Her voice was husky: "You're lovely as spring."

Carolyn reached for her. Luxuriant flesh was under her hands— Val's hips and thighs. Kissing Val, she soon took her mouth away to concentrate on savoring her body.

Shyly, she brushed a palm over crisp-soft hair still damp from the shower. Val's legs opened. In a surge of excitement she caressed between, within warm folds of satin.

Val took her hand away and turned Carolyn onto her back. She parted Carolyn's thighs and then arched her body over Carolyn, fitting her dark thatch of hair between Carolyn's legs. With a soft sound, her eyes closed, Val lowered her body.

Welcoming her, wanting her, wanting to fully enclose her, Carolyn raised her legs high and wrapped her arms and legs around her.

The sound in Val's throat was helpless, as if she could not control her body. Carolyn's arms tightened. Connected to the pulsing rhythms of Val's body, her hips gradually became undulant, synchronized.

Val sucked in her breath, and Carolyn could see her hands grip and release the towel as if powerless to sustain either the grip or the release.

Her own arousal growing and deepening, her hips still undulant, Carolyn lowered her legs to spread them fully. Val's hands began a spastic fluttering. A thought passed through Carolyn that her body was being used so very lightly to give such great pleasure. Then there was only Val in her arms and the brilliance of her own sensations.

Val's body was rigid, her hands gripping with white-knuckled fierceness. Her body was quivering stillness, as if consumed. Then the hands relaxed; Val's body eased and once more blended softly into Carolyn's.

Still absorbed in her own sensations, her hips continuing to undulate, Carolyn arched as the big soft hand cupped between her legs.

She was fully embraced in warmth and softness, knowing that she must somehow extricate herself and knowing she could not. She lay on Val's body aware of one hand that caressed her hips, squeezing and releasing them, but focused on the pleasure from the other hand, the fingers enclosed in her. She moved only slightly, her pleasure a luminous constant, until she could not prevent the rhythm of her body. Afterward the hand did not leave her; the fingers lay intimately within.

The clock chimed seven. She dragged herself from Val.

She composed her excuse to Paul as she dressed, then pushed further thought of that from her mind.

As they drove to the Valley, Val seemed remote, her silence like a cloak around her. Carolyn was grateful; she did not want to use either her voice or her mind. She sat quietly, in pure contemplation of the exquisite satiation and euphoria of her body.

ꙮ 29 ꙮ

She called her father. She would pick up Neal early in the morning and take him to school, if that was all right. Yes, she was okay; she just needed more time for herself. She spoke briefly, lovingly to Neal, then hung up knowing her father thought she was with a man. Not that he would be judgmental: *poppycock* was his most frequently expressed opinion of religious moral strictures. But his concept of sexual normalcy was standard male; he would consider the events of this day equivalent to her taking up with an orangutan.

She opened a can of pork and beans, eating from the pan as the beans heated, too ravenous to wait. Holding the pan insulated in several thicknesses of dishtowel, she took it into the living room and sat on her sofa and wolfed down the rest. She placed the pan, still wrapped in its towel, on the coffee table and sat for several minutes unmoving, the sounds of traffic on the street below washing over her. Its rhythms, she realized, were like ocean rhythms . . .

Leaning back, she extended her hands to examine them. She touched a fingertip to her lips and inhaled the scent of Carolyn Blake.

She wondered sardonically who would laugh harder, Paul Blake or Alix Sommers? Probably Paul Blake. Whatever the trouble was with the Blake marriage, he would scorn the idea that lesbian sex could pretend to compete with good old heterosex. So his wife had amused herself with another woman, had indulged in a little mutual masturbation, so what?

What *had* Carolyn Blake felt? Surely nothing like what she knew in her marriage bed. Yes, she had enjoyed the sex . . . more than enjoyed it. But she, Val, could hardly accept congratulations for Carolyn Blake's exhausted sleep; undoubtedly it was the number of times, not the intensity of each experience.

Val walked into the kitchen. As she heated water for a cup of instant coffee, she addressed the sneering face of Paul Blake: *I'll lay odds you've never put her to sleep. I'll lay odds you're like most men, just shoot your wad off and fall asleep.*

She returned to the living room with her coffee, thinking about Alix. Alix would laugh at her too. Short and knowing and bitter laughter.

How old had Alix been when they lived together? Richard had left the year before . . . Neal was four . . . She remembered how Alix had leaped at the opportunity to live with her. After years of capricious affairs with men, of feeling like an object of prey even more exposed because of her blondeness, a nonmale domestic situation had seemed to Alix somehow a measure of protection. Twenty-six. Alix had been twenty-six. The same age as Carolyn Blake.

For Alix, falling in love with a woman was a clear answer, an explanation for the previous incoherence of her life, an answer she accepted with alacrity even if it brought along with it complications and anguish. In rebellious exhilaration she quit her conventional office job, and when she would no longer accept the physical frustrations of living with Val, Alix moved out. There had been a succession of jobs and women lovers, each welcomed with fresh belief, each lover abandoned with little evident regret and no apparent damage or acrimony on either side. All of Alix's lovers were still her friends, a circumstance Val had viewed as proof that sexual love between women lacked true visceral power.

After Alix's departure Val had decided not to live with anyone else. For Neal's sake as well as her own she would not risk repeating her debilitating marital wars, and the idea of living with another woman she had rejected without examination of the issue.

But she knew why. She would not live with a lesbian, and a heterosexual woman could not follow Alix, could not duplicate that smoldering sexual tension between herself and Alix.

Yes, they had touched, Alix continually seducing her into brief embraces, each time trying to break the barrier Val had circumscribed for herself, each time Val pushing her away. Val had known that if she lived with another woman she would want a woman like Alix again.

She had believed Alix should be grateful for whatever she chose to give her. Clearly, Alix's brand of love was inferior. Hadn't Andy and Richard shown the same attitude toward her? She was a freak among women; she should be grateful they were willing to marry her.

And she *had* been grateful. Then she dared to assert herself, ask for more, even expect a measure of equality. Unlike Alix, she did not walk out; the pitiful men she married were the ones to walk out, never to return.

Of her lovers, casual or serious, only Alix had remained her friend. Even limited touching of Alix, she conceded now, qualified Alix as a lover. And she herself was one of Alix's ex-lovers—one of a select group Alix chose not to abandon.

She lay back on her sofa and opened her memory to Carolyn Blake, her body filling with heat as she relived their long slow love, as the vivid images became more and more intimate.

In the performance of her art, she reflected, nothing would be more foolish or self-defeating than to deny her artistic instincts. Yet in the performance of her life she had denied the life-giving sustenance of her sexual instincts. To have a woman in her arms was as right for her as the integration of the right color onto canvas.

Again she raised her fingers to her lips and inhaled their scent. Her want was raw and exposed: to take taste from those fingers as well. Carolyn Blake had been naked in her arms, open to her; yet she, Val, had been too timid to explore beyond what had seemed safe. Once again she had not dared to push beyond self-imposed limits.

Self-imposed limits. Her entire life had been a matter of self-imposed limits.

She asked herself the question again: Given again that year with Alix, knowing what she knew tonight, would they have spent their days and nights as lovers?

Yes, she answered. And maybe they would be together today. And she would not have become enmeshed with Carolyn Blake.

Alix was right. Withdrawing from the world of men never meant that she, Val, was living by her own rules. She had lived her entire life by their rules. Thirty-six years. All those wasted years.

She inhaled the smell of Carolyn Blake again. Mixing powerfully with her desire was the added heat of anger. What about Carolyn Blake? Would Carolyn Blake want to see her again? Would Carolyn Blake even want to face her tomorrow?

She would not allow Carolyn Blake that decision. She would confront her. Their relationship would evolve or it would end, but one way or the other, tomorrow she would know.

In sharp hunger she inhaled the scent from her fingers. The image of Paul Blake rose into her mind. She thrust the fingers into her mouth.

❧ 30 ❧

"Of course I wanted to phone," Carolyn said for the third time. "But we were in no-man's-land. There was no phone around."

He was confronting her in the living room, standing with his hands shoved deep in the pockets of his sweatpants and balled into fists—she could see the outline of his knuckles in the fabric.

He stated, "I *told* you that rattletrap of hers would break down."

His comment of this morning had been the genesis of her concocted story. She said wearily, wanting this to be over, wanting to retreat into her own thoughts again, "Yes, you did."

"You could have called afterward." His voice was grating, his lips stiff on his pale face.

"We came home without stopping. It's only a little after eight. I'm two hours later than I said I'd be."

His stare impaled her. "You said you'd be home this afternoon."

"I said I'd be home around dinnertime," she replied without conviction; she could not remember.

"No, Carolyn. I started expecting you around three." His voice rose. "Things happen to women, even if what's her name does look like Queen of the Amazons."

Ire worked its way into her weariness. "I don't think that way, Paul."

"Someday you'll learn the world's a fucking jungle and then it'll be too late."

She was offended as well as irked; he knew she detested that word. "I didn't mean to have you worry. I didn't," she insisted guiltily, knowing she had scarcely given him a thought. "Did you eat?"

"No," he sulked. "How could I? I was too upset even to watch Reagan debate Mondale."

She toasted bread and fried ham for sandwiches. Tantalized by the smells, ravenous, she forced herself to eat slowly under his alert gaze.

"Did you have any luck?" he asked. He added impatiently as she looked at him in bewilderment, "With the art gallery."

"Oh. Yes, they're taking her work."

With a smothered snort he bit into his sandwich. His voice was surly: "Why didn't you take your car like I wanted?"

"Her paintings were packed. It's best to move them as little as possible."

He did not reply. In the silence of the house there was only the sound of their eating. She knew he was still angry and looking for another opening to attack. "Paul," she said, "why don't we make peace?"

"Okay by me." His face was suddenly eager, his voice vibrant.

Her choice of words had been unfortunate; he had read extra meaning into them. In sharp annoyance she rose from the table. "Why don't I turn on the TV? Angela Lansbury's new show is on—you really like her." She felt his eyes burn into her as she switched on the set.

He said, "This guest room stuff—it's all over, then."

"No," she said shortly, feeling whipsawed by her guilt and her compelling need to have this night to herself. She could not bear the thought of his touch.

"Princess, why not?" His voice had softened to persuasiveness. "Princess, we're not getting divorced over any of this, are we? Right or wrong, what's done is done. If we're to have a marriage we've got to go on from here."

She gave him the concession of a nod. "For now I'm not ready for . . . the sex part of our marriage. My feeling right now about that isn't . . . right."

"You don't love me anymore, is that what you're trying to say?"

She knew the question was rhetorical, but she answered soberly, "No, I do love you. I just don't feel terribly loving." *I need tonight. God, just give me tonight—I'll never ask for another thing.*

For long moments his gaze was on her. Then, as if he had seen something in her face that satisfied him, his eyes moved to the television screen.

At ten o'clock she went gratefully toward the guest room. He got up from his armchair to intercept her, gripping her shoulders.

She could not prevent her reaction: she twisted away to throw his hands from her. As he stood gaping she said hastily, in distress, "I'm sorry. I'm sorry, honey, I—I'm just so very tired—"

The shock on his face was replaced by rage. He raised a hand, and for an unbelieving instant she thought he would strike her.

He lowered the hand. "For God's sake, Carolyn." He turned away from her. "I only wanted our good-night kiss." His voice dropped to a whisper: "Like always." He stalked toward the bedroom.

As she lay in her bed his angry presence seemed to radiate through the walls of the house. But he had every right to be angry, she reflected . . . and she would make it up to him tomorrow, somehow.

She turned her thoughts from him, but her mind retreated again, from analysis of what had happened today, from its meaning. There was one distilled fact—that she longed to be in Val's arms now, against her softness.

Images of Val's body, memories of her surrender to that powerful nudity coursed through her. Her body aching with want, she rolled over onto her stomach and buried her face in her pillow.

❧ 31 ❧

Carolyn drove to her house by rote, her hands gripping the steering wheel, a thickness in her throat she could scarcely swallow past. The day's work seemed in the remote past; she had performed her job automatically, her mind skimming over its surface. As she turned onto her block she felt momentarily dizzy from the surge of adrenalin. Would Val be there, would she be in the backyard swimming as she always was?

She glimpsed Val, in cutoffs and a white T-shirt, sitting at the top of the three small brick steps that led to her front door.

She parked carefully, using the electronic door opener to close the garage behind her. Faintly, shakily, she walked out onto the driveway and to her front door.

Unrestricted by a bra, Val's breasts strained against the thin fabric of the T-shirt, flattened slightly by the cloth barrier, the taut nipples starkly outlined. Carolyn reached to her, to take the opulence in her hands. Val stopped her, taking Carolyn's hands in hers. She removed the set of keys from the side of Carolyn's shoulder bag, examined them, unerringly chose the house key.

Carolyn dropped her purse onto the small table in the entryway and walked through the cool house knowing Val was following. In the guest room she turned and again reached for what she wanted, tugging the T-shirt up to clasp the bare breasts in her hands, then burying her face in them, opening her mouth to take the soft warm flesh into her, her tongue avid on a swollen nipple. She felt Val's hands at the zipper of her dress, felt clothing being loosened, falling from her, felt Val's hands slide inside her pantyhose to pull them over her hips. She stepped from Val, stripping the pantyhose off as she tugged at Val's cutoffs.

She was shocked by the heat of Val's body. The strength of Val's arms forced the breath from her. She arched into the heated softness and pulled Val's mouth to hers and wrapped her arms around the thickest part of her back, craving that heated flesh in all the hollows of her body; and as Val lowered her to the bed, she raised her legs to lock them around her.

Val's tongue thrust in and out of her mouth, the bed rocked and creaked. She answered the gradual but ever-increasing tempo of Val's body with her own urgent rhythm, writhing under Val with the brilliance of her own sensations, the fierce throbbing between her legs. In shuddering intensity Val pressed herself fully into her, and Carolyn's body absorbed the quivering height of her coming.

They lay fused together. Then Val lifted her body away.

As cool air struck her nudity Carolyn felt exposed beyond nakedness, rigid with want, aching between her legs, her nipples so taut that the first touch of Val's mouth on her breasts was unbearable and she pulled Val's mouth away. Val lay down between her legs, her palms sliding up Carolyn's thighs.

Her eyes squeezed shut in her need, she did not understand what would happen to her until Val's mouth came to her. Instantly remembering Paul's revulsion, she froze.

There was a smothered, choking sound from Val, and her hands released Carolyn's thighs to grip the bedspread. Carolyn felt her mouth as a roughness, a hungry searching. Val's hands came to her again, to press Carolyn's thighs tightly up against her warm face. There was the sound again from Val's throat and then Val's mouth softened, stilled, opened.

She was melting from each stroke, she was in the very heart of pleasure, each stroke on the jeweled center of her was perfect and she spread her legs fully; she would die if the strokes stopped. The strokes moved, just slightly, and frenzied in her diminished pleasure she seized Val's hair, her two hands holding Val's head viselike as the strokes quickened and created new and greater ecstasy. On the very edge of orgasm she hovered exquisitely, knowing that in the next instant she would come, the next instant, the next instant—and then she did come, from the roots of her hair, from everywhere, consumed with her coming.

She settled slowly onto the bed, her body light and so utterly empty she thought she would float.

Val's disembodied voice vibrated above her, speaking the first words between them: "God, you love that—you absolutely love it."

Carolyn spoke with difficulty, her mind a thickening gray swirl of cotton. "I don't . . . want you ever . . . to do that again."

She awakened at four-thirty. The bedspread had been pulled up around her; her dress had been hung in the closet, her other clothing lay folded neatly on a chair. She sat up to read a note propped on the dresser: I'LL BE AT THE BEACH HOUSE ALL DAY TOMORROW.

I won't, she thought, *I can't let this happen again.*

She had an hour before she had to begin preparations for dinner. She lay back, and then rolled over, tears leaking from her eyes into the pillow as she remembered, the euphoria of her body dissipating in the heat of reawakened desire.

๑ 32 ๑

Paul watched Carolyn stare at the TV screen as if she were newly converted to the ritual of Monday Night Football. "So they had to call off the presidential election," he said.

Her response was an absent nod.

"Goddammit, Carolyn." She looked up at him in alarm. "You haven't heard one thing I said since I got home."

She shook the ice cubes in the drink she had not touched, placed it on the coaster, and rubbed her eyes.

"Bad enough you don't sleep with me, you don't even listen when I talk." Her sigh pushed his anger higher. "You say you need time— how *much* time?"

"I don't know . . . till it's right again." The green eyes looking into his were wide and grave. "How can you want me when I feel like this?"

"I always want you." He added pointedly, "If you committed murder I'd forgive you. And want you."

"That's crazy. You can't mean that."

He considered his statement only briefly. "I do mean it. Whatever you did, I'd love you and want you."

"But I don't want you to love me like that. It's as if nothing about me matters. As if your love has nothing to do with anything about me. I don't want that from anyone."

"Everything matters about you, that's just the point," he said, shaking his head at her vehemence, smiling at her silly logic. Women were such a goddamn pain in the ass. "You're stuck with how I love you. Believe me, a lot of women—"

There was a buzzing sound in the kitchen and she went off to see about the microwave and their dinner. He sat down in the blue armchair and propped his feet on the ottoman, admiring his slippers—

deep brown leather, ridiculously expensive—she had given them to him last Christmas.

After dinner he divided his attention between the football game and a competitive report he was formulating for a new product line of featherweight tubing. He raised his voice to ask, "Princess, what are you doing?"

"Just straightening up," she called from the kitchen, banging a cupboard door in emphasis.

All she did these days was clean and tidy. Or go over to that Amazon bitch's house. Come to think of it—why hadn't she gone over there tonight? She always went there on Monday nights, part of her justification being that she'd leave him to his football game.

For a moment he allowed himself to hope; then he realized that if there were a breach with the Amazon, Carolyn would be back sleeping with him again. Probably the Amazon had plans tonight, maybe with her bratty kid. That Amazon bitch, still laughing up her sleeve at him—knowing he hated all this time Carolyn was spending with her and there wasn't a goddamn thing he could do about it.

Eight miserable nights. Nine, now that tonight looked to be no different. She missed it too, goddammit. Look at her—nervous, jumpy, hardly eating any dinner. Bad day at the office, she says. *Bullshit,* I say. *After eight years I should know. She needs it just like Rita needed it, just like I need it.*

"Princess," he called, "you can come out now, football game's almost over."

When would she stop this craziness? The image came to him of the way he lifted Carolyn's hips off the bed as he slid into her, and he squeezed his eyes shut to drive off the vision, stirring uncomfortably with his partial erection.

She came into the living room and glanced at her watch. "Merv Griffin's on." She went toward the guest room.

Her watch—fourteen carat gold, two small diamonds, seven hundred wholesale. Four years ago this Christmas—or was it five? He had been so sure she wouldn't like it, wouldn't approve somehow, would make him take it back . . . but she had fastened it onto her wrist and that had been that. He concentrated on his report again.

She came out of the guest room tying the belt of a white terry cloth robe, face cream glistening on the warm tan of her face. She curled up in her usual corner of the sofa and began to brush her hair.

Why had he ever stopped brushing her hair at night? It had been years. . . . He longed to feel the silk running through his hands again.

His attention was absorbed by a chase scene on the television screen. When the scene faded into a commercial he glanced at her, about to speak, and saw that she lay with her head on the sofa back, gazing at the gray painting.

He glared balefully at it. What was there, what did she see? He could do as well by collecting gray ash and smearing it over canvas. He returned his attention to his report.

When next he looked at her she was asleep, her head tucked into the corner of the sofa, arms hugging her body. He waited until the program ended, and then through the ten o'clock news, wanting to keep her with him even asleep. He went to her, knelt before her.

"Princess," he whispered, aching with love and desire, kissing her forehead.

She awakened reluctantly. Her eyes heavy-lidded, she gathered her robe around her. Almost as an afterthought she kissed him on the cheek—he grieved that it was unshaven—and then she got up; he watched her walk slowly, yawning, into the guest room.

❧ 33 ❧

She awoke at two o'clock. Quietly, she made herself a cup of coffee, and turned on a small lamp in the living room and sat on the sofa, reflecting wryly that unlike Scarlett O'Hara she would prefer never having to think about anything, ever. Surely not about Paul, and surely not about Val.

She curled up in the corner of the sofa and contemplated her painting in the chill of the dim room, sipping her coffee, imagining the sound and smell of rain.

She rinsed her cup and returned to bed. Like oncoming rain, drowsiness descended in a gradual enveloping. Her pillow was soft against her face, like Val's breasts; she pressed her face into the softness.

The only way to bring normalcy back into her life, she decided, was to do all the things that were routine and normal. Like going to work today and concentrating on her job—and ignoring these images and feelings that were compelling her to go to the beach house instead. She yanked the pillow out from under her head, pressed her face into the firm mattress.

When she rose for work she walked grimly into the shower and turned the cold water tap.

She drove to her office in the gray overcast, considering whether she should call Val and tell her she could not come to the beach house that day. But the wording in the note was not an invitation, just a statement of where Val would be—and her own resolve was not so strong that the sound of Val's voice . . . Val would know soon enough that she would not be there.

She honked furiously at a jogger who had stepped off the curb. He cast a frightened glance at her, rapidly backpedaled, and sped around the corner.

At work, she concentrated with some success on the computer-generated figures she was assessing for the quarterly employment forecast. The office Muzak, which she had become used to and seldom consciously heard, began a disemboweled version of a song that nagged at her with its familiarity. She put the computer sheets aside to listen, determined to remember. And she did remember: "Every Breath You Take." She had last heard it on the radio coming back from Santa Barbara with Val, on the way to the beach house. . . .

She bent over her desk, as defenseless as if caught in a sudden deluge, flooded with the memory of Val's mouth, memory so intimate and detailed and vivid that her legs trembled and opened and spread apart, her knees pressing feverishly into the hard edge of the desk, the throbbing between her legs of unendurable intensity, as if she were again feeling that warm delicate tongue.

"Carolyn?"

She started violently, feeling the color drain from her face. She stared at her boss, amazed and mortified; she had been fumbling with the belt of her pants, and if he had come in only moments later he would have discovered her with her hand inside . . .

"Carolyn, you're as white as a sheet. Are you coming down with something?"

A few minutes later she left her office, having agreed that she should go home to fend off what must surely be an onslaught of the flu.

❧ 34 ❧

By nine o'clock she was certain Carolyn would not appear, but still she strained to hear the sounds of a car over the pounding and hissing of the surf. It was too dark with cloud and mist to paint, and she had not expected to paint; the thought of what she had anticipated for this day sent a searing over the surfaces of her skin. Carolyn still might show; it was remotely possible . . . If not, perhaps it would be bright enough later to work.

Despondently, she worked on a finished canvas—the light lay well enough across it for varnishing—applying a thin coat to one small square at a time. She propped the canvas against a wall facing a window. The plants were watered, she'd dusted, done all the things she had intended to do Sunday. Her restless glance lingered on the painting of Carolyn; she had brought it with her to finish drying here where they had made love. Pulling a sketch pad from the travel case Carolyn had given her, she sat near the window apathetically sketching sets of waves.

She had miscalculated, misinterpreted yesterday—what could be more obvious? Just as she herself had reacted to Alix, Carolyn apparently considered this new venture into lovemaking a perilous foreign border she did not intend to cross again. The words Carolyn had whispered yesterday before she had fallen asleep, so puzzling after her passion, were now clear and meaningful.

Val turned the page, began a new set of waves, her pencil marks thick on the page. Probably the chance was gone to explore this new aspect of herself—this capacity to initiate and create pleasure in a woman she desired, a woman she had learned over the past months to treasure. And to possess Carolyn again was to learn more of those mysteries of her that Paul Blake knew. What she had discovered yesterday gave her a measure of equality with Paul Blake; the ecstasy

Carolyn had felt was a weapon Paul Blake could truly fear. Now that weapon literally had vanished from her hands.

Was that a car outside? Wishful thinking, she decided as a wave obliterated all sound with its thunderous arrival. Adding a rock to her sketch and smoothing its edges, she continued her reverie, smiling at the image of Carolyn asleep yesterday and her enchanting quality of innocence. Each time, even at the uninhibited height of passion, she seemed freshly overwhelmed, as if experiencing all her sensations for the first time. And she fell asleep with the suddenness of a child. . . .

The house reverberated with the chime of the doorbell. Val dropped her sketch pad.

Framed in the doorway Carolyn looked young and vulnerable in her white wool jacket and pants. She stared at Val. "It took me a while to—to . . ."

Val cupped Carolyn's face in her hands. "Are you all right? Your color seems high."

Carolyn's eyes closed; she bit her lips as if fighting back tears. Val pulled her close, her lips brushing Carolyn's ear. "What's wrong?"

"I . . . just want you." Carolyn's arms tightened around her; her body molded itself to Val's.

In churning excitement at Carolyn's desire, exulting in her sense of control, Val led her to the sofa. For a long time she kissed her, holding Carolyn's body close into hers, savoring the ardent response. Kissing her with slow deep strokes, she unbuttoned Carolyn's pants and slid a hand down into soft wet hair and began an equally slow stroking. Her hips undulant, Carolyn gasped into Val's shoulder.

She knelt beside Carolyn, slid clothing down unhurriedly, touching her cheek to the pale hair, brushing her lips through it. She slid her palms over Carolyn's stomach and under her hips, clasping and lifting them, kissing high inside her thighs, intoxicated by the heady sexual scent and the exquisite flesh quivering under her tongue.

Carolyn's hands, rigid and imperious, gripped her hair; she fastened Val's mouth to her.

The sounds of the room were muffled by the soft trembling thighs that cushioned her face and the heavy thudding of her own heartbeats. Carolyn's thighs opened, and the sounds were more distinct but oddly distorted: As from a great distance she heard a wave break; the ticktock of the clock was sharp as pistol shots. Carolyn's breathing seemed like sobbing, and her legs spread apart, one leg high up on the sofa back, the other brushing objects across the surface of the coffee table. A second wave broke, a third, and as the fourth broke Carolyn's body was arched stillness. The transfixed hands relaxed and took Val's mouth away.

Val dabbed at the wetness of her face with an edge of her sweatshirt, regretting the quickness of Carolyn's climax. Carolyn's eyes were closed; Val knew from her erratic breathing she had not fallen asleep. She took the blanket from the foot of the sofa and covered her legs.

Moving purposefully, she gathered up Carolyn's clothing. She packed up the traveling case, elated that she would have no further use for it this day. She glanced only briefly at the fireplace. The floor might be all right for Carolyn's young body but she was not yet ready for another afternoon there. She removed the blanket from Carolyn's legs. She said softly, "Let's go upstairs."

She pulled the spread off the bed and finished undressing Carolyn. With Carolyn silently watching, she stripped off her own clothing.

"Are you going to do that to me again?" Carolyn's tone was plaintive as Val came to her.

"Do you want me to?" She stopped any reply with her kiss, then picked her up in her arms to lay her on the bed.

A long leisurely time later Val murmured, "Tell me now."

"Yes," Carolyn uttered.

Afterward, as Val took her into her arms, Carolyn mumbled, "It's like dying . . . Never, I've never felt . . ." With her usual abruptness she fell asleep.

He doesn't do that to her. He never has. No one ever has. She was amazed. *All the man does is fuck her.*

Gently she released Carolyn, and went into the bathroom to towel her face, to stare at her visage in the mirror. She went downstairs and returned with her sketch pad.

Carolyn's body lay in an arc, one leg drawn up over the other, an arm flung up over her head. Thinking Carolyn might shift, she quickly sketched the attitude of her body, then lingered over the lines and curves, warm in her desire, yearning for the woman on the bed and in her sketches to awaken. Finally, Carolyn stirred, and Val put aside the sketch pad.

This time her mouth on Carolyn was a long, slow searching, with different pressures, exploring every crevice, her tongue stroking all the swollen folds of flesh before she took the tiny hardness between her lips.

You don't have this. She remembered Paul Blake grabbing his crotch, spitting the words at her. *You want one.*

Carolyn gasped and her head thrashed back and forth on the bed as the tip of Val's tongue vibrated.

I don't need one, she hurled back at Paul Blake.

In uninterrupted joy, again and again, unrelenting, she lay between Carolyn's legs, her hands on the quivering thighs to feel them spreading fully open to her, projecting taunts at the image of Paul Blake: *She's never felt you like she feels me now.*

To Carolyn's question, asked twice, she answered, "I don't need to."

And she did not. Carolyn's orgasms were like coming herself, and she could not feel the sensations enough. And late that afternoon when Carolyn's response had all but ceased and she uttered that she couldn't anymore, still she came again with a protracted shuddering that left her tearful in Val's arms. And Val understood that if she made Carolyn come a hundred times it would not extinguish her own fire.

Carolyn had been silent as they dressed, remote, unresponsive to Val's questions. When Val took her into her arms, Carolyn turned her cheek to Val's lips.

Val looked at her in sudden knowledge and an apprehension that became deepening fear. Instead of making tender love with the precious woman she passionately desired, she had been in bed attacking the man she hated.

"Carrie," she breathed in terror, in cold sobriety, like a drunk awakening to realize the damage of the riotous night before.

"I'm so very tired," Carolyn whispered. "I've never been so tired."

❧ 35 ❧

Carolyn walked into her house and went straight to bed. When Paul came home she called out weakly from the guest room, "Could you get your own dinner? I think I've got the flu."

He sat on the bed, felt her forehead, brushed at the tears that leaked from the corners of her eyes. Exhausted, shamed, she would not look at him. She felt ravished by Val's passion, humiliated and diminished by her raw need. In a depression so black and deep she did not care if she lived or died, she fell asleep.

At nine o'clock Paul awakened her. An arm supporting her, he fed her soup as if she were a child. She fell asleep again.

The next morning when she got out of bed she nearly collapsed from the weakness of her limbs. She realized that she had a fever—that she did, in fact, have the flu. When Paul came in later offering coffee she waved him away, mumbling instructions to call her office.

Throughout the day the phone rang. Either Paul or Val, she supposed, without caring.

Sometime that day there was a knocking on first the front door, then the back. She pushed the pillow against her ears.

Paul came home from work early. "I called a doctor," he told her. Docilely she accepted the pill he gave her along with some broth, but refused solid food.

Again the phone rang. Paul came in to ask brusquely, "Do you want to talk to anybody?"

"Not even God," she whispered.

She could hear him in the other room, his voice raised and harsh, "No, she doesn't. Yes I asked her. I don't have to tell you anything, you can—" He slammed the phone down. "Dyke bitch," he snarled.

Time distorted, days and nights passed in a haze of phantasmagoric dreams and occasional awareness of sound: the phone ringing, knocks at the door. She somehow knew that Paul was leaving late for work and coming home early.

Except for liquids, she refused food. In the evenings Paul sat with her and watched the small portable television he had moved into her room. During one of those evenings the vice-presidential debate occurred; she slept through it. Afterward, in response to her sleepy-voiced question, she heard in Paul's tone his condescending opinion of Geraldine Ferraro's performance; she did not listen to his words.

On a Thursday, eight days after she had last been with Val, her temperature finally normal, her strength and her appetite for food having returned, she sat outside in warm afternoon sun for more than an hour, contemplating the still surface of the pool, the thin striations of cloud in clear, pale sky.

She supposed she was crazy. Why else had she allowed herself to be pulled into this vortex? Why else was she now repelled by the loving touch of her husband? How else could she explain this passion she felt for another woman, sensations unlike anything she had ever known with anyone, a sexual depth in herself she had never dreamed she possessed?

There was no one in her life she could turn to, whom she could trust with this confidence. Her weekly conversations with her mother were always inconsequential; her mother was helpless and usually tearful in the face of the smallest difficulty.

She thought of her father and smiled in affection as she remembered his ever-present billowing cloud of pipe smoke, a smell delicious to her to this day, evoking images of his huge physical size and strength and energy, his bearhugs and laughter. Like the expected death of a loved one, his defection from her life had not really surprised her. He had always seemed bored and impatient with any problem relating to her. She knew she was a mere diversion in his world—an exciting world, a masculine world of significant activities. With her father, she was beyond receiving or inflicting hurt; she had understood her precarious place in his hierarchy of value.

Why should Paul and Val suffer unhappiness now because of her? Why should either of them care this much? Both had succeeded in professions where comparatively few achieved success. They had more to give each other than she could ever offer either of them. Why did they want her? Why would anyone want her?

If she did not understand her desperate sexual need of Val, did it really matter? Did addicts understand their addiction? The one essential was that they understand and avoid the destructive source of their problems.

Perhaps she and Val could go on, be friends again—just friends. For that she needed distance and time to learn control over this sharp new hunger of her body. The fire of fever and a purging illness which had stripped away seven pounds had not reduced the capacity of her body to betray her. Even now, just the image of Val . . .

What Paul had done to Val was despicable. But he had sensed danger, had realized that her defiant friendship with Val Hunter threatened the foundations of their marriage, strained the bond of their love. *Dyke,* he had called Val Hunter. It had never occurred to him to apply the same label to his own wife.

Eight peaceful, contented, conventional years of marriage, with the promise of greater professional success for Paul. How could any alternative be better, more acceptable? Why this confusion, this distress, this rebellion without rational cause? What was *wrong* with her?

She heard the glass door behind her slide open: Paul had come home. He bent to one knee on the grass beside her and took her hands. "You look so much better, Princess."

"I am. I think I can go back to work tomorrow."

"Monday," he stated firmly, "and don't argue. Tomorrow's Friday, what's one more day? You'll be at full strength Monday." He added, "I won't let you go back tomorrow."

She smiled, grateful for his love. "All right, honey."

"Some news, Princess. I've been trying to catch up with Dick Jensen's performance numbers ever since the company transferred me here. I finally did it. My district won the third-quarter sales contest."

"Paul, that's wonderful! I'm so very proud of you." A suspicion dawned and she asked, "Did you just get the news?"

"Last Wednesday."

She looked away from him, guilt descending. The trouble between them, combined with her illness, had caused him to carry this triumph unshared for more than a week.

"It's a good news–bad news kind of thing," he said ruefully. "We get a real nice bonus—something over five thousand, I'll get the exact number tomorrow. But it means entertaining the sales group. Think we can . . . get it together for a week from Saturday? Afternoon and evening, there'll be wives and kids—"

"Honey, I see no problem." She squeezed his hand, her mind gratefully at work on the logistics of a party for twenty or so. "Let me see about our dinner." She started to get up.

He took her by the shoulders and gently settled her back into the lawn chair. "Woman, leave it to me, tomorrow night's dinner, too. I'm getting good at this. I'll put the chicken in the oven till we're ready to eat. You stay out here where it's nice. The sun is good for you."

He went back through the glass door and she turned her thoughts again to the party. They would barbecue, of course . . . vegetable trays and cold pastas. She would buy some of that already made up. With any luck it would still be warm enough and the children could play in the pool and not be underfoot. Saturday would be the end of October, she reflected; people here were actually swimming outdoors in October. . . . How very different it was to live in California.

Memories of Paul came to her, of when they had first moved to this city. He had been like an endearing country bumpkin the way he had gaped at the more outlandish citizens and the city's unique landscape. He had been a little boy who held her hand and laughed in wonder and enchantment as they explored Disneyland together; he gawked like a ten-year-old at the sound stages and back lots of Universal Studios, the fairy-tale estates of Beverly Hills and Bel Air. But when she had coaxed him into further exploration of the city, into Chinatown and Griffith Park and the beach cities, he had become increasingly reluctant, wanting to retreat behind the walls of their new house, just as he had in the last two cities where they had lived.

A lonely, wistful little prince, she thought tenderly. *Needing only his castle and trusting only his Princess. . . .* No one knew as she did how his cool demeanor and graying hair disguised a solitary and needy little boy. She did love him. How could she not love him? she asked herself as he came into the yard with a tall, frosted drink for her.

"Orange juice," he told her. "Lots of vitamins. Just a tiny bit of vodka—that's good for you too." He touched her drink with his martini glass: "To your perfect health."

She said slowly, "I thought . . . I'd come back to our bedroom tonight."

As his eyes widened in happiness she glanced away, out over the pool where she had first found Val Hunter four months ago, to the fence Val Hunter had leaped over to come into her life.

Yes I love him, she thought, *but I can't have him touch me yet. Not yet.*

She said, "But that's all. I'm not a hundred percent about everything, about us. But I'd like to be back in our bedroom again if that's okay."

"It's okay." He started to say something else, and paused; then he said simply, "I'm glad."

✑ 36 ✍

Carolyn had moved her clothes into their bedroom and then gone to bed. He sat with a magazine in his lap, watching television unseeingly, forcing himself to wait until his usual hour for bed.

Freshly showered and shaved, he slipped into bed beside her, uncertain whether she was asleep and not really caring. Moving close enough to feel her warmth but careful not to touch her, he lay awake for some time; and he awakened frequently during the night, the perfume of her presence washing over him. They had been apart eighteen days.

The next day he sent roses to the house and made reservations at a restaurant they had gone to months ago, its decor too fussy for his taste but one she had pronounced charming. He brought home a bottle of champagne. "What is all this?" Carolyn asked, smiling and shaking her head, "Christmas?"

He stripped the wire fastening and foil from the champagne bottle and worked at the cork with his thumbs. "Feel well enough to go out tomorrow for just a couple of hours? To some of those fancy stores in Beverly Hills?"

"Sure. But not to buy anything. It's ridiculous to pay a fortune when—"

"Indulge me. The bonus is just short of six thousand—more than I expected." He poured the foaming gold liquid, handed her a glass, and lifted his own in a toast: "Princess, let's celebrate—let's go spend money!"

Saturday they walked the crowded streets of Beverly Hills hand in hand, looking in shop windows, chuckling at mannequins costumed in army fatigues and wrinkled cotton. "Get rich so you can look elegantly poor," Carolyn joked. She refused his urging to go into the Rodeo Drive shops but she did go into Neiman Marcus.

Happily reminding himself of the bonus money, he talked her into trying on the well-cut gabardine pants and green silk shirts she was admiring. Stroking the fabrics as if hypnotized, she surrendered to his insistent coaxing and chose two pairs of pants, a skirt, two silk shirts. The saleswoman disinterestedly charged seven hundred and forty-six dollars to his American Express card.

As he carried the packages out to the car he thought exuberantly that he wasn't through yet. He'd get them out of that house in the Valley next. Maybe buy a place in the South Bay. And only a month or so to go on Carolyn's new job—he'd make damn sure that company of hers kept its promise about changing her hours back. Now that his marriage was returning to normal, now that that damned woman seemed to have lost her grip on Carolyn—he wouldn't make the mistake of banking on it but it sure looked that way—he wanted Carolyn as far removed from her as he could possibly manage.

❧ 37 ❧

Val was snatched from her desultory reading of the paper by Carolyn's name. Neal had asked, "Do you think Carolyn's getting better by now?" He was sitting beside her on the sofa.

"I hope so," she answered, sliding an arm around his shoulders.

Monday Night Football ended to staccato shouts by the announcer and statistics across the screen. "Homework time," Val said, squeezing his shoulders again. "What've you got?"

"Math."

"Ugh. Be a good kid and do it out of my sight."

Neal obediently went off to his room, and as she had for days, she went to bed early. Sleeping meant the absence of thought, and she ached with the misery of her thoughts. Amid the desolation of all the recent days, this day had contained a bleakness all its own: the phone call from Carolyn.

"I want you to know," Carolyn had said slowly, "that I'm fine . . . but I need time. I need to get myself back together. To sort things out."

She could visualize Carolyn; she had seen her speak on the phone several times with that unconscious habit of clasping a hand to her throat as if to physically control the tone of her voice. Val answered carefully, "I understand. I should tell Neal something. He asks, he—"

"Say I've gone away to recuperate for a while. It's the truth, anyway."

"Will you let me say one thing?"

"Right now I just—"

"One thing, that's all. The last time we were together I was . . . I damaged whatever we—"

"Please, Val."

Her body weakened at the soft sound of her name, with memory of the beach house, of Carolyn breathing that name. "Carrie—"

"Please don't. I can't talk anymore." And she had hung up.

She could never have imagined this need—that Carolyn's absence would bring her to the desperation of repeated phone calls, even laying siege to Carolyn's house. That she would so totally abandon pride. And now it was over. Carolyn was gone.

There was no one to whom she could voice her anguish, except perhaps Alix, who had returned from Houston four days ago—surprisingly, still with her Helen. She had spent a long evening with Alix, had spoken of Carolyn—how could she not, when Neal would talk about little else? But she had not revealed herself. Why submit to further mortification, debase herself by confessing to Alix how stupidly she had lost Carolyn?

That she was totally responsible was beyond challenge. The accumulated humiliation of a lifetime had driven her into a heedless resolve to somehow trample Paul Blake; instead she had damaged the tender shoots of the love Carolyn had offered her, and her own emergent new self.

She must end this paralysis, somehow function again. Her work? Yes, that was always there. She could not and would not stop working; financial necessity as well as ingrained professional habit dictated that she work daily at her craft. But the usual controlled excitement of applying paint to canvas had paled into effortful drudgery.

What about Susan's suggestion that she conduct evening classes at the gallery? She had refused then; an art class was a minimal source of income at best, not worth the time involved; and her approach to art was probably too iconoclastic and personally focused. But the assertiveness in her work that Susan had spoken of as a frequently missing ingredient in women's art—perhaps that could somehow be communicated to novice painters. She could explore Susan's ideas further, at least . . . She might even come into contact citing new talent . . . other women . . .

Tomorrow she would call her father, go see him. Take Alix with her. Dad had always liked Alix. Renew acquaintance with artists and art-loving friends scarcely seen since she had moved into the Robinson's guest house. Jacques, Monica, David . . . She smiled, thinking of how the Robinsons would have viewed with slack-jawed amazement her artist friends, especially Monica with her graveyard makeup.

Yes, she had been neglecting her friends and that whole aspect of her life for months. Ever since Carolyn.

Why not a party? As soon as possible? This Saturday, she decided. Planning a party and contacting old friends might help distract her from this pain. Oh God, this pain . . .

❦ 38 ❦

On Friday afternoon after work, the day before the party for Paul's office staff, Carolyn drove to Venice, to the Austin Art Gallery. Located three blocks from the ocean amid a cheerful clutter of small antique shops and specialty stores, the gallery appeared from its front room to be a labyrinth of smaller back rooms. With a sense of obligatory propriety, Carolyn paused to inspect a series of pleasant if bland seascapes.

A trim, dark-haired woman ventured partway into the room. "Let me know if I can answer any questions."

Carolyn looked at her curiously. The textured white wool skirt and sweater looked expensive. Could this be the Susan whose parents owned the beach house? "Thank you," she said, "I'd like to stroll around."

"Stay the afternoon." The woman's smile was easy and attractive. "You'll find coffee in the back room."

With decorous slowness, in mounting anticipation, Carolyn moved through a room of cheerful geometric mobiles, then through impressionistic landscapes, glossy acrylic miniatures, paper collages, huge watercolor flowers. She knew she had found Val's work before she saw HUNTER in firm upright strokes in the lower corner of the first painting.

Five oversize paintings, the only contents of a room lighted by angled fluorescent ceiling fixtures, seemed to reflect their own light. She stopped before a canvas of glowing viridian, its dust-colored background shot through with what she judged to be cobalt yellow. In a seemingly haphazard fusion of tropical foliage she identified palm fronds. Other leafy shapes tugged at her mind in vague familiarity. An inked card beside the painting stated:

GREENERY, SOUTHERN CALIFORNIA
V. Hunter, Los Angeles, California

She studied the painting for a long time, held by the hot vital greens, the fluid rendering of leaves and plants she had seen every day along the streets and freeways of Los Angeles without really seeing.

The next canvas poured warm cadmium oranges and yellows over her. Suggestive of the composition of her own rain painting, vaguely symmetrical shapes of burnt sienna conveyed building tops at the horizon level. The card read: SUMMER SUNRISE, LOS ANGELES.

Reluctant to leave the incandescence of this painting, eventually she turned her gaze to two large canvases which presented different perspectives of the same subject: an angular, cerulean blue body of water tightly surrounded by dusty hills whose sparse cover was dry, brittle, dying. The controlled shape of the body of water was somehow comforting, its strong blue color tranquil and clear—cool reassurance amid the encroaching desolation of the arid hills. The card beside each painting was identical: RESERVOIR AT CASTAIC: SEPTEMBER.

"I see you've found an artist you like."

So immersed in the paintings she had forgotten where she was, Carolyn whirled at the sound of the voice.

"I didn't mean to startle you," the woman apologized softly. "I noticed you'd been in here awhile so I thought I'd mention that this artist is selling quite steadily. She's an exceptional talent."

The woman stepped to a painting Carolyn had not looked at yet—a scarlet vase, the flowers it contained suggested by splashes of color so brilliant they seemed to move, to dance. "Her work is distinctive, very bold. And her use of color—look how she's put light colors against a dark background, very difficult to do well. Incredible use of color."

Carolyn passed her cool hands over her face; she knew she was flushing in her pride for Val.

"This painting of the sunrise is a particular favorite of mine—how she builds up the color effects. And it has such optimism."

"Yes, yes it does," Carolyn said, her gaze again captured by it.

The woman left, and Carolyn's contemplation of the paintings continued until a glance at her watch told her she scarcely had time in rush-hour traffic to arrive home before Paul.

She found the woman seated at a small desk making notations in a ledger. "The sunrise painting," Carolyn said, "how much is that?"

The woman smiled. "Obviously I think that's a fine choice." She consulted a chart. "Five-fifty."

Carolyn wrote a check. She thought: *Paul will go berserk.*

In traffic that inched along the San Diego Freeway she made her way out to the Valley, penetrated by her awareness of the landscape beside the freeway, watching soft hills dense with foliage darken and deepen in their greenness as dusk descended. Taking her exit from the Ventura Freeway she gazed at distant palm trees black against the horizon, their bushy heads swaying in the slight evening breeze. She remembered films she had seen of palms bent parallel to the ground in hurricanes, their suppleness granting survival.

Palm trees are odd compared to most trees, she reflected; they're like people who lack conventional beauty yet possess strong individuality. All things have beauty—that's what Val celebrates in her art.

She drove slowly down her block looking at the houses. Like the vast majority of structures in Los Angeles, they were stucco or frame or both. This great city has no fear, she thought; it lies so fragile in the sun, confident that nothing will ever happen to it. . . . Only the palm trees really know about living in sunlit cities.

Paul had arrived home before her. When he saw the wrapped painting in her arms his face darkened; he looked away from her and his shoulders adjusted, as if he were squaring them. He said, "One of hers?"

That name is never mentioned in this house, Carolyn thought. She nodded.

"I thought—I got the idea when you were sick that you two were on the outs more or less." His voice came from deep in his chest, heavy with a resonance that seemed almost menacing.

"Not on the outs. But she's finally settled into her new place," she said smoothly. "She has things going on in her life right now." She placed the painting on the bar. "This is from the gallery, I went there just on impulse. I was curious," she added truthfully. "I didn't intend to buy a thing. You may even like this—it's quite different from the one we have."

"How much?"

"Five-fifty."

He heaved a sigh. "We're spending money like drunken sailors, Princess. The trip, this party—"

No longer listening to his words she stripped the paper off and propped the painting on the bar for him. He stood back, arms crossed, in lengthy appraisal.

"I do prefer it to the one in here," he said. "The brightness will be good and—"

"I want it in the guest room," she stated.

He flicked a surprised glance at her. "If it's in there you'll hardly ever see it." His tone was not argumentative, and he added, grinning, his hands raised in mock-terror, "Will you?"

She chuckled. "I expect I won't see it very often. But that's where I want it."

He said promptly, "Let's hang it."

She carried the painting toward the guest room. "Not now. I don't feel like it," she improvised. She did not want him touching, handling it.

She leaned the painting against the wall. After the party she would hang it. Sunday, when Paul was at the Raider game. When she was alone in the house.

❧ 39 ❧

Early Saturday afternoon, while Carolyn showered and dressed, he roamed the house and yard on a final inspection tour. Soon his office staff and their wives and children would arrive. And Will—later of course, after the sales staff.

All was in readiness. Flowers everywhere. The bar stocked, the refrigerator stuffed with prepared food, the meat ready for the barbecue. Ample towels in both bathrooms, a dozen extra laid out in the backyard for swimmers. Nice. Everything perfect. Carolyn always did this kind of thing so well.

He whistled his admiration as she came out of the bedroom in her new dark green pants and emerald shirt. He took her silken shoulders caressingly in his hands. "Princess, you look absolutely gorgeous."

She smiled, pecked his cheek. "For what this outfit cost I should." She moved past him, toward the kitchen. "Time to put ice on the bar."

At two-thirty the five salesmen and their families began to arrive, all of them assembling within a five-minute period; soon afterward all seven children were shrieking in the pool, the wives taking up position in lawn chairs along the decking. At three, Will and Annie Trask arrived. Annie, fiftyish, earth-motherly, and bossy, immediately tucked a kitchen towel in the band of her broad white pants and took charge of the barbecue, cooking hotdogs for the kids. Paul assisted, teasing and flirting with her; Annie liked him and he knew it. He was watchful of the scene in his yard, and of Will, who finally left his seat among the women to join the salesmen on the patio.

The wives changed from sports clothes into bathing suits and brief terry robes, and posed self-consciously on towels, drinking mai tais, applying Coppertone and chattering among themselves with birdlike animation, admonishing their children whenever the decibel level in the pool rose. The men, wearing college T-shirts over their shorts or cotton pants, sat around the picnic table playing poker. Percussive music pulsed from stereo speakers on either side of the patio.

Refilling wine glasses, emptying ashtrays, offering snacks, Carolyn circulated continuously, stopping occasionally and briefly to chat. Paul sipped a martini and glanced at her often and proudly.

Carrying a weak scotch and water, Will finally strolled over to him. Will's paunch, usually minimized by good tailoring and dark colors, bulged under gray sweatpants and a USC T-shirt. Paul knew that Will's clothes today were as much for effect as when he was in the office. He was here to set the company's seal of approval on the men who had exceeded the company's objectives, and on Paul, who had gotten it done with his leadership. Will must mix with his subordinates, look casual, be relaxed, comfortable, democratic.

"Fine party, my boy," Will said, shaking his hand.

Paul basked in the approval. He knew he already stood in high favor with Will; this party could only enhance him.

"You know how to do things right. You and Carolyn," Will said, his eyes darting over the yard and coming to rest on her as she brought a carafe of wine to the wives beside the pool. He winked at Paul and clapped him on the shoulder. "Whatever you do, my boy, don't get old." He strolled off toward the poker game as Paul laughed loudly.

Someone had turned the stereo up, and the general noise level gradually rose as the afternoon wore into early evening. Paul congratulated himself that he had thought to warn the Robinsons. Jerry was not pleased with him these days; Dorothy still would not forgive him for evicting the Hunter woman. The older couple who had rented the guest house had turned out to be indefatigable complainers. He would smooth all this over tomorrow; he was taking Jerry to the Raider game as final payment in the deal to evict Val Hunter.

He began cooking steak and chicken on skewers, the smell of barbecue smoke and teriyaki permeating the evening air. By seven-thirty dinner was over. Under patio lights the poker game resumed, more boisterous than ever. Several wives, apparently grown bold from the consumption of mai tais and wine, heedless of hairdos and makeup, splashed in the pool, its night lights turning the water milky aquamarine. He helped Carolyn carry stacks of paper plates and plastic glasses into the kitchen.

"Everything's terrific, Princess." Heady with vodka and his jubilation, he kissed the top of her head. "Will's impressed."

She rinsed a casserole, poking baked beans down the disposal with a serving spoon. "I'm truly thrilled that Will's impressed."

His euphoria vanished as a clear warning sounded. He glanced at his watch. It would be ten-thirty, eleven before the party broke up. "Tell you what," he said lightly, "stick it out a few more hours and I promise never to win a sales contest again."

"Paul," she said, "why do you love me?"

He stared at her. Her tone had seemed normal, even conversational. She was working efficiently, picking silverware out of paper plates, discarding the plates into a plastic trash bag. "You need to know that right now?"

"Right now. It's important."

He heard a woman shriek, "Jimmy don't *do* that!" Had one of those brats done something to the yard? He said as patiently as he could, "You're my Princess. You're sweet . . ."

He suddenly realized that she had not looked at him since he came into the kitchen. "And you're so beautiful . . ." She hadn't been drinking, of that he was certain. Could it be her period? They hadn't had sex for so long he'd lost track.

"Princess," he said, "what's this all about?" He dumped the contents of half-consumed drinks into the sink and tossed the plastic cups into the trash bag. "A party's no place for this, to discuss—"

"What else?" she asked. "Besides sweet and beautiful."

Anger flared. He was tired, goddamn sick and tired of putting up with all this crap. Weeks, months of it from her. Nothing but crap from her. "We used to have good sex. We even used to be able to talk about things, to—"

"What things?"

An idiot, she was acting like a neurotic *idiot*. "Carolyn, for chrissake—everything," he said in exasperation. "About our jobs, about—"

"You talk about where you went for lunch, office gossip. Not about your work." She scraped potato salad down the disposal. "I don't even know exactly what contest you won to have us deserve this wonderful party." She flipped the disposal switch.

The alcohol he had consumed seemed to burn along his veins, up through his head. A cupboard door was slightly ajar and he slammed it, wanting to beat on it with his fists. She switched off the disposal.

"If we ever have to do this again, my dear and loyal wife," he grated, "you can spend the day at a fucking hotel."

She looked at him then, and her eyes were opaque, as if his words had deflected off her, had not registered. That remoteness, he had seen it before. . . . He pushed the thought away before it was completed.

She said, "You like sports, you like cards and games. I don't. I like movies and dancing, other people, going out. You don't. You like—"

Another shriek rose from the backyard. "Stop it," he said. "Jesus Christ, my wits are floating in booze, we have a houseful of people, and you pick this time for a dissection of our marriage. Three more hours, they'll all be gone. Three hours, then we'll talk. We've got to get back out there, Carolyn. These people work for me, Carolyn . . ."

She leaned against the sink, her body slack, her shoulders slumped.

"You're just tired," he said in sudden understanding. "It's not that long since you were sick, it's been a long day. Princess, don't worry, we'll—"

Will Trask walked into the kitchen. "You and Carolyn get out there, enjoy yourselves, relax. You've worked hard enough." He clapped Paul on the shoulder. "Get some of those wives out there to clean this up."

"I don't want any help from the wives," Carolyn said, and turned on the disposal—unnecessarily, Paul knew. He managed a grin and a shrug, as if saying to Will, *Who can understand women?*

"Paul my boy," Will said when it was finally quiet, "why don't you get the wives more wine and leave your lovely wife to me?"

It was the last thing he wanted to do. He looked apprehensively at Carolyn who was swabbing the counter with paper towels. What could he say to Will—that his wife was having a momentary breakdown? He winced as Will unexpectedly clapped him on the shoulder again. If the day ever came when this old fart worked for him, the next time he laid a hand on him would be his last.

"Right, Will," he said with forced heartiness. "See if you can talk her into leaving this mess till later."

With a final glance at Carolyn he went to the bar to get the wine, his chest constricted. Somehow, in a way he did not understand, everything had again gone out of control.

⤖ 40 ⤖

"Been a long day for you," Will Trask said. "Shouldn't have to clean up all this mess besides."

She said sarcastically, knowing he would not hear the sarcasm, "You know how we wives hate a messy kitchen."

"Some of the wives've gone in swimming," he said. "How about you joining them? I remember that little bikini you had on, what was it, a year ago?"

She looked at him. Arms crossed above his stomach, he was regarding her complacently, half-smiling and impervious, certain she would not react in any way disadvantageous to Paul.

She turned her back squarely on him and walked from the kitchen. In the bathroom she brushed her hair and stared into the mirror for long minutes.

She went out toward the bar. Two of Paul's salesmen, their backs to her, sauntered toward the door to the backyard carrying fresh scotches.

"A Reagan landslide," Larry Keating was saying. "The man held off Mondale; Bush put it right up Ferraro's ass."

Following Keating out the door onto the patio, Fred O'Brien laughed. "How about the IRA trying to blow Maggie Thatcher's pussy off? Not a very good year for the women, hey?"

The men's laughter faded as they moved out into the yard. Carolyn poured herself a vodka and tonic, understanding with perfect clarity that she could not possibly get through the next several hours without perpetrating some spectacular outrage. Pleasurably, she contemplated various acts of mayhem: grinding a bowl of vegetable dip into Larry Keating's smug face; pouring a pitcher of orange juice over the careful coiffure of Fred O'Brien's conceited wife; aiming a well-placed foot at Will Trask's backside and propelling him into the pool.

She looked at the bottle of scotch on the bar, then inspected the cabinet below. She removed the two remaining quarts of scotch, carried them into the kitchen, poured them simultaneously down the drain, and tossed the bottles into the trash bag.

She found Paul in the yard. "We're out of scotch," she told him. "There's less than half a quart."

"Can't be. Jesus." He scowled. "I can switch the guys to bourbon, save the rest for Will—"

"I'll get more." She spoke emphatically. "Just a few minutes break from here and I'll be fine the rest of the night. I promise."

"Okay. Good. Two more quarts, Princess."

She noticed Will Trask at the poker game watching her; his eyes were uncertain, gauging.

"Have Annie be your hostess while I'm gone," she said. "It'll be good for your career."

"Do hurry back," he said glumly.

"Carrie . . ."

Val's body seemed to fill the doorway of her flat, her black dress a copy of the white one she had worn the night she met Paul. From behind her came music and the mixed cadence of party conversation.

Carolyn backed away. "I'm sorry, it never occurred—I never thought—"

"A few friends—just a small party."

Carolyn laughed, aware of the hysterical edge in her laughter. This was the final absurdity in this entire absurd day. "I can't stay. We're having our own party—Paul's office staff. I escaped for a few minutes."

"Come in, we'll go to Neal's room."

"Neal, is he—"

"At his grandfather's. He'll be so upset he missed you. Come in. Please."

Carolyn entered the flat. Her glance took in four women and five men, unconventionally garbed compared to her own guests, elegantly arranged on Val's furniture like exotic birds. She met the intelligent brown eyes of the woman from the gallery; the woman made no sign of acknowledgment.

"A friend. We need to talk a few minutes," Val said to the group. "Alix, would you and Helen take care of things? David needs a fresh drink."

A pretty blonde woman in tight black pants, a red tie hanging in loose nonchalance from the neck of her white shirt, nodded to Val, her eyes drifting down Carolyn in cool appraisal.

Carolyn followed Val into Neal's bedroom, sat on the narrow bed. She said quietly, "I don't know what's happening to me."

Val sat down beside her, her hands crossed in her lap.

Carolyn continued slowly, "I'm not sure about more and more things in my life . . . I feel scattered in a thousand pieces. But I want to be with you and Neal again, I do know that."

"I'm glad," Val said. "I hoped . . . I'm glad, Carrie."

They sat in silence. Carolyn ached with a restless, indefinable yearning she remembered from when she was small, when the relentless winter cold first began to release its grip on Chicago. Early spring fever, her mother had called her mercurial moodiness.

Val raised her hands, turned them over, looked at the palms. She said, "Am I not to touch you?"

Carolyn reached for the hands, placed them around her waist. She pressed her face into the soft flesh of Val's throat. Val's hands began to move, to shape her body. Sliding her hands across Val's shoulders until the breadth of them was enclosed in her arms, Carolyn knew that she had come here only to have this again, to speak any words that would let her have it again.

Val's face was against her hair; she could feel her breath warm on her ear. Val's hand came to her breasts. Her nipples hard, she strained against the caressing palm. *This is insanity,* she thought, *anyone could come in here.*

The hand moved down her, to her thighs. Desire was suddenly an electric current so vivid and precisely focused that she could not bear it another moment. As Val's hand cupped between her legs she fumbled with the belt of her pants; gasping, she struggled with the zipper. Val lifted her onto her lap, slid her hand down inside the pants.

The wetly stroking fingers were excruciating, too slow for her need. Her hips gyrated in urgent seeking, directing a fingertip into the swift motions she needed. Rigid, shuddering, her jaw clenched to smother the gathering sound in her throat, she came with exquisite sharpness.

Val lifted her from her lap. Breathing rapidly, Carolyn lay docile on the bed while Val tucked the shirt back inside Carolyn's pants and fastened them.

"I have to go," Carolyn mumbled in utter bleakness, her eyes closed.

"I love you," Val said.

Carolyn flung an arm across her eyes. The words were expelled from her: "For God's sake, why?"

Silence followed.

"Never mind," she said to Val. *Why can't I die,* she thought. *I wish to God I were dead.*

"I'm looking for the words," Val said, "the way to tell you. I think it's because you . . . react. To me. To my life . . . to my son . . . my art, everything. You make me feel . . . defined. In good ways I never dreamed I could be. You make me feel . . . strong. And whole."

With a sensation that was almost palpable, Carolyn felt the disorientation of the past weeks leave her as if a layer of skin had fallen away.

"I feel whole," Val repeated. "There're other reasons, lots of superficial things. Physical ways you have, the angle of your back, crazy things. Smells of you, your skin and hair . . ." She raised her hand, inhaled from her fingers, smiled. "Cocaine couldn't be any better."

Energy surging through her, Carolyn sat up. "Come over tomorrow. Paul's going to a football game. We'll have the afternoon."

Gazing at Val, wanting her, she felt assertive, in control of her want, euphoric with the sense of possibility. Thoughts, images, plans were forming rapidly in her mind. "Come at noon," she said.

She got up, her glance falling on painting paraphernalia and stacks of sketch pads usually kept in the front room but moved in here because of the party. She picked up a sketch pad. "May I borrow this?"

"Sure." Val circled her with an arm. "You're thinner. Too thin."

"From being sick." Was she less desirable to Val? She added hurriedly, "I'll gain it back."

"You're so lovely, Carrie. That shirt is wonderful on you."

Reassured, she smiled at Val, wanting to tell her she was beautiful, knowing she could only tell her when she could show her.

Paul said crossly, "Where did you buy the scotch, San Diego?"

"The moon," she said happily.

"Will wanted to go looking for you."

"Did he?" she said, entertained by the idea that Will Trask thought he personally had driven her out of the house. She pushed the bag containing the scotch into his hands. "I'll go be charming to our guests. I did promise, remember?" In the chill of the evening the wives had again donned sports clothes. The party had quieted, was moving indoors. Carolyn mediated several arguments among children grown querulous, and put the O'Brien's daughter to bed in the guest room. Overflowing with her private joy, she bestowed smiles and chatter on her guests, avoiding Will Trask, whose eyes were on her each time she glanced at him, his expression baffled and irritated.

The party broke up at midnight. Afterward, helping her empty glasses and ashtrays, Paul said tiredly, "I can't figure you out and neither can anybody else. Will actually asked if you take uppers. We can't have people thinking that."

"I suppose not," Carolyn agreed, yawning, thinking she would wear the other new silk shirt for Val.

With Paul heavily asleep beside her, Carolyn rose and donned a robe and slippers. Quietly, she let herself out of the house and retrieved the sketch pad from her car.

Curling up on the sofa, she opened the pad—to a sketch of herself. Transfixed, she turned over two more pages of drawings, all recent—she recognized background details of Val's flat. In the first sketch she was sitting on Val's sofa frowning down into the pages of a book in her lap; in the other two she was playing cards with Neal.

There were three more drawings. In each of these she lay on a bed, nude. On her stomach, a leg drawn up. On her side, her back to the artist. With her body in an arc, an outstretched arm pulling her breasts upward.

She knew when the sketches had been made; heat came to her face and waves of warmth spread over her breasts, down her stomach, as if she were being slowly caressed. She looked at the three sketches again, at the catlike languor and contentment of her body which had come from more than sleep.

She opened the pad to the unused pages. She worked hesitantly on her pencil drawing, pulling four attempts from the pad before one satisfied her; she worked for some time improving it.

She went back to bed. As sleep enveloped her she wondered why she felt so happy. She still did not know what to do about herself, or Paul. She only knew what she would do with Val tomorrow, not what she would say to her.

❧ 41 ❧

At noon precisely Val got out of her car and walked across the street to the Blake house.

Carolyn's eyes were sea-green against the green print of her shirt, her hair was brushed to sunlit silk. Choked by the loveliness of her, Val touched her cheek to Carolyn's and walked into the house without speaking, thrusting a note from Neal into her hands.

Carolyn opened and read the note as she walked to the sofa. She chuckled. "According to this I've agreed to see him tomorrow night."

Val sighed. Convincing Neal that he could not accompany her today had been difficult. "I had to tell him something. I hoped I could talk you into it."

"You have." Carolyn put the note into the pocket of her shirt and sat on the sofa, tucking her legs up under her.

Awkwardly, Val sat beside her. She decided to plunge into what she had rehearsed. Not looking at Carolyn, she began, "I want you to know I understand about . . . I want you to take the time you need to—" She broke off. The words were clumsy, inadequate.

She turned to Carolyn. "There was a woman at the party last night, four years ago I lived with her. There was an attraction, I—"

"The blonde?"

Val gaped at her. "How did you know?"

"The way she looked at me. And we're physically similar."

"You are?" Again she was astonished. "You're not remotely alike. Well, maybe a little, but—" She would not be sidetracked into this issue. "Anyway, I wasn't ready, I couldn't handle my feelings—No, that's not true, I didn't *want* to handle my feelings, not like now, not like—"

Carolyn took her hands, interrupted her stumbling ramble. "Val, I know I haven't worked through everything yet. I haven't had time. I know I'm in a new place. It doesn't scare me—but it's strange to me."

Squeezing her hands, Carolyn peered anxiously into her face. "For a while I need to be . . . not with you. Or Paul, either." She spoke her words slowly, as if each were being newly minted. "I need to be somewhere between you both. For a while. I need to be by myself. Maybe not for long, but for a while. Can you understand that?"

"Yes," she answered.

It was far from the worst scenario. Immeasurably better than her belief of these past days that she had lost Carolyn irrevocably. "I'll be here," she said. "For whatever you want, anything you need."

Carolyn rubbed Val's hands between hers. "As long as I know that." Then she said softly, "I have something to show you."

She pulled a sheet from the sketch pad lying on the coffee table. Val held the edges between her palms and studied the drawing.

A series of finely drawn links were interlocked in a curving, delicate chain, appearing to rise from the bottom to the top of the paper. The links at the bottom were subtly shaded but distinct, darkening as the chain rose toward the center of the page. The shading of the links briefly varied between dark and light, then gradually and uniformly darkened until there were two links of solid black. The chain then dissolved into whiteness.

"Pure emotion," Val mused, "locked into itself, blocking out everything. Wavering, then gaining strength. Most powerful at the two black links. Ending suddenly."

"You're so good." Carolyn was smiling but her eyes were shy. "It's sensation rather than emotion. I was trying to show how I felt you." Her fingers traced over the drawing. "How you took everything away except feeling you. I felt you more and more, then it changed a little. Then it became strong and perfect. Stronger, then strongest." She paused. "I tried to keep it longer but it was gone."

Val cleared her throat. "Was it a particular time?"

"My first." Carolyn's voice was quiet, uninflected.

Her first? Did she mean . . . She was too orgasmic, she couldn't mean . . . Val asked, "May I have this?"

"Yes, if you want it."

"I want it. Sign it."

Carolyn took the drawing to the desk, signed it with a pencil, handed it to her. Val looked at the signature: CARRIE in tiny letters in the lower corner.

Carolyn said, "I'll give you this in exchange for the sketch pad I borrowed. I found six drawings of me in it."

"I didn't realize you took . . . that's the pad with . . ."

She looked at Carolyn, remembering, heat flowing through her body. Carolyn held her gaze. Desire, thick and sweet and heavy, hung between them.

"You asked me once to humor you," Carolyn said huskily. "Now do that for me."

Val pushed off the wall at the deep end of the pool, glided to the bottom and somersaulted. Arms extended, she floated to the surface, cool currents sluicing deliciously against her bare breasts, her thighs. Drawing breath deeply into her, she submerged again, twisting, turning, stroking her breasts and thighs, intoxicated by the sensuality of her body.

She surfaced at the shallow end close to Carolyn, who clung to the wall gently flutter-kicking currents up around her own nude body. Val sidestroked over to her, reveling in her litheness; water was the one place where she never felt awkward. She flung her hair out of her eyes and said in exhilaration, "I love you Carrie; don't ever be afraid that I love you."

"Nothing about you frightens me; not anymore."

The voice was quiet. Cool hands slid over Val's shoulders, caressing, smoothing the water off. Carolyn said, "I think this may be my favorite place on you." Her lips were soft and warm, kissing across Val's shoulders; the cool hands slid down over her back. "I love your strength. I've always loved watching you walk, swim . . . do the most ordinary things."

Carolyn took her hands, entwined their fingers. "I love your hands. I love watching you fix things . . . when you work with your hands . . ."

She drew Carolyn to her, held her, needing her substantiality; she felt a giving way within herself, a dismantling.

Carolyn said, "I remember seeing great statues of women in a park when I was small . . . and loving them." Her hands, featherlight, caressed down Val's hips; her lips brushed Val's throat. "I think I loved women even before that. I think I've always wanted to be loved by a woman, a woman like you. I can't imagine making love with a woman more beautiful than you."

She could not reply; she was helpless from these inconceivable words.

Carolyn's body was sinuous against her, Carolyn's warm lips moved down her, to her breasts. Val shuddered as a nipple, cold and rock-hard from the water currents, was taken and warmly savored.

Carolyn took the other nipple into her, the soft tongue slowly stroking, and Val gripped the edge of the pool. Carolyn touched between her legs; Val's body tensed to rigidity as a fingertip began its own slow strokes.

Groaning from her sensations, Val seized Carolyn's hips, pulling them into her. Carolyn's arms slid around her, Carolyn's mouth was under hers. Dimly aware of the growing turbulence in the water around them, she pressed Carolyn fully up into her in rising ecstasy, rotating the rich flesh clasped in her hands, her tongue pulsing in the softness of Carolyn's mouth as if it were the satin between her legs. The first spasms shook her; "Carrie," she moaned, and was engulfed in orgasm.

Naked, they lay inches apart on towels spread over the grass.

"God, I want you," Carolyn said.

"I tried," Val reminded her. "You stopped me."

"I want this." Carolyn touched a corner of Val's lips, traced over them. "But not wet hair."

"Let me wrap it in a towel, Carrie," she whispered, aching to love the woman so tantalizingly close to her.

"I want to feel your hair; I want everything. It should dry fast in the sun."

Val ran her fingers impatiently through the crown of her hair. "Soon."

Carolyn said, "I bought *Summer Sunrise*."

"Susan told me. After you left last night. I was surprised. You're becoming a woman of wonderful impulses," she teased.

"Paul didn't even fuss very much. I think he's learned to roll with the punches. Except for the one that's coming," she added, her eyes suddenly remote.

Val regretted the change of mood, the deflection of Carolyn's thoughts from her. But she asked, "What'll you say to him?" Surely nothing about their own relationship . . .

Carolyn said somberly, "Only that I want a separation."

Val realized that her hatred of Paul Blake had extinguished without a wisp of smoke. Her one concern was Carolyn's pain. "When will you tell him? Have you decided?"

Carolyn's face was grave. "I haven't thought any of this through, Val. My instinct is to tell him now. If I wait he'll misread it to mean the trouble between us is healing. He loves me so much. If I delay, if I think about it . . ."

Dwelling on this now would cause Carolyn's resolve to begin weakening immediately. Better to speak as if she assumed Carolyn would carry through her intention. "I understand why you won't move in with Neal and me. But you need a place—"

"I'll find one, it won't take long. I can afford decent rent. I have a good job; I'm entitled to part of our savings. . . ."

Carolyn looked away. "Know something? I've never been alone. I lived with Mother and then I married Paul." Her eyes met Val's again; they were lighted with eagerness. She said cautiously, as if in guilt that she had allowed herself such anticipation, "Maybe I'll hate it."

"You might—but it'll be good for you," Val assured her emphatically. "Everyone should be alone for a time in their lives." She grinned. "Just don't like it too much. I can visit once in a while, can't I?"

Carolyn's smile was quick and flirtatious; her gaze drifted down Val's body. "Once in a while. I'll have a rule in my new place. Certain visitors must leave their clothes at the door."

Val laughed. "A terrific rule." She was enjoying Carolyn's growing boldness.

They lay quietly, looking at each other. Val felt weak with her want, a sensation containing none of the helplessness she had known in the pool, and purely pleasurable.

Carolyn's eyes were heavy-lidded. "Your hair's dry enough," she whispered. "Let's go in."

The painting in the guest room cast its warm colors over the room. "Until I take it with me," Carolyn said huskily, "it stays in here."

"I love it being in here. I love you having it." Val turned to her.

Carolyn raised a hand for silence, her head cocked to listen.

After a moment Val asked, "What did you hear?"

"I don't know. A metallic sound. From the garage, I think."

"I'll check."

"No, it's just a cat, I'm sure. They jump onto the garage roof all the time," she breathed as Val took her into her arms. "The neighborhood is full of . . ." She closed her eyes. "Val," she whispered.

Val lifted her onto the bed. Her body poised over her, she gently kissed her face and explored the exquisite breasts, the tender body arching in her slow savoring hands. A hand cradling Carolyn's head, she brought Carolyn's mouth to hers and lowered her body onto her. Carolyn moaned, and seized her. Carolyn arched again to the quickening strokes of Val's tongue in her, as Val's hand cupped and caressed in sweet soft damp. Carolyn moaned her want; Carolyn's arms released her. Blood pounded in Val's ears as she moved down, between the soft open thighs.

❧ 42 ❧

They had gone almost three miles on the Golden State Freeway when the engine of Jerry's Chrysler coughed and stalled. Paul braced himself as traffic behind them braked and screeched and Jerry jabbed at the emergency flasher and drifted the car perilously over one lane and onto the shoulder.

"Shit," Jerry spat. "The goddamn thing just out of the shop, new generator—goddammit! Wish we'd of taken your car like you offered."

Wryly remembering when he had wanted Carolyn to take her car instead of Val Hunter's, Paul shrugged. "Happen to anybody, Jerry. Maybe it's something simple."

They examined the engine connections, found no obvious problem. "Goddammit, shit. Sorry Brother, always swear my head off when I'm mad."

"Relax." Paul gripped his shoulder. "There's a call box right behind us."

An auto-service truck arrived an hour later on that Sunday afternoon. The burly young driver buried his head under the hood of Jerry's car and emerged to announce, "Carburetor."

"Shit," Jerry said. "Goddammit." He kicked at a tire in rhythmic fury.

"Know a place you can tow it?" Paul grinned at the young driver, who was chewing gum and gazing indifferently at Jerry.

"Yup. Get it fixed up for you today." He jerked a thumb at Jerry's car. "Only take a minute to hook her up."

With the Raider game blasting in the cab of the truck, they rode down Western Avenue in Hollywood, Jerry's Chrysler rattling behind them. Jerry peered out at peeling billboards, dilapidated buildings. "Shit, this don't look too good."

"You want a mechanic on Sunday," the driver said imperturbably, "you take what you can get." He turned into an ARCO station.

A few minutes later a tall, gaunt man, the name Lamont stitched on the breast pocket of his coveralls, toweled grease from his hands and stated, "Need to take the carburetor apart, see what's choking that baby. Cost you a hundred-forty."

"Holy Jesus shit," Jerry sputtered.

"No checks. Cash or credit card. Up to you—take it someplace else. Ten bucks a day storage till you get it out of here."

Jerry glared at him, turned to Paul. Paul shrugged. Jerry's shoulders sagged. "How long will it take?"

"Be ready after five." He waved at the neon words blinking under the ARCO sign. "We're open twenty-four hours."

To circumvent further profanity, Paul said hurriedly to the mechanic, "You have a loaner we could have? To rent?" he added.

"Nope, last one's gone."

"Shit," Jerry said. "There goes the goddamn Raider game."

The mechanic was filling out a form attached to a clipboard. He touched a foot to Jerry's car, to the license frame which read North Hollywood Chrysler-Plymouth. "You guys from the Valley?"

"Burbank, close by Glendale," Paul answered, looking around for a pay phone. He would call Carolyn.

"Let me check with Mike; he's the morning man. Lives out that way. He'll drop you if he's going straight home."

"No big deal, Jerry," Paul said soothingly as Jerry pulled his Raider ticket from his shirt pocket and waved it in disgust. "We'll get out to another game." *Fat chance,* he thought. "Maybe see a better team than Denver."

"I wanted to see Elway," Jerry said mournfully, accepting the clipboard from the mechanic and signing the paperwork. "Brother, you mind running me back in here to pick up the car? I hate to ask."

Mentally, Paul cursed. "Sure, Jerry."

"You're a hell of a guy, Brother. Damn good neighbor." Jerry crumpled his Raider ticket and threw it into a trash receptacle.

Sitting in the high cab of Mike's pickup, Paul glimpsed Val Hunter's battered tan Volkswagen as soon as the truck turned onto his street. His chest constricted; the pain was swift and crushing.

Jerry said, "Come on in, Brother. We'll have some beers and watch Dallas on the tube."

"Don't think so, Jerry." His temples throbbed, his chest hurt. He nodded thanks to Mike and dispiritedly walked down the driveway and let himself into the garage. He would take his car, go for a drive.

No, goddammit. He slammed a fist on the roof of his Buick. Why should he go anywhere? It was his house, his wife, that Amazon bitch wasn't driving him away from his own house and his own wife. But he walked around the car several times in frustration and indecision, then bent down to finger a chip on the door of Carolyn's Sunbird. He straightened. He would stay outside—assuming they were inside— and work on the pool, maybe go for a swim. He went out through the side door of the garage into the yard.

He heard a sound from the slightly raised window of the guest room. He had never heard such a sound before, yet he knew with a prickling sensation along his scalp that it was Carolyn's voice. The sill was at eye level, only two steps away.

For an instant he thought Carolyn was being attacked, and in that moment he rose onto the balls of his feet from the force of the adrenaline rushing through him. Then he saw that Carolyn's arms were locked in fierce embrace around the massive nude body of Val Hunter, that Carolyn's mouth was fastened to hers, that Val Hunter's hand was within Carolyn's legs.

Hair stirred on the back of his neck; his head swam with vertigo.

Carolyn made the same sound, a moan from deep in her throat; and her arms released Val Hunter. Val Hunter moved down her body. Carolyn's thighs rose to imprison Val Hunter's face between them; then her body arched as if struck by an electrical charge.

He steadied himself with a shaking hand against the side of the house, and looked around, his eyes momentarily dazzled by sunlight glancing off the blue water in the pool. He walked a few steps away, conscious of the ground yielding slightly under his feet, remembering that he had watered the grass only this morning. He stared at towels on the grass above the pool decking, imprinted by two bodies which had lain close together; and clothing in careless disarray on a chaise— jeans and a T-shirt, Carolyn's new silk shirt, her new pants; and beside the steps at the shallow end, panties and bras.

"God oh *God* . . ."

As if hypnotized, as if his feet were lead weights dragging him, he returned to the window.

Carolyn's body was spread-eagled, Val Hunter's hair a disheveled darkness between her thighs. Val Hunter's hands were under Carolyn's hips, slowly rotating them; Carolyn's head was flinging from side to side, her hands clutching at the bedspread, her breathing like sobs.

"Val . . ."

Her body stilled, drawing into itself, her shoulders rising, her head bending back between the shoulder blades, clenched fists lifting the spread from the bed. A sound began, was choked off. Her face was a rictus of ecstasy.

The hands released the bedspread; she sank back onto the bed. Val Hunter lay motionless, her face resting on Carolyn's thigh. She wiped her face on the bedspread as Carolyn reached down for her, groping blindly.

She gathered Carolyn into her arms, rocked her. Carolyn gasped something he could not hear and Val Hunter murmured back indecipherably.

"Yes," Carolyn uttered. "That. Now."

He squeezed his eyes shut, stood swaying.

"Beautiful . . . Val . . ."

Seemingly of themselves, his eyes opened.

Val Hunter, hugely naked, knelt astride Carolyn's delicate shoulders. Carolyn's hands avidly gripped, glided over the white globes of hip; she reached up with both hands to seize with rough eagerness the massive breasts. Her arms circled Val Hunter's hips, convulsively tightened. Val Hunter's hands cradled the head between her columns of thigh. Carolyn's arms pulled Val Hunter down to her. Carolyn's rigid legs rose slightly from the bed, the toes pointed, the feet quivering.

Val Hunter flung her head back. The powerful hips became undulant. "Carrie," she moaned, "darling Carrie . . ."

The words galvanized him into motion. He pulled himself away from the window and strode quickly across the yard.

He sat before the television set in Jerry Robinson's family room holding a beer, staring at a football game, remembering accounts he had read of people declared clinically dead on the operating table who claimed later that they had hovered over themselves before their vital signs returned. He seemed to be somewhere outside himself, watching as he sat in the Robinson house looking calmly at the TV and speaking normally.

He found himself on his street with no memory of leaving the Robinsons, or of any conversation exchanged with them. He belched the sour taste of beer he could not remember drinking. How long had he been with the Robinsons? He peered at his watch, could not focus on the gold hands. What difference did it make? Val Hunter's car was still outside his house.

He crossed the street. He paced with long even strides as if he were an automaton, and watched his house. When the front door finally opened he stepped quickly behind the broad peeling trunk of a palm tree.

The figure of Val Hunter shimmered in his vision, outlined in red. He blinked rapidly but still the redness framed her. She strode across the street, her faded jeans riding low on her hips, a manila envelope under her arm.

How she would sneer if she could see him hiding from her. How she must be gloating, he raged as he watched her jaunty stride. She had been laughing at him for months—how she would love to laugh in his face. She—a woman—*she* had seduced his wife.

He rocked savagely back and forth as he watched her, visualizing her face under the soles of his jogging shoes. He stared unblinkingly as she opened her car door, as she bent to fold her burly body within.

A leviathan, a freak. She was no woman—look at that hard elephant ass on her. Real women were soft, vulnerable. Soft skin, velvet pussies, wonderful soft asses. Men's asses were flat and solid but a woman's ass was lush, the epitome of everything soft and vulnerable. She was grotesque—a mutation of a woman.

A vampire. She was a pseudo-woman who seduced real women into her despicable ranks to perform her despicable practices.

Words reverberated through him: *Beautiful . . . Val . . .*

The tan Volkswagen started with an authoritative roar and moved off down the block, out of sight.

He was pacing again, around his block, around and around.

More words: *Yes. That. Now.*

A voice, low and resonant: *Carrie . . . darling Carrie.*

A vampire. But she was real, not a legend. She was lethal. Not enough that she had her own kind, she had to corrupt real women, prey on his innocent Princess.

He paced until his calves cramped. Then he opened the front door of his house, holding for a long moment the warm smooth brass door-knob, thinking of Carolyn's breasts, how tenderly he had always held them.

All I ever did was love you.

She sat in her usual corner of the sofa, a book in her lap. The heavy blonde hair was groomed, the lips lightly lipsticked. The neat pants and shirt were those he had seen in a discarded heap in the yard.

She was looking at him with a puzzled frown. "Jerry was over a few minutes ago looking for you. You had trouble today with his car? What's going on?"

"Nothing." He was amazed; his voice was normal. "Nothing important."

She glanced at the clock over the fireplace. "Where've you been? Jerry said you left their house an hour ago."

An hour? Had it been an hour? "Walking," he said. "Thinking."

"I've been thinking too."

Her voice was cautious, her face turned so that her glance at him was sidelong, a mannerism he knew well. He knew so many things about her so well, her facial expressions, her gestures, the fidgety, intense way she led up to a discussion of anything important to her: all her mannerisms. He had thought he knew her completely.

"Yes," he said.

"We've been having our problems over these past months, Paul."

The formal use of his name, emphasizing that this issue was of unusual significance. She waited now—as he knew she would—for his reaction to the ball she had lobbed so carefully into his court.

"Yes," he said, and leaned against the bar.

A minimal return, but sufficient. She said forcefully, "The last thing I want in this world is to go on hurting you. I think . . . I think a separation would be wise." She took a deep breath, exhaled.

An image seared his mind: Her body, spread-eagled.

"Wise for both of us, Paul. To give us more breathing space." A note of pleading came into her voice. "To give us a chance to . . . get things straightened out. If you'd like us to see a marriage counselor I'd agree to that."

He shook his head, trying to drive off the images of her. "Tell me something," he said, and his mind was swept clear as if speaking had been an exorcism. "The whole time we've been married, did you ever have an orgasm?"

The words had come from a molten depth. Focused acutely on her, he saw first the shocked glance, then the jaw that dropped almost comically, then the eye-shift. Then heard the words: "What, why—" she blurted, "of course."

"All the time? Or some of the time?"

"Why are you asking? If you think—"

"You've answered the question." Congratulating himself on the pleasantness of his tone, he smiled.

She frowned; two distinct creases centered between her eyes, "I have *not* answered the question," she stated. "It's an impossible question—whatever I say you'll challenge or take the wrong way. If you could understand that that's not an issue. Yes, I wish we could have talked . . . but even so—Paul, if you think my wanting a separation is because of—it's got nothing to do with—"

He cut in sharply, "What this is all about is the same thing that's been going on for months. You'd rather be with that Amazon than with me."

"That's not true." Some of the color had left her face.

"It is true. You'd rather be with her than me. You'd rather be with a woman than a man."

"What I want at this moment is to be by myself." Her voice was as flat and definite as her statement. "And you'll soon find out that that's exactly the truth."

His head suddenly throbbed fiercely. She had spoken with perfect conviction, as if the evidence of his own eyes, her passionate loving of that creature in a room not a dozen steps from him, were a nonfact. It was the same device she had used these past months to deceive him, confuse him, make him crazy. She had drawn him into a realm of irrationality where lies were made into truth.

The game was over.

He looked at her. The green eyes were veiled, impenetrable. He remembered trying vainly to see into them after lovemaking, to penetrate the barrier that limited, ended intimacy.

Another image flash-froze behind his eyes: Her body arched, her face contorted.

"The truth is," she said, "I simply want a separation. I'll do anything I can to—to . . ."

She looked away from him. Her hands were clenched tightly in her lap, a mannerism he had seen rarely in his marriage, its meaning clear: the finality of her decision.

"I want a separation now," she said quietly. "I think it's best."

THIS IS BEST.

Every woman in his life had defrauded and betrayed him, punished him.

Why?

Why had she abandoned him? Those long evenings away from him. That Saturday she had been gone all day claiming the car had broken down. Months of afternoons to herself because of that job she'd insisted on having. Refusing to let him touch her, making him think it was all his fault. All that time pretending she loved him, when she was in the arms of that . . . that . . . All the time that creature was sneering at him, knowing she'd won.

All women were vampires, all of them treacherous, their rules unfathomable. They were all vampires, feeding off him, draining him.

Every last living one of them—even the woman he had chosen as the most precious among women, the woman he had thought would be his Princess forever.

"All I ever did was love you," he said, and walked toward her, the knowledge of what he would do growing in him, cold and implacable.

As he saw the fear gathering in her, as she shrank back into the sofa cushions, he slowed his pace deliberately, wanting to examine the dimensions of this unexplored power.

Unhurriedly, he reached down for her, pulled her from the sofa by her silk shirt, and with deep satisfaction heard the fabric rend in his hands.

"Paul," she said in an appalled whisper.

There was a sharp snap of sound; the flesh of her cheek stung his palm. Again there was the snap of sound, and his raised hand threatened her a third time; he would not listen again to that voice saying his name. The voice choked off; the eyes were wide and stunned with shock.

This was her fault. It was her fault she had ever had to know that this was in him.

He flung her backward. Her body glanced off the coffee table, landed heavily on the floor. He lifted her by the shoulders, spun her, propelled her toward the bedroom. She hit the doorframe, fell again.

He picked her up and sent her sprawling across the bed. With her nails clawing at his face he tore the silk blouse into tatters. Seizing her bare shoulders he shook her; her head flopped like a puppet's head, the blonde hair churning across her face. When he released her she lay limp; but he took her wrists and held them in one hand and clamped her legs down with a knee; and with his free hand proceeded with his task, pulling her pants down over her hips.

In a moment he would be in her; he was hard, stone hard knowing that nothing could stop him, he would do anything he wished, she was helpless beneath him. He unzipped his pants to free his erection. He had never known such power and potency; he would rear like a stallion in her. She had never felt anything from anyone as she would feel him now.

Her face was contorted from the force of her screams. The image formed of her arched body, that face . . . The imprinted images flooded him, as if through a rent in his mind. He forced her clothing down to her knees.

He clapped a hand over her mouth and his voice hissed from him: "I saw you today. I saw you I saw you. . . ." He turned her over onto her stomach. "I saw you I saw you I saw you . . ."

"Paul don't do this. God oh God—"

The words impaled him: God oh *God.*

He plunged into her. A hand clawed back at him. He grasped her wrists again, pulled them around behind her. Hearing her shrill screams, forcing his way into the unyielding flesh tensed in revulsion of him, he yanked her head up by her hair and roared his rage. She *had* to receive him, to *feel* him.

Her face was a hideous mask of horror. He slammed her head down, screaming with the flaming pain that engulfed him, pushing the face and its horror with all his force into the pillow.

"Paul! Paul!"

It was not her voice. There was a piercing, insistent shrill—the doorbell.

"Paul! Brother, what's going on in there?" The doorbell shrilled continuously.

Carolyn was limp beneath him. He rolled off her, ripped the pillow away. Her head lolled; she lay utterly still.

"Paul! Answer me, Brother! Do you need me to get help?"

He understood that if he did not answer the door Jerry would call the police. He leaped from the bed, pulling his pants closed, yanking his shirt down as he ran to the front door.

Jerry Robinson took a rapid stride backward. "Uh, Brother is everything . . . I uh, heard uh—" He was staring at Paul's cheek. "I mean all these weirdos around, uh—God, the things you hear—"

Paul brushed at his cheek, saw a faint smear of blood on his palm. *Carolyn . . . Carolyn . . . did I . . .*

"None of my business, didn't mean to disturb but I never knew you two to—" Jerry Robinson backed down the steps. "Forget the car, I'll—"

Paul threw the door closed, ran back into the bedroom.

The bed was empty. He staggered, faint with relief; then looked wildly around. Where was she? He glanced in the bathroom, then ran into the living room. She was in the house—somewhere, hiding from him.

The drapes over the glass door to the backyard were swaying. He hesitated. Had the door been open when he first came into the house? She often left it open . . . Were the swaying drapes from the breeze or—

He jerked the drapes aside and ran into the yard. It was empty. But she could have gone out the gate and down the path alongside the house . . . Her instinct would be to run but she couldn't be far.

He raced into the house, into the bedroom. The sight of green silk shreds scattered over the bed and carpet filled him with sick dread. *Christ, she must have run out of the gate while Jerry was here.* She was out in the neighborhood half naked. *Jerry saw blood . . . . Christ, let me find her.*

Yanking his keys from his pocket he ran for the garage, flinging the front door shut behind him. As the electronic garage door slowly rose, as he backed the Buick down the driveway, he glimpsed Jerry Robinson on the Robinsons' front lawn. Rolling down the electric window on the passenger's side he yelled, "You see Carolyn?"

Jerry gaped at him, his face pale.

An idiot, the man was a fucking moron. All this was his fucking fault, if he hadn't rented that fucking guest house . . . He backed out with a squeal of tires.

He cruised slowly down the block, turned at the corner, cursing in his impatience, his anxiety, straining for any sign of a moving figure. She could be anywhere, behind any tree or shrub, in someone's backyard . . . Maybe she'd already run into someone's house or found someone to pick her up. All he could do was look, and hope. If he couldn't find her in the next few minutes he might as well go home and wait for the police, wait for the whole goddamn fucking world to come to an end.

❧ 43 ❧

She regained consciousness hearing Paul's voice in the living room.
Groggily, she sat up, rose weakly and painfully to her feet, struggling
to pull up her pants.

She had to get out, get away . . . She heard the front door slam.

He was coming back.

She fled into the bathroom, stepped behind the door, flattened herself into the wall, squeezed her eyes shut as he came toward her and
into the room. She heard the thud of his footsteps running into the living room.

Sidling out from behind the door she decided she would make a run
for it, get past him and out on the street. She heard his footsteps
again, coming toward her, and she retreated again.

There was a jingling sound: keys. And his footsteps running into
the living room, the slam of the front door.

He thinks I've left . . .

She was out of the bathroom, pulling a sweater from a drawer. She
heard his car start. She ran into the living room, seizing her purse as
she fled out the patio door. Hearing his car roar down the driveway
she let herself into the garage from the backyard door.

He would look for her on the street and soon know she was here.
He would be back. She had to get away now, get away from him . . .

She pulled the sweater down over her head, jamming her arms into
the sleeves. With one shaking hand supporting the other she unlocked the car, inserted the key into the ignition. She backed out
heedlessly, striking the garage door that was slowly descending after
Paul's departure, and skidded off the driveway into the Robinsons'
front yard. She glimpsed Jerry Robinson's stupefied face, saw him
dash across his yard as if she were coming after him. Reaching the

street, she straightened the car and floored the accelerator, the tires spinning and shrieking, the smell of burned rubber in her nostrils.

She careened around the corner, braked sharply at the sight of slow-moving taillights. Twisting the wheel violently to turn around, she skidded across the intersection. The car behind her had stopped, was beginning to turn; it was Paul's gray Buick. Again she floored the accelerator. The car leaped ahead on the empty street.

She sped up and down streets devoid of traffic on this early Sunday evening, too terrified to look in the rearview mirror, zigzagging erratically until her vision was caught by a green freeway sign. She roared up the on-ramp, knowing that other cars were her best concealment. Finding the courage to look in the rearview mirror, she drove an outside lane of the Ventura Freeway, exiting several miles later.

Taking a circuitous route, she drove to Val's flat, circled the block, parked two blocks away.

Glancing fearfully around for any sign of Paul or his car, she walked the two blocks.

Val answered her knock. Carolyn stepped over the threshold and collapsed.

๑ 44 ๑

Val stood frozen over the crumpled body. Neal spoke in an awed voice, words she did not hear; but the sound impelled her to action. She fell to her knees, cradled Carolyn's head. "Carrie," she whispered through her terror.

She pressed her fingers to the side of Carolyn's neck; the pulse was faint and rapid. Carolyn's face shone with perspiration. Her eyes fluttered open. They were dull, unfocused.

"Ma," Neal said, "should I call the paramedics?"

"No." Carolyn's voice was weak, but she reached out to him. "No honey, don't do that. I'm okay, honest."

She struggled to get up. Val supported her, then lifted her into her arms, feeling dampness in the clothing. She noticed that the pants and sweater were badly mismatched—pink with deep green.

"Bring some hand towels," she instructed Neal as she carried Carolyn into the bedroom. "Wring one out in cold water."

She lay Carolyn on the bed, sat beside her. "Carrie," she said, her dread huge and shapeless, "what did he do?"

Carolyn looked at her in seeming incomprehension. There were rounded patches of redness on her cheekbones, as if from a fever.

Val said, "I'm taking you to a hospital."

Carolyn clutched at her. "No. No, Val."

Neal came in with the towels. "You sure you're okay, Carolyn?"

Carolyn whispered, "Now that I'm here I'll be fine." She smiled weakly at him.

Feeling a small degree of relief, Val gently patted Carolyn's face dry. "Honey," she said to Neal, "would you leave me alone with Carolyn for a few minutes?"

"Sure."

Carolyn's face had again beaded over with perspiration. Her breathing was shallow; Val could see the rapid pulse beat in her throat.

"Carrie, tell me what he did."

Carolyn turned her face away. "Just let me stay here," she whispered, taking Val's hand in both of hers.

The hands were clammy. Val said, "You're cold; you're soaking wet. I'm putting you to bed."

From the dresser she removed flannel pajamas she kept for camping trips. Supporting Carolyn with an arm, she pulled the sweater over her head, and with a lurching sensation saw that Carolyn's bra was twisted up around her shoulders and the shoulders were darkly latticed with bruises.

Carefully, she unfastened and pulled off Carolyn's pants, her panties. There were red welts merging with the dark hues of bruises in a patchwork over her hips and thighs.

Gingerly, Val dressed her in the pajamas. Dampness quickly permeated the flannel. Val pulled the blanket up, sat beside her. She took Carolyn's head in her hands. The red marks on the cheeks, she saw, had a purplish tinge. "You told Paul," she said quietly.

Carolyn closed her eyes.

Val said, "This is what he did."

Tears leaked from the closed eyes.

"Carrie." She succeeded in controlling her voice. "Something could be broken. You could be bleeding inside. I'm taking you to a hospital."

Carolyn's hands flew out from under the covers to clutch at her. "Please no. I know I'm okay. I can tell. Please, just let me stay here with you."

"Don't worry," Val said in profound anguish, "you'll be staying with me." Afraid to touch Carolyn's body, afraid she might hurt her, Val again cradled her head and murmured endearments to her, seeing the tension in her face subtly diminish; but when she tried to get up from the bed Carolyn pulled her back. Val whispered, "Let me see about Neal a moment."

In the living room she said softly to Neal, "Go in and watch her. Tell her I've gone to the bathroom if she asks. I need to make a quick phone call."

She dialed Alix's number. She said without preamble, "It's Val and I need help. I have someone here; she's hurt. She won't let me take her to a hospital—"

"What happened?" Alix asked in a quiet voice. "Is she badly hurt?"

"God, Alix, I think he—" Val's voice broke. "Can you just come over?"

"I'll try to do better than that. Be there as soon as I can." Alix hung up.

Val shuddered, buried her face in her hands. She straightened, cleared her throat, rubbed her face vigorously. She dialed Marion Berman in the pink apartment building across the street, with whom she had arranged reciprocal child care. She spoke briefly, thanked her, hung up. "Neal, honey," she called, "come here, will you?"

She took him into the kitchen. "I want you to take yourself and your homework over to Mrs. Berman's and bunk with Marty tonight."

Neal said softly, "Carolyn . . . he hurt her, didn't he?"

She hesitated. "Yes," she said, "he did." She looked into his serious, intelligent eyes.

"Ma," he said, "let's not let her go back . . . to that Frankenstein."

In spite of herself she grinned. "Okay. But I need to see about her, what needs to be done to have her stay with us. Now get out of here. Be back first thing in the morning, and I do mean first thing or your name will be Munchkin."

He bowed. "Yes, oh great and powerful Oz."

Carolyn's face was pale, shiny with moisture; she appeared to be dozing. Val smoothed damp hair from her forehead, sat beside the bed, and waited for Alix to arrive from West Hollywood.

Forty-five minutes later, as she was directing silent but continuous curses at Alix, there was a knock at the door.

Alix introduced the woman accompanying her. Short and fat, with iron gray hair, Irene Donovan appeared to be in her early fifties. She wore shapeless gold corduroy trousers, a brown plaid shirt, and the formidably competent manner of an operating room nurse.

"Fortunately Irene was off duty," Alix said. "Unfortunately she had three friends over for dinner. They're now cooking their own dinner."

"I'm truly sorry," Val said, "but I'm grateful."

Irene shrugged. "It's happened before." She spoke in a breathy baritone. "What's the problem, as if I couldn't guess."

Val gestured to the bedroom door. "Her husband . . . she won't talk about what he did to her."

Irene shrugged again. "Typical. It's a defense mechanism, Val. All I can do is look at her. See what the situation is."

"That's all I ask. I need to know if she belongs in a hospital."

"Even if she does you can't make her go," Alix said. "You can't make her do anything."

"In our free country," Irene said wryly, "you can be as crazy as you want to be."

"I'll make her go," Val said quietly. "If she needs to be there I'll make her go. Irene, give me a minute with her. To tell her you're here."

Heedless of the women watching from the doorway, Val leaned down and touched her cheek lightly to Carolyn's. She felt Carolyn's arms slide around her. "Irene is here. She's a nurse, Carrie, a friend. I want you to let her look at you."

"No." Carolyn pushed Val away and shook her head, wincing with the effort. "I told you I'm okay."

"Carrie, you have to do this, I have to know you're all right—how to take care of you. Otherwise I have no choice, I'll take you to a hospital. Trust me, Carrie dearest, do this for me."

Carolyn's arms fell away; she lay with her eyes closed. Val rose and nodded to Irene. Alix, standing with her hands on her slim blue-jeaned hips, stared at Val with perceptive blue-green eyes.

Irene picked up Carolyn's wrist, scowled at the watch on her own plump wrist. She removed the pillow from under Carolyn's head, pulled the covers down, folded the pillow and slid it under Carolyn's feet. She felt Carolyn's forehead, then knelt on the bed; it creaked alarmingly under her bulk. She lifted the flannel top and curved large, blunt-fingered hands over Carolyn's rib cage.

"Breathe, sweetie." She pressed her ear to Carolyn's chest. "Again, sweetie, deeper. Good. Once more now." She addressed Val and Alix. "I'm taking the pajamas off now, why don't you—"

"Val," Carolyn pleaded, "don't leave me."

"So stay," Irene said to Val, "since she wants you here."

Alix slid an arm around Val, quickly released her. "I'll go get a glass of water." She sauntered off, the heels of her boots resounding on the wood floor.

Efficiently but gently, Irene removed the pajamas, inspected the bruises without comment. Again she pressed her hands up and down Carolyn's rib cage, then she took Carolyn's hands. "Push against me. Hard as you can. Again." She took Carolyn's feet in her hands and repeated the instruction. "Good," she murmured, "very good."

Slowly she kneaded Carolyn's stomach, studying her face. "Good," she said. "Will you turn over now, sweetie?"

Irene placed her hands on Carolyn's hips; then she straightened abruptly and pulled the covers up over Carolyn's body. "Stay just as you are," she ordered her sternly. "I'll be right back." Beckoning to Val, she left the room and pulled the door shut behind them.

She strode into the bathroom and scrubbed her hands vigorously with soap and hot water. "I need antiseptic, alcohol, whatever you have."

"What, what—" Val stammered, reaching for the medicine cabinet.

"Here, let me," Irene said, shouldering her aside. "Fine, you've got everything I need . . . There's rectal bleeding." She poured alcohol over her hands. "Pretty well dried from what I see but I need to clean it up and take a look . . . Let's hope it's external, that he didn't puncture her inside."

"You mean—"

"Let's hope he only used a penis. And do leave me alone with her now. I'll ask some questions she may not answer with you in the room."

Val sat on the edge of the sofa, a hand at her throat, feeling her chest rise and fall as she breathed. Alix sat in the armchair sipping orange juice, contemplating her, the sleeves of her gray sweater pushed up to her elbows, her legs crossed, a slim, booted foot swinging back and forth.

Alix said, "She was here last night. She's the Carolyn that Neal talks about."

Her eyes fixed on the bedroom door, Val nodded.

"This woman and you—is this what I think it is, Val?"

Val smiled thinly. "Probably."

"I had a feeling about her last night," Alix said. "We look alike."

Val's eyes swung to her. "That's what she says too. I don't see it."

Alix half-smiled. "Well, you're slow to see a lot of things, aren't you, Val?"

"I suppose I am, Alix."

Alix sighed. "Somewhere in this I think I've won a moral victory. For whatever that's worth." She lapsed into silence.

The minutes ticked by interminably. Indistinct voices came from within the bedroom. When Irene emerged Val followed her.

Irene washed her hands; Val could smell the acrid odor of alcohol. Irene said, "The bleeding appears external. *Appears,*" she emphasized. "But if there's blood in her urine, if her stools are black . . . Her bowel movements will be painful for a few days. No broken bones so far as I can tell—that's all the good news. The bruises are extensive and deep. Her breathing's shallow, she's perspiring, clammy to the touch. She'll be in a lot of pain tomorrow."

Drying her hands, Irene looked carefully at Val. "Her pulse rate's high. Too high. But it's slowing just a bit. If it hadn't started going down I'd have had to say it's too dangerous to keep her here. She's sleeping now, which is good. You'll need to watch her closely tonight."

Val followed Irene into the living room, sat beside her on the sofa. Irene said, "Then there's her mental state to consider. Alix can give you good advice on the aftermath of sexual assault and battery."

Val remembered listening many times to accounts of Alix's work on a rape hotline, and always with only cursory interest—indeed, with detachment, believing herself so far removed as a potential victim that the issue itself had seemed equally far removed.

Alix asked, "What about the husband?"

"He's a dead man," Val stated. "I'll take care of him myself. Smash him to a bloody pulp."

"That'll be very helpful, Val," Irene said in her deep bass voice. "The husband a bloody pulp, you in jail, her staring into the wall of a psychiatric ward."

Val slammed a hand onto the arm of the sofa. "I have to do something."

"No you don't," Irene said. "Only one person can do something."

Alix gestured toward the bedroom. "This may be difficult to accept, Val, but it's entirely up to her. It's her assault. She's the only one who can decide what she should do—if anything."

"I did talk to her," Irene said as Val began a belligerent protest. "Told her if she'd go to a hospital and report this I'd go with her, stay with her every minute, make sure she got special treatment. I told her she could file charges, that husbands aren't any different from street thugs when it comes to this." She shrugged. "But they are, of course. Anyway, she refused. Most women refuse."

"I'll call the police myself," Val grated. "Report the—"

"You can do that," Irene said. "They'll take a report but they won't be much interested. You're not the victim. And when they hear it's marital they'll be too bored to yawn. Even if she reports it they won't much care. Almost always the wife drops the charges. It's a waste of time and effort, and nothing ever goes to court. And if it does, you have no idea how hard it is; it's even more devastating for the victim—"

"I'll get him," Val said.

"For God's sake, Val." Alix expelled the words. "A man like this is real trouble. What do you know about him?"

"Not much. It's hard to believe he'd do this. He's your white-collar, *Wall Street Journal* type."

"Any type's the type," Alix said grimly. "Maybe he's done his deed; maybe right now he feels like total shit. But then again—"

"Then again," Irene finished, "he may think this is just a good start. And he's looking for her."

"I hope he is. I'll take care of him."

Alix said disgustedly, "Val, stop this insanity and use your brain. A man who could do this—he could be more dangerous than a mad dog. Does he know where she is? How to find her?"

Val considered. "I'll have to ask Carrie but I don't think so. My phone's not listed."

"If he wants to find you he will," Alix said. "You need to take her somewhere else and not just for that reason. Val, listen to me. Believe what I'm telling you. When the shock wears off she'll be terrified. I mean petrified. She'll be looking for him under the wallpaper. She needs to be somewhere she feels safe till she can put herself back together. She can stay with me or—"

"I'll call Susan," Val said. "Maybe I could use the beach house. . . . Regardless, I'll have her out of here tomorrow. I won't have her afraid." She turned to Irene. "What do I do to take care of her?"

"Keep her warm tonight. Get something into her if she's willing—milk, broth, anything. Keep those feet elevated till her body warms. No matter how much she hurts don't give her aspirin, any medication at all. All those bruises, there's too much unclotted blood. Tomorrow you can use ice or cold towels, that'll help with the pain and swelling, especially on bruises near bones—they'll swell quite a bit overnight. Stay with her tonight, watch her pulse. If it rises, call me. If there's any problem, call me. Stay with her. She needs that more than anything else."

Alix got up and opened the shoulder bag she had tossed on a chair when she came in. "I'll give you Jean Bowman's number," she said. "Call her tomorrow. She's a lawyer who's worked with a lot of battered women. Her fees are reasonable—usually whatever the woman can pay, whenever she can pay it. She's terrific and she'll take care of the husband. Believe me—he'll think he's come up against Attila the Hun. Stay away from the bastard, Val. Let Jean advise you. Let her handle this."

Val looked at her silently. After tomorrow Paul Blake would not be able to find Carolyn. But she, Val, would know exactly where to find him . . . when the time was right.

Alix sat beside her. "Now you need to listen to me for a while. I'll tell you what to expect when the shock starts wearing off for your Carolyn."

Val sat between Alix and Irene. Feeling protected by these women in a way she had never before experienced, she extended a hand to each of them. Clasping their hands she said, "Thank you. Thank you both."

Alix squeezed her hand, smiled at her. "Welcome to the lesbian community, Val."

❧ 45 ❧

Alix and Irene left at eleven o'clock. Shortly after midnight Carolyn awakened. She limped to the bathroom and closed the door against Val's insistent pleas to come in with her. Val went into the kitchen.

A few minutes later, back in the bedroom, an arm gingerly around the damaged shoulders, Val held a mug of broth to Carolyn's lips; Carolyn took several sips, muttered, "Don't leave me," and fell asleep.

Sitting in a kitchen chair beside the bed under a small but bright lamp, knowing the lolling of her head would jerk her awake every few minutes, Val held Carolyn's hand and allowed herself to doze. She needed her full strength for the coming day.

Carolyn's body had warmed; she was no longer perspiring, but she uttered tiny whimpers at any slight movement of her body. The red-purple patches on her face were swelling and had acquired a bluish tint. Her pulse continued to slow.

At seven o'clock that morning, as Carolyn fitfully slept, Neal returned to the flat. Val had decided that she must keep him out of school today. They would leave as soon as possible for the beach house, she told him, and warned him of Carolyn's appearance, that she would be in pain. He listened somberly, asked no questions. He sat down at the card table to organize a list of what they should take with them.

She had called Susan the previous night, giving her necessary details including Carolyn's identity. Remote as the possibility seemed, it might occur to Paul Blake to find his wife by locating Val through the gallery showing her work. "I need a safe place," she told Susan, "maybe as long as two weeks."

"Use the beach house," Susan said immediately. "I would think you should stay there at least that long."

Neal took a load of clothing down to the car. Val called Carolyn's office. Identifying herself as a friend of Carolyn Blake's, she told Bob Simpson that Carolyn had left for Chicago—her mother was seriously ill; she would be away indefinitely.

Val picked up Neal's list and resumed packing. Sooner or later Paul Blake would contact Carolyn's office—possibly even today. But she had done all she could to protect Carolyn's job.

Carolyn awakened and went into the bathroom, her misshapen face a mask of pain. Afterward, she labored to remove her pajamas. "God," she said faintly, looking down at herself. The bruises were newly huge and grotesque.

Val dressed her in an old wash-softened sweatshirt and sweatpants, wincing at Carolyn's sharp intakes of breath. The clothing hung from her in shapeless folds.

Neal stared, visibly swallowed. Then he reached behind him as if to push down an imaginary tail and spoke in the voice of the Cowardly Lion: "Shucks, folks, I'm speechless."

Val chuckled; Carolyn smiled and said weakly, "Right now, honey, I'm a horse of a really different color."

Val and Neal alternated carrying loads down to the car; Carolyn stood in silence beside the window staring down into the street.

"Where did you park your car, Carrie?" Val asked. "I don't see it anywhere."

Carolyn blinked in bewilderment; her damaged face contorted and tears welled. "I can't remember."

The keys were not in her purse nor in the pockets of the green pants. "I'll find your car," she told Carolyn, "it has to be close."

Carolyn burst into tears. "He could be out there. Waiting for you to leave."

She'll be terrified. I mean petrified. She'll be looking for him under the wallpaper.

"Don't worry, I'll keep you safe—I promise," Val soothed, knowing better than to reason with her.

"Stay with her," she whispered to Neal as she prepared to take the last load down to the car. "Talk to her, tell her I'll be right back."

But it took ten minutes to locate the Sunbird two blocks away, its front wheel jammed into the curb, the keys still in the ignition. She drove it back and parked it in the alley behind her building.

Slipping a thermal jacket around Carolyn, she led her on a slow and painful trek downstairs to the Volkswagen.

"Where are we going?" Carolyn asked, sitting on a bed of pillows in the backseat and looking fearfully at the parked cars and traffic around them.

"Emerald City," Neal said, kneeling on the front seat and leaning over to talk to her. Val watched Carolyn in the rearview mirror in concern; she had told her their destination twice before.

Travel required two hours of slow, careful driving to minimize Carolyn's pain. At the beach house, while Neal unpacked, Val made her comfortable on the sofa and applied ice wrapped in hand towels. Exhausted, Carolyn fell deeply asleep.

Val left the house and drove to a J. C. Penney in Santa Monica. She quickly chose a feather-soft nightgown and a fleecy robe, drawstring sweatpants, sweatshirts, tennis shoes and socks, panties and bras— selecting sizes in certain knowledge of Carolyn's body. Swearing at the price tag, she bought a Raider T-shirt Neal had been coveting. Amid all the packages for Carolyn she must have something for him.

She called Jean Bowman from a pay phone in the store.

With well-modulated crispness Jean Bowman agreed to do what she could—but not before direct preliminary contact with the client herself.

"Of course I realize the physical and emotional shape she's in." Jean Bowman's voice lowered, acquired harshness. "She needs time, she can't make clearheaded decisions right now. But we can use some of that time to her advantage. My advice is to take no action at all for the next several days. He won't know what's going on; he won't be able to find her; he'll have no idea what she might do. He'll be crazy. When I do contact him, I'll have the advantage. And these next few days may turn out to be the most damage we inflict on the son of a bitch."

Fat chance, Val thought. "We'll do as you say," she answered. She liked Jean Bowman—the brisk confidence of the voice, the distinct edge of steeliness. Alix had not said that this lawyer was a lesbian, but presumably she was. Irene Donovan. Jean Bowman. Some impressive women were lesbians. "I'll be back to you in a few days," Val said. "Thank you," she added.

That night, with Neal bedded down on the sofa, Val lay in the upstairs bedroom listening to the sounds of the ocean, a calming hand on the body next to hers as it convulsed in brief tremors. Her own sleep thwarted by anxiety, Val spoke softly and reassuringly throughout the night as Carolyn whimpered with her pain and her dreams.

Expect her to sleep badly. Expect night terrors, even violent nightmares.

The next morning Carolyn's eyes were dark hollows in her discolored face. Unwilling to leave her or subject her to another trip in the car, Val kept Neal out of school again. He went down to the beach for the day, telling Val, "I know for sure she doesn't want me around her today."

Wearing her nightgown and robe Carolyn lay on the sofa apathetically watching the television screen or staring out to sea. She drank orange juice and ate a few slices of apple from the tray of cheese and fruit Val had placed on the coffee table.

Expect loss of appetite. All you can do is put food around that might tempt her.

Carolyn spoke only once, and sharply: "Leave me alone. Stop watching me."

Obviously, Val thought, *Neal has better sense about her than I do.*

The next day Val drove Neal to school with Carolyn in the back of the car on her bed of pillows. Carolyn mumbled monosyllabic responses to questions and soon would not speak at all. As soon as Neal disappeared from view tears streamed down her face. Alarmed, watching her anxiously in the rearview mirror, Val drove quickly back to Malibu. In the house Carolyn lay huddled on the sofa, her tears soaking the pillow.

That evening Alix called to inquire about Carolyn. "Physically she's better," Val said grimly. "Emotionally . . ."

"Nobody I know is jumping for joy right now," Alix said dispiritedly.

"What do you mean?"

"For God's sake, Val. You're really out of it. The country had an election today. The networks projected a Reagan landslide about four seconds after the Eastern polls closed. Don't turn on the TV unless you're a real masochist."

Alix continued to talk about the election, about West Hollywood becoming a city with a gay majority city council. Val listened absently, remembering that on Sunday she and Carolyn had decided to vote together this day, to cast proud votes for the first woman vice presidential candidate. Val was compiling a list in her mind under the heading of Paul Blake. She added another item.

That night in bed Carolyn's silent tears continued, her face pressed into Val's shoulder, the tears soaking Val's nightshirt. When Carolyn fell asleep it was to whimper and cry out with the torment of her dreams.

The next morning, with the bruises less painful but in full violent color, Val dressed Carolyn in new navy blue sweatpants and a white sweatshirt, then brushed her hair. Carolyn accepted these attentions indifferently, and ate a scrambled egg and a piece of toast without interest.

The day was cool. Val built a fire, then carried a sturdy rocking chair down from the upstairs bedroom. She cushioned its hard seat and positioned it in front of the fire.

Looking out to sea, she held Carolyn in her arms and rocked her for hours. Carolyn dozed; periodically she turned her face into Val and soaked her shirt with the silent tears. Val rocked Carolyn and thought about what had been precipitated by her meeting with Paul Blake, and continued to add items to what she now called The List.

That night Carolyn cried again, aloud, with words and phrases meaningless to Val: "Wood, wood, like wood, nothing there . . . wood, wood, wood, couldn't hear . . . wood, wood . . ." Clutching Val's hands, she sobbed into her shoulder.

Expect emotional extremes. Expect apathy, irrationality, tears, deep depression. Don't allow her to feel isolated.

The next morning, after they had taken Neal to school, Carolyn said, "Can't you put the car in the garage? He could drive down this highway, he could—"

"You're right," Val said. "Carrie, it's time for you to call someone, a woman who can help us . . ."

Smiling, Carolyn hung up from Jean Bowman. "I do like her. I feel much better now." Then she sighed deeply. "I need to do something about my job."

"What do you want to do?"

Carolyn moved to the window, gazed out over the ocean. "What else is there to do besides quit? I can't go back. But I don't know how to explain to Bob Simpson."

Knowing how much Carolyn had loved her job and respected the man she worked for, Val added another item to The List. "Don't explain at all," she suggested softly. "Write a simple letter. Apologize for the lack of notice. Let it go at that. It's best all the way around, Carrie."

Sitting beside the fire, Carolyn said, "I hurt him. I hurt him so bad."

Don't be surprised if she blames herself. Victims often believe that some flaw in themselves caused the assault. If she starts to talk try to keep her talking. If she can verbalize her thoughts and feelings she'll begin working out of the trauma much faster; she'll start the process of integration.

Val asked cautiously, "How did you hurt him?"

"I didn't love him enough. He needed me to love him. He thought I loved him. He *believed* in my love."

"But you *did* love him, Carrie. For years you had love between you."

"You don't understand," Carolyn said dully. "You don't know."

"Then help me to know. I want to understand."

"I don't want to talk about it anymore."

Jean Bowman called for Carolyn, then talked to Val. "My client has given permission to speak to you," she said only half-jokingly.

Her voice acquired briskness. "I called this morning, at his office. It was good strategy to wait and a good place to call him. I laid a few things out—no lies mind you, just some heavy suggestions that we have no hesitation about informing the world about this episode in its entirety. I suggested that he had exactly one chance to do business in a civilized manner in contrast to his previous behavior, and only if he was totally cooperative. He showed his cooperation a few minutes ago—three bank books arrived by special messenger."

Val chuckled. "Jean, you're wonderful."

"What I want you to do, Val, is be certain Carolyn capitalizes right now on this generous impulse." Jean Bowman's tone was acid. "Before he recovers from it. Have her immediately open an account and deduct from those bank books what she considers community property—and make her be generous with herself. We can argue all this out with the husband later. The bank books are en route to you by special messenger."

"I'll take care of it," Val said.

"He's different, Val, this man. It wasn't that he didn't ask about her—it wasn't anything he said or didn't say. Just something in his voice. He sent ice down to my shoes."

Carolyn, her sweatpants rolled to her knees, walked out to calf-high water. "I like my new clothes," she said, adjusting the sweatshirt around her hips.

"I'm glad," Val said simply. It was the first notice Carolyn had taken of herself.

Carolyn walked back to her, reaching to her. Holding hands, they walked along the surf, picking their way among the rocks. Carolyn said slowly, "I was never the person Paul thought I was."

Val retorted, "Was he the person you thought he was?"

A breaking wave became a carpet of foam. Carolyn kicked at it as if to break its pattern. "You don't know that. What he did—that wasn't him. And you met him only once."

"I saw the person you were around him. And I know how you talked about him. You never saw the narrowness in your lives together."

"Yes I did," Carolyn insisted. "After I knew you."

As a wave sucked away sand from under her feet Val said, "Even then, I wonder if you fully saw his compulsion to control you. He never felt threatened about you before me. He and I hated each other instinctively. I think he panicked at the whole idea of me."

"You have no idea. He . . ."

As she trailed off, Val looked at her wondering what Carolyn was not telling her. Val said softly, "I have the same needs and fears he does. All of us do. But I'll never need to subvert someone to prove my worth."

"That's not fair. Or even right. He loved me; his loving made me feel worth something to myself. I never understood exactly how to cope with his love or his need. But I always felt . . . grateful."

Val winced. Gratitude: The prime component of her own two marriages.

Carolyn fought for balance in powerful eddies that pulled at her feet. Val watched her.

She's been utterly honest with me. She's never told me she loves me. Maybe she's not ready. Maybe she doesn't. Maybe she never will. I grew to love her only from wanting to hurt him. And what he did to her was to hurt me. How insane that she blames herself. She should hate us both.

"Let's go back," Carolyn said. "The fog's coming in."

Carolyn rested on pillows before the fire; Val sat beside her, legs crossed yoga style.

"He found out I was a fraud," Carolyn said in a voice filled with pain.

Val waited, but Carolyn did not speak again. "A fraud?" she prompted.

"I don't think I really want to talk about this now." She propped herself on her elbows. "Maybe later." She smoothed a pattern in the carpet with slow, pensive strokes of a hand.

Amid the sounds of surf the silence between herself and Carolyn seemed to gather weight and substance. Deliberately, she waited.

"Val," Carolyn said in a barely audible voice, "he saw us. He came home early last Sunday and saw us—I think through the yard window."

Val felt exposed, invaded and desecrated. She struggled against enveloping fury, fighting for control; it was crucial that she focus not on herself but entirely on Carolyn.

"Val, he saw . . . how I was with you. And I was never like that with him. I was a fraud. That's why he—"

"It doesn't *matter,* Carrie," she exploded. She slammed her hands on her thighs in her vehemence. "Whatever he saw, whatever we were doing, he had no right—"

"I was a fraud."

About to vent more anger, Val broke off, the full meaning of Carolyn's words sinking in. "But he was good for you in bed . . . wasn't he? With me you're so—"

"It's different with you. With him it was . . . I loved him. At times it was . . . Until the first time with you. Then, going to bed with him was—I couldn't bring myself to do it anymore."

Astounded, Val stared at her.

Still propped on her elbows, Carolyn was gazing into the fire. "The drawing I gave you, I never felt anything like that before you. I didn't think I was much of a woman."

Val found her voice. "What you felt with me you could feel with anyone."

There was no reaction to the words, as if they had not registered. Carolyn said, "I needed all those things about being married to him but I never really needed *him.* I never felt what he thought I felt. I was a fraud."

Carolyn was looking up at her. Val rubbed her hands across her face and concentrated on maintaining an even tone. "I wasted years of my life, Carrie. I did feel the physical things with men. But never such exact rightness—" She broke off, seeing Carolyn's nod.

Carolyn whispered, "That's how I feel with you—exact rightness."

"Carrie, tell me," Val asked, "besides Paul how many men were there?"

"Enough. Eight."

Val heard the number with surprise, remembering that Carolyn had married at nineteen. "Was it good with any of them?"

Carolyn smiled. "Compared to you?" She paused. "I don't know how to answer you. I was looking, I didn't know what I was looking for. It was as good as it ever got with Paul. The thing is, I made commitments I believed in when I married him. He gave me years of his life, he believed—"

"Carrie," she interrupted, "it happens all the time." The taut posture of Carolyn's body told Val how vitally important this conversation was to her. Yet it was all so clear—why did Carolyn have to hear what was so obvious? "People make the most solemn commitments and then events change their whole lives around. What more can we do than the best we can do? It's one thing to feel guilt at promises you couldn't keep but—"

"Val?" Carolyn sat up to look at her. "He didn't want to hurt me, he wanted to kill me. He tried to *kill* me."

No, it was me he wanted to kill. "Then why aren't you angry? Why do you blame yourself? You gave all you knew to give; you did the best you could for eight years. Did you deserve to have him *kill* you? Why are you blaming yourself? Carrie, why aren't you *angry?*"

Carolyn worked her wedding ring over her knuckle and dropped it onto the carpet. Val slid the ring into her pocket.

Little by little, over the next three days, Val patiently drew out every detail of Paul Blake's assault, made Carolyn verbalize every moment of the terror. She added many more items to The List, including Paul Blake's hand in her eviction from the Robinson guest house.

She wondered how much of Carolyn's feeling for her had had its roots in simple guilt at her husband's behavior. But then, did it matter? Her own love for Carolyn had evolved accidentally . . .

Each night Carolyn slept in her arms, but there was no sexuality in the act. Skittish about being touched even casually, she seemed to lack all sensual awareness.

Val could hear Alix's words: *This will be difficult for you when she's so new and wonderful, but she may have very little interest in lovemaking. You'll have to understand that it's not rejection of you; it's another way she's been damaged. You'll have to be patient and wait, Val. And it's impossible to predict for how long . . .*

Carolyn was spending more and more time on the beach, her healing face turning bronze in the November sun. Sitting by herself on the rocks or playing with Neal when he was home from school, she built sandcastles, waded in the surf, walked with Neal hand in hand along the shore.

Val set up a painting table beside the front windows and occupied herself with her profession, the two people she most valued often in sight on the beach below as she worked. She was working well; the break to take care of Carolyn seemed to have brought a fresh infusion of creativity.

Her mind unceasingly occupied with Paul Blake, again and again she ordered herself to be patient. He would be there when the time was right.

Jean Bowman called while Carolyn was down on the beach. Paul Blake wanted to put the house on the market; there were papers for Carolyn to sign. He had filed for divorce, asking a fifty-fifty split on community property. Settlement seemed no problem.

"One more thing, Val. He did request a meeting with either or both of you. To personally return unspecified possessions. Of course I told him no. He requested that I relay the message anyway."

"Thank you, Jean," she said evenly, knowing Paul Blake's "message" was intended for her. But why? Surely it was not physical harm he intended if he would go through Carolyn's lawyer to arrange a meeting . . . and he could have assaulted her on that Sunday when she had been with Carolyn. "I'll relay all this to Carolyn," Val said, "and get back to you, Jean. Except his request for a meeting, of course. That would only upset her."

"Still no word of concern about her or what he did to her," Jean Bowman said. "Know something, Val? It's not only this man—after fifteen years in this business I'm convinced men think we're making it up or exaggerating when we talk about psychic scars of rape and battery. I think it's an unbridgeable gulf between men and women."

When Val hung up she was elated, but annoyed that the proposed meeting had been Paul Blake's initiative and not hers.

Carolyn shrugged. "I don't care what he does as long as I don't have to see him. I do want your paintings and my clothes, personal things—my degree, photos of my parents, things like that." She looked at Val miserably. "We could go there when he's not around but I'd be petrified he might show up. I think if I saw him I'd go completely to pieces."

"You'll never have to see him again," Val stated. She would take care of that. "Make a list of what you want. We'll give it to Jean."

Val called Jean Bowman and relayed Carolyn's agreement to sale of the house and the conditions for an uncontested divorce. "If he'll have everything on Carolyn's list delivered to Bekins Storage, I'll take care of it from there."

"Fine. I'll tell him he can deliver his so-called unspecified possessions to me. Any response, however profane, you'd like me to add about the proposed meeting?"

"No. Nothing."

Jean Bowman might feel duty bound to report back to Carolyn that Val had sent word through Paul Blake's office when she would meet him.

❧ 46 ❧

Val drove to the Blake house and parked. Paul Blake, pacing his front yard, his hands in the pockets of his gray jogging suit, watched her for several moments as she crossed the street, then he strode into his house.

Unhurriedly she walked up the driveway, noting the Century 21 for-sale sign on a lawn which was not yet unkempt but overdue for mowing. The front door was ajar; she left it open behind her. Footprints were tracked on the parquet floor of the entryway, a thick coat of dust dulled the glass-topped hall table. There was a mustiness in the house, an air of abandonment.

Paul Blake sat in the white armchair, his gray jogging shoes propped carelessly on the matching ottoman. His blue eyes seemed transparently pale against the light background. "Sit down," he said.

The voice was cool, the posture self-possessed. Her instincts told her that she need not make any statement about precautions she had taken; and only then did she concede the real depth of her fear in coming here.

"I'll stand," she told him with the insolence of her newfound confidence. "This can't take long."

His gaze drifted down her. "You've got guts, I'll say that. Too bad you can't be the man you wish you were. Too bad you can't give her what a man can—a good house, good food, good clothes, protection."

"Protection. I heard the man say protection."

His expression did not change.

She said, "At her age I was married too. I had all those things."

Again his gaze drifted down her. "Yes, I remember. Someone actually married you."

She smiled. "Twice."

"We're the same age . . . How tragic that women live longer than men when the law of gravity is so much crueler to you. Look at you—you've already begun to sag. A few decent years, that's all you've got. I'm nowhere near my prime."

So this was why he wanted this meeting—or at least one of the reasons. To reclaim his territorial rights by assuring her that she had won no victory, that her gains were short term and illusory.

The List etched itself clearly in her mind. She crossed her arms. "She's with me," she said slowly, with relish. "Where she wants to be."

He said evenly, "Queer is such a perfect word for you. You *are* queer. A freak. She's been with men, she'll go back to men when she gets tired of being fucked by a queer."

There was an almost palpable sensation of the words caroming off her, off the impervious armor of her confidence. Never again would she allow the best of herself to be diminished. Why had she ever allowed it?

"I have her now." She spread her feet and said with deep pleasure, drawing out the words, "I'll have her a good long time, all that sweetness of her to enjoy . . . to the fullest. You'll never have her again."

He stared at her with his transparent eyes. "You're pathetic. An imitation man. A perversion of a man. A dyke, a cuntsucking—"

"She doesn't like to be sucked." Her voice was soft, containing none of the exhilaration she felt. "I start by putting my tongue just up inside and circling her. Her hips rock, she goes crazy."

The transparent eyes froze on her.

"I know all the ways to move my tongue, how to make her moan and want to come, but not let her come."

As his face blanched, she watched with the most savage joy she had ever known, the adrenaline surging through her.

He rose. She squared her shoulders and stood to her full height.

She said, gauging him, "You saw us that Sunday—did you watch the whole afternoon? Did you see all those times? Did you watch all those ways she loved me?"

She braced as he moved toward her; she would slash the edge of one hand across his throat, drive the knuckles of the other hand into his eyes.

"Every night from now on I'll have her. Every night she'll be fucked by this queer."

She stopped, not because he had halted a few feet from her, but because she was finished, and because every item was gone from The List.

She stared into his white face. She could smell alcohol on his breath.

He moved around her, past her, and into the guest room.

Her euphoria vanished. Fear took cold shape. Had he gone in there for a weapon? Nonplussed, unsure, she hesitated, then took two steps toward the door she had left open.

"Wait," he commanded from behind her.

A painting under each arm, he walked up to her and placed them on the floor, turned their faces out to her. "These are what I wanted to return."

In sick dread, understanding what she would see, she forced her eyes downward.

Across the grays of the rain painting, the slashes were diagonal and ragged, as if the blade had deliberately paused to inflict deeper damage. In *Summer Sunrise* the slashes were vertical and so close together that fragments of the canvas hung from the frame; the thin gaps in the bright oranges of the canvas were dark and jagged, as if the sun were bleeding black blood.

"A vandal," he said.

She wrenched her anguished eyes away from the corpses of her paintings to meet his pale blue stare.

"I wanted to give them to you personally," he said. "You see how it feels to have some pervert destroy what another person values."

"Pervert," she repeated. "Perversion is destroying what you yourself value. Especially when it can never be replaced."

Unable to look down, she gestured to the paintings. "Other things can be replaced. Like these."

He would not know that she could only make replicas, that the creative spark and urgency that gave force and depth to these paintings had been used up and was gone.

She reached into the pocket of her jeans and he stepped quickly back. She realized in sharp exultation that they were equals in their apprehensive mistrust of each other.

"I have something to return to you, too." She raised her hand and let the ring fall onto the carpet.

Their eyes locked.

She said, "If you come near us I'll kill you." To say these words was the reason she had come here.

He smiled, and she was the one to take an involuntary step backward. A memory flashed through her—the same memory as the night she had first met Paul Blake—of being in the desert with Neal, and retreating in dread revulsion from the shiny rattler patrolling its territory with easy and deadly efficiency.

"Why should I come near you?" His eyes held the arctic cold of a shark. He said softly, "There are other women."

He pushed the paintings toward her. "Take these and get out."

She closed the door of the Blake house behind her, wishing she could hermetically seal it.

~ 47 ~

Quietly, Val let herself into the beach house. Neal was watching television. Carolyn, he told her, was upstairs reading in bed.

Sorting through the mail she had picked up at her flat, Val opened an envelope from Hopestead Gallery in Santa Barbara. A letter from Hilda Green asked her to please note the enclosed check for twenty-one hundred dollars, and testily enumerated attempts to reach Val to discuss additional paintings for the gallery.

Carolyn was propped up in bed, her hair fanned over the pillow. She lowered her book. "You were gone a long time."

The reason for leaving the beach house had been to go to the flat. "I took care of a few things," Val said easily, sitting on the bed. She handed Carolyn the check from Hilda Green. "You weren't really worried, were you?"

As she hoped, Carolyn was distracted by the check, gazing at it with a slowly widening smile. Eventually, Val reflected, she would have to tell Carolyn about the destruction of the paintings. She had never allowed Carolyn to watch her work; perhaps she could manage to secretly duplicate them.

"Dear, wonderful Val," Carolyn murmured. "I'm so proud of you."

Val began to unbutton her shirt. "Let me do that," Carolyn said in soft command, sitting up.

Val submitted to the warm hands, steeling herself against the heavy silk hair that brushed her throat and shoulders, the enveloping gentleness. Carolyn slid her arms around her and buried her face in Val's bare breasts.

Succumbing, her desire sharpening as a nipple hardened in Carolyn's tender mouth, she pressed Carolyn's mouth into her. Was desire finally surfacing in Carolyn, or did she still want her breasts for comforting, as a mother's breasts?

Carolyn took her mouth away but did not release her. "God, you're so beautiful. But—"

"I understand," Val said quickly. Her question answered, she was heartened by the words and by what had just happened between them.

"I need just a little more time to—to . . ."

"I know."

"You truly are so beautiful." Carolyn released her, moved her hands caressingly over Val's shoulders. "Much as I hate to leave this wonderful house, I think I'm ready. But not to go back to your place, Val. I'm uneasy about that. I think—well, I don't know, I haven't thought this through, but I've got a little money now. . . ."

"We've both got money." Val picked up the check, let it flutter down to the bed.

Just a little more time with you . . . I need a little more time, too. To be everything I can, to do everything I can . . .

She smiled into Carolyn's green eyes. "I think I've definitely entered a green period. I'd like to be in a place where it's all green. What do you think about going up to Oregon for a while?"

"You crazy woman." Carolyn shook her head. "It's the worst possible time for a trip to the Northwest." She said dreamily, "All that rain and mist and fog, all those green trees . . . it sounds like absolute heaven."

Exultant, Val said, "Dad'll leap at the chance to spoil his grandson."

"Can't Neal come with us? He'd love it. Oregon might even be the real Emerald City."

"Yes, it might be," Val said musingly. "But it's too close to the end of the school term, Carrie. Believe me, he'll love being with his grandfather. They'll take in every sports event on TV and in town besides. You'll have to put up with just me."

"I think I could adjust to the idea," Carolyn teased. Her expression sobered, her eyes grew distant. "It is a good idea, Val, getting away from here. I know I'd stop being afraid. Completely."

Val nodded, thinking somberly that other women would inherit her fear.

Carolyn said, "And when we come back—"

"If we come back," Val said quietly.

"That's another idea," Carolyn said, and slid her arms around Val again.

"Everything's changing so fast." Carolyn rested her head on Val's shoulder. "Every day things look different to me. I look different to myself. I want to be with you now, I do know that—while the real Carolyn emerges. Will you wait for me? Is it enough?"

"Yes," Val said, holding her closely. "It's enough."

The Art of Katherine V. Forrest: An Afterword

Victoria A. Brownworth

It's easy to enjoy the works of Katherine V. Forrest. Written in accessible, colloquial prose, peopled with believable and (except for, of necessity, some of the villains) likable characters, well plotted and well situated in terms of both place and time, Forrest's novels read quickly and well. Reading and writing are, by their very nature, acts of sharing, and Forrest writes like a woman who wants to share, writes as if she wants the reader there with her in the place and time of and with the people in her stories.

Of course many writers embrace their audiences, and the concomitant desire and ability to do so can most often be found in genre writing—romance, mystery, science fiction—and at each of these Forrest is equivalently deft. But some readers privately and many critics publicly sneer at genre writing; somehow it doesn't measure up to the standards set by serious literary fiction. Those who make such facile determinations, however, forget about romances such as Tolstoy's *Anna Karenina,* mysteries such as Dostoevsky's *The Brothers Karamazov,* and science fiction such as Orwell's *1984*—all very much, in addition to their genre niches, the most serious and classic of literary fiction.

As someone who has taught the art of genre writing at the college level for two decades, I know what the best of genre fiction does: it addresses the most fundamental struggles of Voltaire's "condition humaine." A good mystery (and all of Forrest's are) succinctly pits Good against Evil and most often allows Good to win in the form of justice served, even if shaded by many a moral gray area. A well-crafted mystery does what real life so rarely can: provides vicarious justice for all that is wrong in the world (or a given milieu) as exemplified by the crimes therein and explicated by the characters in the given story. A writer such as the "grande dame" of mystery, P. D. James, escorts the reader through a Byzantine maze of moral quandaries, divides, and certitudes in the course of one of her novels, yet leads that reader to the exit where Good wins out, if only just barely, and justice is proffered, if not always before a magistrate.

In her novels, regardless of their genre, Forrest writes the lesbian and queer landscape, charting territory that isn't in itself new but that in her capable hands still remains fresh. In books such as the Kate Delafield mysteries, *Murder at the Nightwood Bar* and *The Beverly Malibu*, Forrest takes her readers into decidedly queer territory where murder grimly underscores the political subtext the author delineates as she explores the differences between how queers and straights live and how the seemingly simple difference of sexual orientation can create an atmosphere of physical and psychological danger.

Similar to classic detectives of the genre, such as James's Adam Dalgleish, Delafield herself is a complex character who daily navigates her own difficult emotional terrain (her lover was killed in a terrible accident that left Delafield with brutal memories, a deeply scarred heart, and an ineffable yearning for her lost love), as do many of those with whom she comes in contact in her role as a homicide detective in the Los Angeles Police Department. Delafield is in the closet but, as *Murder at the Nightwood Bar* explicates, walks the carefully nuanced line so many queer professionals do between keeping a low profile and being true to one's self.

In her mysteries, Forrest declaims the niche that queers are often forced to fit into in a heterosexually dominant society. Delafield exemplifies what it is to cope with the conflicts burdening a majority of queers as they struggle against bias and stereotypes while attempting to live authentic and gratifying lives in what for many remains an alien culture to their own. Delafield's relationship with her bigoted partner, Ed Taylor, makes her work life that much more difficult. These are the subtleties that Forrest elucidates in her novels: Life for queers is, inexorably, far different from that of heterosexuals, not because they wish it to be (although some of the denizens of *The Beverly Malibu* do), but because straight society—even as epitomized by a grudgingly respectful partner like Ed Taylor—force the issue and make it so. Thus the mere day-to-day wears at one's psyche as it does for Delafield, irrespective of and in addition to the profound difficulties wrought by the horrors of her job.

Forrest does not skirt the sexual facet of her queer characters, either. Despite the loss of her lover, Delafield remains a deeply sexual creature, and in each of Forrest's novels in which she appears, she engages in affairs of the heart that are also very much of the body. Sexuality—and the eroticism it engenders—forms a thematic nexus throughout all of Forrest's work, and although it is subtly woven into her mysteries and science fiction rather than being their focus, sexuality and its partner, sensuality, are given full throttle when Forrest's characters move to the bedroom (or its amorous equivalent). Sex is not just a practiced art in Forrest's writing that always yields up a subliminal eroticism, it is a practicable art, by which I mean Forrest's characters need sex as much as they need love and acceptance; there is no lesbian bed death in a Forrest novel, no matter what the genre. Sexuality is explicit and explicatable and Forrest often uses a character's sexuality—Kate Delafield's in the Delafield series or Carolyn Blake's in *An Emergence of Green*—to illumine other aspects of that character. Thus the frisson Carolyn Blake experiences in her first meetings with Val Hunter is a palpable element of what lies within Carolyn herself; this is a sexual woman, a woman with desires who wants to open herself sensually to another. Forrest elucidates Carolyn's sexual desire in oblique asides throughout the novel, making it clear to the reader that her sexual passion for Val isn't the first she's experienced, it is merely the most fulfilling and complete. Carolyn Blake is no fictional or even political stereotype; she is most definitely *not* a woman who was devoid of sexual feelings before her first woman lover, and in stating this as clearly (if subtly) as she does, Forrest takes a risk with a lesbian-feminist audience but also makes Carolyn more realistic. Carolyn's sexual passion for Val is actually intensified by the fact of her preexisting sexual desire. Carolyn married Paul Blake, a man nearly ten years her senior, when she was only nineteen. But she had had several lovers prior to him, even at that young age. Carolyn is thus portrayed as a woman who desires sexual intimacy.

That Forrest continually writes her female characters as women for whom sex is as necessary as any other need makes her work that much more provocative, particularly when considering the time line for that work. For more than twenty years Forrest has written characters such as Carolyn Blake for whom desire is as palpable as love.

Forrest also explores the range of lesbian and female sexuality in her work. Forrest's women have varied sexual tastes. Thus when Paul Blake accusatorially suggests to Val Hunter that all his wife was seeking in the arms of another woman was the oral sex he found so distasteful, Val clarifies for him in explicit detail exactly what it is his wife enjoys with her—that it goes well beyond stereotypical male perceptions of what women can and do experience together in bed. Concomitant with that range of sexual choice is also a range of identity choice. Are Carolyn and Val—two women who had married men and whose only sexual experiences have been with men—lesbians? We read them that way if we are queer, but married women in the suburban enclaves in which these women live may read them as they read themselves—perhaps committed to loving other women, but not yet committed to declaring themselves as queer or even bisexual. Forrest's novels manage to be highly political and definitively queer while not always demanding that the characters self-identify as queer. Sexual identity is a complex and often rough territory for these characters to traverse, and leaving one place—in Carolyn's case, for example, heterosexual marriage—to visit or move to another, such as lesbianism, can be fraught with danger, as it is for Carolyn when Paul assaults, rapes, and sodomizes her.

Although the issue of sexual identity takes a political form in much of Forrest's mystery and science fiction writing, in her romance and literary novels the political recedes to a more nuanced facet and the sexual broadens, and with that broadening, questions of how *lesbian* is defined are raised, but the answers are not always simple. In the twenty-first century, *Sex and the City*fied literary marketplace, the blatant element of active—not pornographic, but definitely explicit—female sexual passion may not seem very dramatic, but one must both quantify and qualify Forrest's place in creating that new milieu of explicated female sexuality, because it is perhaps the most startling aspect of her work.

In the 1970s, two novels shocked audiences with their explicit female sexuality. One was Erica Jong's *Fear of Flying* in which the term *zipless fuck* (which would later become the basis for the actions of many of the *Sex and the City* girls and their retinue of chick-lit followers) was coined. The other, far less widely read when it was published by a small independent press, but which would later be bought and reissued by a mainstream publisher, was *Rubyfruit Jungle* by Rita Mae Brown. What these books had in common was the openness with which their characters expressed and pursued their sexual desires, the one for heterosexual sex, the other for lesbian sex. Although neither book was a stellar literary work, both did something new and therefore shocking: they stated, unequivocally and on the heels of the burgeoning second wave of feminism, that women wanted and moreover *deserved* to have the same kind of sex as men, which was to say at that pre-AIDS time, unencumbered, unabashed, and unrelievedly orgasmic sex with multiple partners of either gender. And, unsurprisingly, the novels became instant classics of a heretofore nonexistent genre, of previously unknown authors. Jong, a graduate of Barnard, had published several books of moderately well-received poetry while Brown, a lesbian activist who had been personally purged from the founding group of the National Organization for Women by none other than Betty Friedan, had written a series of provocative essays collected under the title *The Hand That Cradles the Rock* and was a member of the Furies, an intellectual/political lesbian-feminist literary collective.

Lesbian fiction did not exist as a genre prior to the 1970s and the establishment of small, independent presses such as Daughters, Inc. which published Brown's novel and Naiad Press which would first publish the fledgling Forrest. This is not to say that lesbian novels were not published—they were, but a majority of those, such as the works of Ann Bannon, appeared as pulp paperbacks that were to the minds of many one step from pornography. And indeed many novels of lesbian sex and seduction were published as pseudo-pornography in

the mainstream, but for a decidedly straight male audience by Faw-
cett, Grove Press, Evergreen, Dell, and others throughout the 1950s,
1960s, and 1970s.

Thus the work of Katherine V. Forrest becomes defining in the historical time line of lesbian fiction because it is among the very first to
literarily define lesbian sexuality as distinctly lesbian, that is (as the
lesbian separatists of the 1970s might have noted), for lesbians only.
Not in an effete, off-the-page intellectualization of lesbian sexuality as
Virginia Woolf, Gertrude Stein, Djuna Barnes, Radclyffe Hall, and
other lesbian writers of the early twentieth century had occasionally
written, nor even in an early Second Wave feminist intellectually ob-
fuscating stylistic approach such as the 1970s' work of Bertha Harris
or Monique Wittig, but in a happening here, happening now, we-
know-what-they-are-doing, non-euphemistically overt series of sexual images that were unmistakably about two women making love:
and not just making love but having sex—visceral, grab-the-bed-
posts, scissor-your-thighs sex.

Whereas the lesbian pulp fiction of the past (with the exception of
Ann Bannon and Patricia Highsmith whose work was not overtly sexual but which was distinctly lesbian, not bisexual) had been promul-
gated for a male audience to promote male sexual fantasies about
women together and in which there was frequently, if not always, a
man looming in the doorway of the lesbian bedroom, Forrest's work
presumes a lesbian audience and a lesbian intimacy with lesbian sexual
practices. That presumption is what makes Forrest so significantly
new to the literary landscape, and that openness of sexual expression—not fumbling nor a sexual coming of age as in Isabel Miller's
sweetly sentimental lesbian historical novel *Patience and Sarah,* which
predates Forrest's novels by a few years—is almost shocking in its explicit desire of women for women, absent men altogether.

In Forrest's novels *Curious Wine* and *An Emergence of Green,* the un-
dercurrent of lesbian-feminist revolution is fomenting beneath the
surface of average American suburban life. Here women begin the exploration of each other in an atmosphere that has yet to burgeon in
their own particular milieus. The time in which these novels are
set—the late 1970s to the mid-1980s—are the days when the term

feminist was synonymous with *lesbian* in the lexicons of heterosexuals and, except in the very large urban areas on the East and West Coasts, the concept of *queer* has yet to be conceived, let alone accepted.

Into this world—and from it—Forrest draws her characters: women tentative about myriad aspects of their own lives but for whom passion is more than a yearning, it is a divination, a palpable desire that can propel them forward into the other pathways of their lives. What Forrest does in these novels—part literary, part romance—is to elucidate the interior landscape of women who have never known that they might have options, that a plethora of choices were open to them, that they could, in all probability, live lives as broad and brave and inclusive as men have led for millennia. This is what happens to Carolyn Blake.

At the novel's opening she is twenty-six, having a drink, and trying to decipher how to make her husband less annoyed with her decision to work a different shift at her job. Enter Val Hunter, the literal woman-next-door who has daily leaped the fence between the two properties to swim in the Blake's pool, unbeknownst to them until this first day of Carolyn's new work schedule. From the first day that Carolyn sees Val—a tall, imposing figure of a woman—she is drawn to her. Val, a painter, has a young son from her second marriage and the two live a companionable but hand-to-mouth existence on Val's occasional commissions and gallery sales.

The relationship between the two women—two heterosexually defined women—evolves from their proximity and growing friendship. Val, independent and self-reliant yet also protective of her child, isn't like anyone Carolyn has known before, coming as she has to the California suburbs from her upbringing in the Midwest by way of a miserable foray in Alabama with her husband. Carolyn's life has always been determined by others, dominated by middle-class social standards of what a girl coming of age in the 1970s should do. Thus when Paul moves for his job, first from Illinois where Carolyn is in college and then from Alabama where Carolyn has just begun to be accorded some status at her own job, there can be no question about what Carolyn must do: Follow her man, irrespective of her own desires.

On the surface *An Emergence of Green* appears to be a novel about a friendship between two women that blossoms, slowly, into romantic love. However, the subtext of the novel reads much more deeply: The story of Carolyn Blake's awakening—personal, sexual, feminist—is historic. Similar to Kate Chopin's novel of a century before, *The Awakening,* or the last section of Virginia Woolf's pivotal novel of female independence and interdependence, *To the Lighthouse,* Forrest takes her characters into the heart of history. To paraphrase Bob Dylan, the times were changing and changing with a rapidity that was frightening to many men *and* women. Yet for a select segment of the female population the exhilaration of discovering that the horizon was far broader than one could ever imagine was defining—*self*-defining—and Forrest describes that awakening as it happens while managing to grasp its larger historical significance. *An Emergence of Green* reads now like the just-written novel of an author who has had two decades to review, reflect upon, and cull from the events of another era and then transliterate them for those of *this* era.

Similar to Marilyn French with *The Women's Room,* Forrest takes the reader into every aspect of her characters' lives—personal, political, sexual, familial. No one is a cipher and no one is a stereotype, including Carolyn's husband. Paul Blake is not evil, although his final actions in the book become evil; rather Paul is as much a victim of prefeminist social mores as his wife. He grew up poor and emotionally sundered by the early death of his mother. Threatened by his first wife's voracious sexuality, he still dislikes sexual experimentation (for example, his emotional complexity makes it difficult for him to enjoy either the giving or receiving of oral sexual pleasure). Paul needs control over his world because there was none as he grew up. His desire to control Carolyn is not, initially, malicious. He merely wants his life clearly delineated; he is fastidious and particular in all things, including his requests of his wife.

Paul likes how Carolyn *looks,* he likes her presentation in front of his colleagues, and he likes her seeming malleability and her sexual vulnerability to him. When that malleability begins to dissipate after Carolyn meets Val, Paul becomes unmoored. He *needs* her to need him. When Val and Paul meet over dinner Paul becomes irrationally riven with anger toward Val whom he immediately finds threatening to his life with Carolyn. Paul views Val as a grotesque misfit of a woman—too big, too loud, too opinionated, too independent, and whose impecunious lifestyle somehow damages his perception of what a family should strive for in suburban America, and reflects obliquely on his own penurious upbringing. He refers to her as an Amazon and an Amazon she is—without even realizing it herself Val becomes a warrior that evening, equipping herself to battle with Paul for Carolyn.

As with all battles, the war for Carolyn's heart and cunt gets violent and bloody. Forrest pulls us back and forth in her narrative, explicating the sexual tension between Val and Carolyn (an afternoon together in the pool, holding hands, is fraught with sexual innuendo even though neither woman has acknowledged such feelings) while explicitly detailing what goes on in Paul and Carolyn's bedroom.

Forrest builds to the sexually explosive first lovemaking between Carolyn and Val and refuses to be coy about their sexual heat thereafter. In scene after scene, Carolyn's desire for Val builds and explodes; at one point she leaves a party at her own home for her husband's colleagues and runs to Val's for what can only be described as a quick hand job. Her desire is palpable to the reader.

Paul tries to woo back his wife, taking her away for an island vacation during which he makes love to her so frequently she hurts from it. Yet part of Forrest's deftness in charting Carolyn's sexuality is that the author does not diminish Carolyn's responses to Paul even as she constructs a new set of responses to Val. The realism of these concurrent scenes cannot be undervalued; a majority of women who discover their sexual attraction to women do it exactly as Carolyn does—in stages, withdrawing slowly from the male partner as they engage more deeply with the female partner but being intimate with both in a way that is not so much an expression of bisexuality as it is a process of transition and reevaluation of one's sexual identity.

Val, too, has to come to terms with her sexual self. Forrest details her sexual life prior to Carolyn—men who were satisfying lovers but unsatisfying husbands or partners and another woman with whom Val was reluctant to take her first lesbian plunge. Thus as the story between Val and Carolyn progresses, Forrest reveals Val's increasing interest in a lesbian world, a world outside the heterosexual status quo with which she has always been at odds.

Subscripts of the novel are the politics of feminism and the real politick of the 1984 presidential election in which the first (and to date only) female vice presidential candidate, Geraldine Ferraro, was running with Walter Mondale against incumbent Ronald Reagan. The manner in which Forrest weaves this external political line into the intricate internal politics of the interrelationship of the Paul-Carolyn-Val triad underscores the tension Forrest elucidates about relationships between men and women in a newly feminist era and how those tensions can, given the right or wrong circumstances, become explosive.

Forrest shocks us with the sexually violent denouement of the novel, yet no other denouement would be believable given how she constructs and deconstructs the stories of each of these characters throughout the book. Sex is truly the battleground between Val and Paul. Carolyn has certainly enjoyed her sexual life prior to her liaison with Val, but the intensity of her sexual satisfaction with Val—an intensity that Paul witnesses, shocked and enraged, when he watches the two women through the window of the guest room—is such that she cannot go back to her earlier life. Regardless of her feelings for Paul, Carolyn's future, at least immediately, lies irrevocably with Val. When Paul sees Val bringing *his* wife, Carolyn, to ecstatic orgasm, he has no choice but to try to reclaim her in the bedroom, to metaphorically take up the sword he believes Val has thrown down. Forrest shifts to Paul's vantage point, detailing how his erection intensifies as he becomes increasingly violent with his wife, illumining through example what we already know from psychological and judicial studies—rape is a crime of passion and power. Yet, it makes utter sense that in a tale so fraught with every aspect of sexual expression, sexual violence would demand explication as well.

In *An Emergence of Green,* Forrest renders one of her best and most deftly nuanced novels. Each of the three central characters gets full exposition; we know who these people are, and we believe their actions are realistic and true to both their personalities and their era.

Forrest takes care to shy away from the didacticism of say, Henrik Ib-
sen's *A Doll's House,* in which the husband, Torvald, is so extreme, so
ogreish, as to diminish his weight as a representative literary foil. Paul
isn't unsympathetic until he rapes Carolyn; he doesn't mean to *betray*
his wife when he forces Val's landlord to evict her in an effort to re-
strict her proximity to Carolyn, he merely wants to protect his relationship from outside threat, from competition. But as Forrest makes
clear in her handling of Carolyn and Val's story after Paul's assault,
the "he said/she said" of rape in marriage kept that crime from being
denoted *as* a crime for centuries. As we witness Paul envisioning the
sexual violence even as he is perpetrating it against her, it isn't rape, it
is reclaiming his own territory from the marauding Amazon who is
trying to steal his wife from him.

Examining Forrest's work in its totality, one sees a clearly delineated exposition of sexual politics, sexual stratification, and sexual
identification. All of Forrest's primary characters are women involved
with other women but not all are lesbian-identified, even if they are
living what we think of as lesbian lives. Carolyn Blake never thinks of
lesbianism while Val considers it and rejects it at several points in the
novel—in part because Val has enjoyed sexual relationships with men
and in part because she loves her son so deeply. Forrest turns ironies
upon each other: physically Val is the prototypical Amazon, a lesbian-feminist archetype, but despite her size, her independence, her
politics, and her bohemianism, Val cannot (initially—she begins to
perceive things differently at novel's end) conceptualize having enjoyed sex with men and wanting to have sex with women. Carolyn,
conversely, bypasses the *idea* of lesbianism altogether; when she tells
Val after their initial sexual encounter that Val must never touch her
in that explosive way again, it is because she feels conflicted about her
role as wife and her relationship with Paul, not because she fears being
labeled a lesbian or because she feels uncomfortable about the sex itself. She likes the sex with Val so much that she has to have it every
chance she gets, even if there isn't time to reciprocate.

The sexual freedom that Forrest's characters embody impels a
dynamism that infuses her narratives. The presumptive passion exclu-
sive of men but not denunciative of men in Forrest's novels is icono-

clastic, particularly if one considers the scope and time line of her oeuvre. Revisiting *An Emergence of Green* as I have, twenty years after its initial publication, what strikes me most is how provocative the sexuality is—how it literally begins with sex and the sex ebbs and flows throughout the entire novel. What also struck me is how—except for the literal time references—the novel is not at all dated. Unlike other pivotal works of fiction, for example, Radclyffe Hall's *The Well of Loneliness,* the read is a smooth one despite the years between its writing and this reissue. One does not balk at either the characterizations or the premise. The conflicts between Carolyn, her husband, and her lover remain as true today as they were when they were written. That is the subtle power of Forrest's tale and the resonance of her characterizations.

Over the past three decades, a burgeoning body of lesbian fiction has evolved, emerging in part from the classic literary novels of the early twentieth century and in part from the somewhat lurid pulp fiction of the 1950s and 1960s. In the early twenty-first century we have a vast array of lesbian fiction from which to cull. Yet there remains a strong demarcation between the highly sexual texts still perceived as erotica and the classic literary work which remains, despite its lesbian content, curiously devoid of actual lesbian sexuality. Throughout this literary evolution, however, Forrest's work has remained resolutely sexual, determinedly integrating female sexuality in all its diversity into the fullness of lesbian life and lesbian politics.

An Emergence of Green stands, after decades, as a compelling and provocative novel, a realistic and substantive tale of passion, politics, and personal evolution. Forrest remains, after nearly three decades of writing in every genre, a writer clearly attuned to the panoply of lesbian experience, and one who must be read, reread, and compared, but one who will, undeniably, stand as a keen expositor of lesbian life, past, present, and future.

❧ About the Author ❧

Katherine V. Forrest is the author of fourteen books, including the lesbian classic *Curious Wine* and the Lambda Literary Award-winning Kate Delafield mystery series. She has also authored numerous articles, which have appeared in many publications, including the *Lambda Book Report* and *OUT* magazine. Her book reviews have appeared in the *Los Angeles Times,* the *San Francisco Chronicle,* and other publications. She has been profiled in *USA Today* and the *San Francisco Chronicle,* in addition to virtually every major LGBT publication in the United States and abroad. She was supervising editor at Naiad Press for more than ten years and has taught many classes on the craft of fiction. She is the recipient of the Lambda Literary Foundation's Pioneer Award.

Order a copy of this book with this form or online at:
http://www.haworthpress.com/store/product.asp?sku=5370

AN EMERGENCE OF GREEN

_____in softbound at $16.95 (ISBN-13: 978-1-56023-542-2; ISBN-10: 1-56023-542-X)

Or order online and use special offer code HEC25 in the shopping cart.

COST OF BOOKS_____

POSTAGE & HANDLING_____
(US: $4.00 for first book & $1.50
for each additional book)
(Outside US: $5.00 for first book
& $2.00 for each additional book)

SUBTOTAL_____

IN CANADA: ADD 7% GST_____

STATE TAX_____
(NJ, NY, OH, MN, CA, IL, IN, PA, & SD
residents, add appropriate local sales tax)

FINAL TOTAL_____
(If paying in Canadian funds,
convert using the current
exchange rate, UNESCO
coupons welcome)

☐ **BILL ME LATER:** (Bill-me option is good on
US/Canada/Mexico orders only; not good to
jobbers, wholesalers, or subscription agencies.)

☐ Check here if billing address is different from
shipping address and attach purchase order and
billing address information.

Signature_____

☐ **PAYMENT ENCLOSED: $_____**

☐ **PLEASE CHARGE TO MY CREDIT CARD.**

☐ Visa ☐ MasterCard ☐ AmEx ☐ Discover
☐ Diner's Club ☐ Eurocard ☐ JCB

Account # _____

Exp. Date_____

Signature_____

Prices in US dollars and subject to change without notice.

NAME_____

INSTITUTION_____

ADDRESS_____

CITY_____

STATE/ZIP_____

COUNTRY_____ COUNTY (NY residents only)_____

TEL_____ FAX_____

E-MAIL_____

May we use your e-mail address for confirmations and other types of information? ☐ Yes ☐ No
We appreciate receiving your e-mail address and fax number. Haworth would like to e-mail or fax special
discount offers to you, as a preferred customer. **We will never share, rent, or exchange your e-mail address
or fax number.** We regard such actions as an invasion of your privacy.

Order From Your Local Bookstore or Directly From
The Haworth Press, Inc.
10 Alice Street, Binghamton, New York 13904-1580 • USA
TELEPHONE: 1-800-HAWORTH (1-800-429-6784) / Outside US/Canada: (607) 722-5857
FAX: 1-800-895-0582 / Outside US/Canada: (607) 771-0012
E-mail to: orders@haworthpress.com

For orders outside US and Canada, you may wish to order through your local
sales representative, distributor, or bookseller.
For information, see http://haworthpress.com/distributors

(Discounts are available for individual orders in US and Canada only, not booksellers/distributors.)

PLEASE PHOTOCOPY THIS FORM FOR YOUR PERSONAL USE.
http://www.HaworthPress.com   BOF04